not
My Greek
Wedding

BOOKS BY SUE ROBERTS

My Big Greek Summer
My Very Italian Holiday
You, Me and Italy
A Very French Affair
As Greek as It Gets
Some Like It Greek
Going Greek
Greece Actually
What Happens in Greece
Take a Chance on Greece
There's Something about Greece
All You Need is Greece
The Greek Villa

Christmas at Red Robin Cottage
The Village Christmas Party

SUE ROBERTS

Not
My Greek
Wedding

bookouture

Published by Bookouture in 2025

An imprint of Storyfire Ltd.
Carmelite House
50 Victoria Embankment
London EC4Y 0DZ

www.bookouture.com

The authorised representative in the EEA is Hachette Ireland
8 Castlecourt Centre
Dublin 15 D15 XTP3
Ireland
(email: info@hbgi.ie)

Copyright © Sue Roberts, 2025

Sue Roberts has asserted her right to be identified
as the author of this work.

All rights reserved. No part of this publication may be reproduced, stored in any retrieval system, or transmitted, in any form or by any means, electronic, mechanical, photocopying, recording or otherwise, without the prior written permission of the publishers.

ISBN: 978-1-83618-934-3
eBook ISBN: 978-1-83618-932-9

This book is a work of fiction. Names, characters, businesses, organizations, places and events other than those clearly in the public domain, are either the product of the author's imagination or are used fictitiously. Any resemblance to actual persons, living or dead, events or locales is entirely coincidental.

PROLOGUE

I turn the invitation over in my hand for the umpteenth time as my mind drifts to the prospect of spending time on the idyllic island of Santorini.

It arrived in the post last week, the thick, white embossed card adorned with gold lettering, that suggests a no-expense-spared wedding. I think it is so much nicer to receive an invitation through the post rather than one delivered by email, although I guess a good friend would always post a handwritten invitation.

The wedding invitation is from my oldest friend, Tasha, and the plus-one invite makes my heart sink for a second, as I have no significant other in my life right now. I do have someone in mind who will hopefully be able to join me though.

I'm thrilled for my best friend, I really am, and I am so looking forward to seeing her marry her best friend, Owen. It may sound a little selfish of me, but I hope I am not surrounded by too many loved-up couples while my own heart is still healing.

Santorini though! I had better get browsing some out-of-season sales for an outfit given my current, not so great, financial situation. And you never know, I might be gifted an outfit from a clothing retailer – as I often am – that might be suitable for a wedding. In return I can promote it on my ever-growing TikTok account.

I must start planning something soon, as the wedding is only a month away and time seems to be racing by. If I'm honest, I am not sure why that is as I find myself with a lot more time on my hands these days. At least I now have something marked on the calendar that I can look forward to though. The opportunity for a holiday in Greece and a chance to have a catch-up with my oldest friend is something I am truly grateful for.

ONE

'Mia, would you mind bringing that washing in, love, it looks like it might rain.'

My gran is calling me from the lounge, as I have just finished uploading a video in her guest bedroom.

My last recording of my trip to Ibiza has been popular with my followers, having already chalked up almost a million views in the last week. If only I had that many actual followers.

'Will do,' I call through to the lounge, before heading outside to the garden of Gran's ground-floor flat.

I spend my spare time here, which I have quite a bit of lately, having recently been made redundant. My gran is not too good on her feet, so a couple of carers pop in during the day, along with me and Mum. Admittedly, I am probably here more than Mum, who works part-time but still calls in regularly.

My gran jokes that she hopes I will still come and see her when I am rich and famous, and I reassure her that I will. And while I hope that it will happen one day, I think I am still quite a way from that. But you never know.

Just lately I have lost count of the number of freebies I have received from small businesses, all eager for me to endorse their brands on my page. I have been gifted all manner of things, including gym wear that I practically live in, along with skincare products and even the occasional household item. It isn't really a job as such, at least not at the moment, as I am not paid an actual salary from it. Or from any other employer right now.

I find budget flights and hotels, sometimes only staying in the sunny locations featured on my videos for little more than a couple of days, but my followers do not need to know that. Even the budget hotels will have to be given a miss for a while though, as I save every penny I can for the forthcoming wedding.

I really want to inspire my followers to follow their dreams, even though my own haven't quite come to fruition, but I believe they will do one day. I have been known to do a bit of singing in the past, and it is something I am keen to pick up in the future. You never know, I may even release my singing voice to my followers and the rest of the world, but only when I feel the time is right.

I think of the photo of my toned, white bikini-clad body on a long stretch of beach in Ibiza's San Antonio, my long copper hair cascading down my back that I shared with my followers. That was before I scooped up my towel, and headed back to my apartment, having avoided the hefty sunbed charge.

Fake it until you make it, isn't that what they say? Hopefully one day there will be VIP party invitations with real champagne, instead of supermarket own-brand Prosecco that leaves me with a slightly furry tongue. And okay, maybe I don't have as many followers as those who have hundreds of thousands – millions even – but I try not to let that get me down. What is meant for me will appear in the fullness of time. At least I hope it will. Maybe then I won't need to rely on Gran's generosity, or her company quite so much.

'Oh, and, Mia,' says Gran as I bring in the washing. 'Would

you mind emptying the kitchen bin and putting it outside? The binmen are due tomorrow.'

'Of course, Gran,' I say as her voice pulls me out of my daydream. I snap on some rubber gloves and head towards the pedal bin to remove its contents. If only my followers could see me now!

TWO

I am enjoying a latte in town with my friend Lulu – Louise, but Lulu has been her family name since childhood apparently– who is still working in the place I have recently left. Or should I say been let go from. Surplus to requirements. Redundant. No longer needed.

'It could be worse,' said Lulu, sipping her enormous hot chocolate, dotted with marshmallows.

I'd taken a photo of both of our drinks at this new café that I will upload later to my Instagram account, along with the food we have ordered, and give a little review. 'At least you don't have to buy clothes with all those freebies you get,' she reminds me. 'Or skincare, and that costs a fortune. Or food, as you still live at home and—'

'Yeah, okay, Lu, I get the picture. It could be worse. It just feels a bit weird not having a routine.' I shrug.

I had worked for a fashion catalogue on the mail-order telephone line for four years, when the department announced cuts. Most people had been there far longer than I had, it being the kind of place you never really left, given its proximity to the train station and being surrounded by shops and cafés. I guess I should never have thought of it as a job for life, especially with my vague aspirations to be famous in some way. Even so, my redundancy left me feeling a little panicked at the thought of not having a regular income. Two other newish starters and I had been given the chop as more people continued to order online these days, directly from the warehouse.

With the modest amount of redundancy pay I received I booked another little jaunt, even though I can hear my dad's voice in my ears making no secret of the fact that he thinks I am being irresponsible.

'You should be looking for a proper job instead of going away again, and uploading videos on that internet. That is never going to earn you a decent wage,' he had told me for the umpteenth time.

'Tell that to all the presenters who have become famous after building up a large following, or appearing on reality shows such as *Love Island*,' I'd informed him, but he remained unconvinced.

'Aye, but they are a handful to the millions out there who are trying. It's a bit like becoming a Premiership footballer,' he'd said, in between mouthfuls of a full English breakfast one Sunday morning. 'Even out of all those that go through the footballing academies, only a handful of them make it. I watched a documentary about it.'

He was right, of course, but being a social media influencer is not quite the same thing. Yes, it takes hard work and commitment, but also a certain amount of good fortune. That one post going viral could make the difference between obscurity and recognition. There are makers and bakers out there uploading videos of their food, as well as people posting pictures of their kids, animals, and exercise routines. Some of the ordinary stuff has catapulted people into the realms of celebrity status. Take Joe Wicks and his exercise videos that got us all through lockdown, for example.

'And I don't know why you don't get back into your singing,' Dad had advised. 'Maybe you ought to audition for one of those reality shows you seem to enjoy watching.'

'I agree,' said Mum as she sipped her tea. 'You have always had a lovely voice. *Britain's Got Talent* would be a good show to go on.'

'Hmm maybe, but there is a lot of stiff competition on those shows, I'm not sure I would be good enough.' I shrugged, feeling apprehensive at the thought.

'You're a damn sight better than some of those singers on the radio that sound like a strangled cat when they have to perform live,' said Dad, helping himself to another slice of toast. 'I needed earplugs watching half of them on TV performing at Glastonbury.'

'Well maybe it's only a few singers who make it big, just like those footballers,' I told Dad, wishing I could just focus on one thing.

'You won't know unless you try,' said Dad. 'Besides, you don't actually need to be famous to earn a living as a singer, do you?' he reasoned. 'And as you seem to post all kinds of different things, it beats me why you don't show some footage of you singing,' he said, not for the first time.

Perhaps he has a point, and I did attend a performing arts college for a couple of years after all, even earning some money singing at pubs and occasionally weddings, that sort of thing. For some reason though, I don't really have the confidence to show myself singing online.

Maybe I would not like the criticism, even though some of my posts already attract negative comments anyway. One bikini shot had someone tell me I needed to put some weight on, which I absolutely do not. It prompted a whole online discussion about body shaming. I guess everyone is going to have an opinion and you need to be thick-skinned to accept that.

Perhaps I ought to invest in a microphone and head off to

the city centre and do some busking, instead of booking a holiday. But I just have this feeling that one day I will be successful, maybe even famous, and perhaps then I will reprise my singing career. Maybe Dad's right in saying real success as a social media influencer does only happen to a handful of people. But I am determined to make sure that by working hard enough, I will become one of that handful.

I had been considering Dad's comments, thinking that maybe I should not be going away again, at least until I have secured a new job, when the wedding invitation arrived.

My old high school friend Tasha, now living in Australia, has decided to have her wedding in Santorini so that her family and friends, including some who live in other European destinations, are able to attend.

Tasha always possessed the focus that I lacked, determined that she would make something of her life, even if it meant moving away from her family and friends. I can't imagine being that far away from my own family, especially my gran, who relies on me quite a bit, but maybe I would have to rethink that, if fame and fortune came calling.

Tasha will be marrying Owen, a successful property developer, and they are footing the cost of an apartment, having rented out a whole block. Not in Fira exactly, the most photographed place in Santorini, but in Perissa a twenty-minute drive away. All I will need to pay for are my flights, and a wedding gift as my gran has already insisted on giving me some spending money, with the words 'Who else can I spend my money on?' And 'You do enough for me.'

Finishing our coffees, we head into town so Lulu can buy herself some new trainers, and I need to look for a new bikini.

Lulu and I became friends when Lulu – who is almost twelve years older than my twenty-eight years – took me under her wing when I started working on the catalogue phone line. She patiently trained me, and laughed when my hand would fly to my mouth, mortified after accidentally cutting someone off in the middle of a call, insisting that I would get the hang of it. And I did get the hang of it, and enjoyed every minute of my job that I stayed in for four years.

I'm sad not to be working there anymore, but then I believe everything happens for a reason. Maybe I am destined for bigger and better things.

'I wish I was coming with you,' says Lulu as we walk. 'Santorini looks heavenly, if all those travel programmes are anything to go by.'

'So come,' I urge her. 'You can be my plus-one, I've already told you that,' I remind her.

'I know, but I don't have any holidays left until my new annual leave starts in December.' She sighs. It's currently early June.

'I'm sure you could take a few days. I'm flying out Thursday, but maybe you could get a flight Friday, take an early finish from work? Surely Phil would agree to that? He might even let you take a day or two from next year's holidays to add on to the weekend?' I suggest.

I know that Phil the manager has a soft spot for Lulu, although she doesn't appear to notice.

'I suppose I could ask. Maybe stay for four or five days, including the weekend. That sounds good,' she muses. 'Ooh Santorini. Imagine all that sunshine.' She sighs, looking up at a distinctly dull sky.

'Yes! Oh, Lulu, it will be a lot of fun. And you deserve a break.' I loop my arm through hers, her shoulder-length curly brown hair bouncing as we walk. Lulu is one of those effortlessly stylish people, and today she is rocking a long black dress, with a bright-green blazer thrown over. I am wearing tight gym wear, with a black body warmer over the top, a gift from a local supplier in exchange for an online review.

'That I can't argue with,' she replies with a wide smile.

Lulu had her children young and, by the sound of things, still runs around after her offsprings, who don't seem to lift a finger. He husband buggered off two years ago with a woman he met at the gym after he turned forty and decided he wanted to get in shape.

Heading into a busy department store, I linger at the perfume counter, giving myself a little sample spray. The prices of some of the scents on sale are eye-watering, and I think of the copies I get sent through the post and endorse on my page. They cost a fraction of the price and are pretty good, although the scent can wear off quickly.

A gorgeous bloke in a smart blue suit is looking at the men's colognes, and I toss my long hair over my shoulder. He gives me a little smile, before he is joined by his girlfriend, who kisses him on the cheek. Oh well. I don't suppose the men's cologne counter is a place to flirt with someone anyway. Santorini on the other hand...

'What do you think of this colour?' asks Lulu, showing me a rust-coloured eyeshadow.

'Nice. It will bring out the colour of your eyes.'

'I don't have orange eyes. I'm not the Gruffalo.'

'It isn't orange.' I laugh loudly.

Lulu has light brown, almost amber-coloured eyes.

Heading to the clothes department upstairs, I take advantage of a sale, and buy a turquoise-coloured bikini and sarong set. And I simply can't resist a shorts playsuit in white, especially as it has a thirty per cent discount. I snap some photos to show my followers and will do a little voiceover later, before doing a walk around the shop, showing them some more discounted items.

'Right, are we done then?' asks Lulu when we step outside. It was raining earlier but the sun has come out now, which has pretty much been the same every single day of the summer thus far. Typical British weather that I can't wait to get away from, and only two weeks to go!

'Yep, I'm done. And don't forget to ask Phil in the morning about those days off,' I remind her, before we hug each other goodbye.

'Oh, don't you worry, it will be the first thing I do. I will let you know as soon as I find out.'

We go our separate ways, as Lulu is collecting her daughter from a bottomless brunch date, who, by the sound of her call a short time ago, is a little the worse for wear.

I am catching the number nine bus in the opposite direction to see my gran.

I hear a notification on my phone and open it to find my brother Lewis has sent me a picture of himself and some pals during their downtime from army exercises, all wearing sunglasses and clutching beers, beneath a bright blue sky. I tap out a reply telling him how I will be doing the same at Tasha's wedding soon, and a tingle of excitement ripples through me.

Glancing out of the window at the grey sky, I can't wait to get home and try on my things, and dream of being in Santorini, but first I need to see my gran. It's another week until her podiatry appointment and her toenails need cutting. What a glamorous life I lead!

THREE

Ah, just look at that house, what I wouldn't give to live in a place like that.' I sigh.

I take in the white walls of the house on the television, with floor-to-ceiling windows overlooking a huge garden as I file my gran's toenails.

I could definitely live in a house like that. I would maybe need to employ a cleaner though, and perhaps a part-time nanny if I ever had a child. Possibly a personal trainer for that huge gym?

'Take it easy, love, you're filing my toenail, not my toes,' says Gran, pulling her foot away sharply.

'What? Oh gosh, sorry, Gran. I was miles away there.'

'You've always been a dreamer,' Gran says with a smile.

Maybe she's right. Well, I know she is. Perhaps the time has come for me to work towards an actual goal. Still it's fun to daydream, isn't it?

There are lots of 'wows' from presenter Abbey Clancy as she is shown around the luxurious celebrity home. The upper floor, accessed by a glass lift, is bigger than our family home.

'What would you do, rattling around in a place that size?'

Gran shakes her head. 'And it could do with a bit of colour, everything seems to be in black and white.'

'That's the fashion,' I tell her. 'With a bit of grey thrown in.'

'Hmm. Well, I think a lot of people's houses all look the same these days,' says Gran.

Gran certainly isn't afraid of colour. The red-leather sofa is adorned with brightly coloured cushions and displays of fake flowers are dotted about the lounge.

Family photos adorn a wall covered in pink wallpaper that has a slight sheen, including those of me and my brother Lewis, who is in the army and currently in Gibraltar. Gran worries about him all the time, but he stays in touch with us all, sending regular photos and updates. When he is home on leave, we all enjoy a huge Sunday roast, at my parent's house.

'Well, each to their own taste, I guess,' I say, and Gran gives a little, 'Hmmf.'

I would do anything to live in a house like the one on the TV, I think dreamily, as Abbey is led upstairs by the homeowner. I would have a huge walk-in wardrobe and a gigantic bathroom with a sunken bath. Maybe even a music studio, where I could sing to my heart's content and even try a little songwriting.

My bedroom in my parent's house is modest, to say the least, but the upside is that I don't have to pay an extortionate rent. I moved back home after leaving the rented flat I was sharing with my boyfriend after we split up. I loved that flat, with the large tree outside the bedroom window and the coffee shop on the corner, but there was no way I could afford the rent on my own, so that was that.

It felt weird returning home a year ago, and I cried for days in my old bedroom, clutching Bronte my childhood teddy bear to my chest every evening and swearing off men for life.

There was no cheating involved, but my ex just stopped trying. Truth be told, I think we both did. Our evenings going for beach walks or meeting up with friends at local eateries had been replaced by drinking wine at home and watching TV.

When I became excited by a forthcoming episode of a soap, I realised we were in a rut. I suggested we join a gym together or at least make more effort to see more of our couple friends and family, but I was met with a wall of silence.

It was clear that the relationship was beyond repair and the passion we had enjoyed at the beginning of the relationship had all but burned out. Perhaps I should have heeded Mum's words when she told me she thought we were rushing into things when we moved in together. And thinking about it, we never really had that much in common. I have always loved music and would listen to songs on the radio at home happily singing along to them, something I am sure my ex did not always appreciate.

Even so, I missed him when the inevitable split came, despite things having reached a natural conclusion. I guess three years is quite a long time to be with someone and I can't deny that a part of me felt mad that I had wasted my time in a relationship that was destined to go nowhere.

I turn my attention back to my TV programme.

'*This* is your bathroom,' gasps Abbey as she is shown into a room complete with a jacuzzi, and the biggest shower I have ever seen in my life. You could fit a whole family in there. The celebrity opens a door to reveal a small swimming pool and Abbey's mouth falls open.

'Right, done,' I tell Gran as I put my nail file away.

'Ooh that's better, love, thank you,' she says as she wiggles her toes, before placing her feet back into her fur-lined slippers.

She reaches into her handbag and fishes out a twenty-pound note.

'Absolutely not,' I tell her, pushing it away. 'You have already given me some spends for Santorini, remember.'

Which I accepted reluctantly, but she insisted. And I will pay her back when I start work.

'I've told you,' She says with mild exasperation. 'Who else will I spend it on? Your mum and dad are okay financially, so is your brother, and with your current employment situation being what it is,' she says, reminding me that I am currently jobless and that I really ought to be searching for a job online. 'But it isn't just that,' she continues. 'I'd have paid more than twice that to have my toenails done privately and you are good to me.' She smiles fondly. 'I appreciate everything you do for me.'

I thank her then, and tuck the money into my bag. I don't use a lot of cash these days, but I have my eye on a little blue bag in the shopping precinct for my holiday, so I might buy that. It isn't leather, but you would never know as it's a good dupe.

'Right, I'm off.'

'Alright, love, and be careful crossing the roads, especially if you have those ear bugs in.'

'Earbuds, Gran.' I laugh.

'Yes, whatever. Those electric cars are quiet enough without you wearing earbuds. Make sure you use a crossing,' she advises.

'I always do, Gran, don't worry.'

I peck her on the cheek as the programme credits roll, and a clip is shown of the house Abbey is visiting in the next episode that could not be more different. The Victorian house has a lounge with bold-patterned wallpaper and a huge pink sofa. The room is dotted with large plants in copper pots.

'Now that's more like it,' says Gran, sipping her tea. 'See you soon, love.'

I head off home and fire up my laptop to browse some jobsites. Not before I look at some pictures of Santorini though, and sigh with pleasure at the bright blue skies and white buildings. I can't wait to be there rubbing oil onto my skin and lying on a beach, before heading off in the evening to sample the nightlife. And, of course, the wedding! Tasha will make the most beautiful bride and Owen is so handsome their wedding photos are bound to be just adorable.

Tasha and I were friends throughout high school, although we knew each other even earlier than that as we lived in the same street but went to different primary schools. As young kids we spent summers in and out of each other's gardens, playing in paddling pools when we were little, to enjoying family BBQs as we got older.

After studying interior design Tasha went on holiday to Australia, where she met her husband-to-be, Owen, a property developer. She stayed for a while and designed the interior of one of his building projects as love blossomed. After several long-haul flights back and forth, she eventually gained her visa.

We have had some great times over the years and a bucket load of memories to look back on in the future.

Breaking into my thoughts, as I am sitting daydreaming, Tasha video calls me.

'My friend! How are you?' I ask, thrilled to be looking at her face and speaking to her. 'I have literally just been thinking about you.' I smile.

'I'm great, thanks, getting a bit stressed about the wedding though,' she admits.

'That's only natural, isn't it?' I frown, hoping all is okay.

'It is, so everyone tells me. I don't know why I'm such a bag of nerves, I think it's just excitement,' she says.

'Definitely not cold feet then? Sorry, I must ask.'

'Oh gosh, no, Owen is an absolute dream. He's definitely the one.' Her face breaks into a wide dreamy grin, telling me everything I need to know. 'I'm just worried about everything being perfect. I think people's expectations of a Santorini wedding are going to be pretty sky high.'

Whenever we speak, I can detect more of an Australian accent in her voice.

'And I'm sure it will be perfect,' I reassure her. 'Especially with your attention to detail.'

'Yes, yes, of course.' She grins. 'And we haven't gone over the top, you know, there won't be peacocks wandering about the place or anything like that.'

'Oh, thank goodness, they freak me out a bit.' I laugh.

I find any type of bird a bit unnerving. I think it goes back to a wedding I once attended, where doves were released and one made a beeline for me like a cruise missile, before landing on my head. My ex joked that the hair fascinator I was wearing must have reminded it of a bird's nest.

'We have gone for understated glamour, white tablecloths, black napkins, lemon trees in planters,' she tells me. 'Oh, and an arch of cream roses at the entrance to the restaurant.'

'Sounds wonderful,' I tell her, imagining my gran saying that the place sounds like it could do with a splash of colour.

'I can't wait to see you, and it's so generous, footing the cost of the apartments,' I tell her gratefully.

It's actually a relief really, given my current financial situation.

'Oh, not at all.' She smiles. 'Owen insisted on it. We got a great deal from the hotel chain with it being a block booking. I'm so thrilled you can make it.' She says warmly.

They have also organised transport to take guests the short journey to Fira where they will marry at a luxurious hotel and where the wedding reception will also take place.

'I wouldn't miss it for the world,' I assure my oldest friend. 'I can't wait to see you get married.'

I met Owen a couple of years ago, when Tasha returned to the UK with him for a holiday. Even then I could see that they were made for each other. If I'm honest, the way they looked at each other made me realise that me and my ex never glanced at each other in such a way, apart from in the early stages of our relationship.

We chat for a while longer, and then I go back to perusing the jobs on a recruitment site.

There are a few admin posts including a doctor's receptionist, a post at a plumber's merchant and an assistant for a coffee shop in town. Coffee shops are so popular now I wonder whether I ought to train as a barista. Or maybe I could open an English tea shop, serving afternoon teas. Who am I kidding? I can just about afford a box of teabags never mind anything else!

Uploading my CV for the plumber's merchant job, I cross my fingers as I send it off. Not exactly my dream role, but the money is decent. I spot another one for a receptionist at a local hotel, so I apply for that too.

I head into my bedroom then, to photograph a load of clothes that I can sell on a clothing site. At least it will keep things ticking over, which means I won't need to delve into my modest redundancy fund too much.

I must resist the urge to buy more clothes. I have a ton of casual-wear freebies so I just need to find a dress to impress for the wedding. Maybe a white, off-the-shoulder number. On second thoughts, maybe not white for a wedding but whatever I choose, I want to look and feel good.

I take a final photo of a leather biker jacket that I no longer wear, and hope my haul sells for a good price, then I can buy myself something really special to wear for the wedding.

You just never know who you might meet in a place like Santorini…

FOUR

'I have been given the time off work so it looks like I am coming to Santorini with you,' Lulu squeals down the phone.

'Oh, my goodness! That is the best news ever.' I do a little fast running on the spot, something I always do when I am excited. My gran used to do it too, before her knees went.

'Me neither. I can't remember the last time I had a break away without the kids. Well, I say kids but I suppose they are adults now,' she says, speaking of her eighteen- and almost twenty-year-old offspring. 'Honestly though, you would think I had told them I was going away for a month.'

'I'm sure they will manage. It might even do them some good,' I suggest.

'You never know, although Chloe asked if I was going to leave some money for takeaways. As if!' She laughs. 'I told her I would stock the fridge and freezer and that her and Tom could cook for themselves, which didn't go down well,' she tells me. 'Even though they both know how to at least rustle up some pasta or a stir fry. Especially Tom, who is more than a decent cook. Would you believe Chloe actually sulked?'

'I'm sure she'll get over it,' I say light-heartedly.

I resist the urge to tell her that her 'kids' never think about her being alone when they are off with their friends to Glastonbury or wherever for the weekend, and that she deserves a break from skivvying after them. I recall her being on the phone to me one weekend, slightly the worse for wear, and telling me how selfish Tom was when he never texted her for days or answered his phone when he went on his first lads' holiday abroad. I might remind her of that at some point though, when her misplaced guilt will no doubt kick in when we are in Santorini.

'So what you up to today then?' she asks, having told me she is on her lunch break from work.

'Oh, you know, sifting through job offers, seeing what takes my fancy.' I wish.

'Something will turn up soon, I'm sure,' she says. 'I miss you here at work. We all do. Well, the few of us that remain that is. I have a feeling it won't be too long before we all go.' She sighs.

'I'm sure you will be fine, you have worked there for years. And I told you, Phil has a soft spot for you,' I tease.

After chatting to Lulu, I remember the photos of the food at the new café in town, so upload some photos with a little commentary to my TikTok account. I am delighted to see that my video of the sale in town has chalked up thousands of views and comments, some saying they will nip into the store for a browse.

With Mum and Dad at work and the house empty, I slip into a bikini and head out into the garden, made private with bamboo screens, and soak up some sun. It will probably be cloudy by this afternoon, so I must make the most of it.

Settling down onto the bed and feeling the sun caress my skin, I can't wait to be in Greece, listening to the sound of the waves lapping on the shore, instead of the noise of the bin wagon outside as it reverses around a corner. It really can't come quick enough.

FIVE

I am having Sunday lunch at Mum's, as one thing Mum has continued to do over the years is cook a roast, even though a lot of people go out for one these days. Gran is around and enjoying the food, but feeling bloated after a second helping of apple pie and is now sucking an indigestion tablet.

'I'll miss you when you're in Santorini,' she says as I clear the plates away.

'Ah, I'll miss you too, but it's only for just over a week, Gran,' I remind her.

'And I'll be popping in, don't forget,' my mum tells her.

'I know that, love.' She smiles at my mum. 'I think I just like the energy of young people, and hearing about what they get up to.' She smiles.

'Oh, so I'm boring now that I'm over fifty, am I?' Mum teases.

'Not at all, but you know what I mean.' Gran smiles again. 'It doesn't seem five minutes since I was that age, although the world is so different now. There are so many more opportunities these days,' she laments. 'And everyone seems to be off somewhere travelling, it all seems so exciting.' She sighs.

I suppose it's true. I can't imagine a world without technology, and of course travel, but I guess what you don't have you don't miss. Gran's tales of dance halls, love letters and strolls along the beach with my late grandad sound far more romantic than someone texting and arranging to meet up at Nando's.

Talk turns to football then, following a match on the telly, and Dad is grumbling about the England football team and suggesting they find a new manager.

'They should get that Harry Ramsden,' says Gran.

'What will he do, give them some fish? Build them up a bit?' I giggle. 'Besides, he's been dead for years.'

Gran frowns before she bursts out laughing. 'I mean Harry Redknapp, don't I? Oh Lord help us. Well, the fish man probably could have done a better job,' says Gran, never one to shy away from giving her honest opinion.

'Are you excited about Santorini?' asks Mum as we sip some tea. 'You know I have always fancied going to Greece.' She sighs.

'Have you?' Dad looks a little puzzled. 'I thought you loved Lanzarote?'

'Well, of course I do, you know that, but Greece does look dreamy. And I enjoyed your birthday meal at the Zeus taverna in town last year. The food was lovely.'

The blue and white interior with huge photos of Greek islands on the wall at the taverna, along with Greek music in the background, might make you feel as though you are on a little Greek island. Until you look outside at the pouring rain, that is. There really is no substitute for the real thing, I think to myself, imagining the hot sun washing over my body, cocktail in hand.

'Oh, and I forgot to mention, I have applied for a couple of jobs,' I tell everyone, but looking at Dad.

'Good to hear.' Dad nods. 'Oh, and Joe at the corner shop was saying that the Royal Oak is opening again soon. It has been sold and the new owner is keen to have live music, so you might get a couple of singing opportunities there,' suggests Dad.

'Maybe.' I shrug.

I know he's right really. More and more pubs are having live music nights and paying singers and bands, especially local talent. And the Royal Oak is a decent pub, so it might be something to consider.

It was at a pub gig that I met my ex. I could feel his eyes transfixed on me as I belted out a cover of a current chart hit. He approached me later, and bought me a drink, and that was that. For three years at least.

Before I know it, it's two days before I leave for Santorini and I am packing my suitcase. I carefully pack the gift I have bought, a beautiful wooden sculpture I found online of two friends embracing that I hope Tasha will love.

After I bought it though, I realised it wasn't really a present for Tasha and her husband-to-be if it represented our friendship, so I hurried out yesterday and bought a small, mosaic-framed mirror in bright colours that was an absolute steal from an antique shop. I have wrapped the mirror in goodness knows how many layers of bubble wrap, before placing it into my case.

Tasha and Owen are not having bridesmaids at their wedding, which I won't lie is kind of a relief as I like to choose my own clothes, although I would have gone along with whatever she chose for my bridesmaid's outfit, of course, as it is her special day.

Instead, I am to be her maid of honour, but as all preparations are in hand, I don't have the traditional role of actually arranging anything.

'So, you kind of don't have to do anything, other than sip champagne with me and keep me calm while I get ready,' she had told me when we chatted.

Tasha's mum passed away a year ago, and I know she will miss her presence, but luckily she has a close relationship with her dad. I've let her know that my friend Lulu will be my plus-one, and I just can't wait as I know the wedding will be a lot of fun.

I check my socials and the upload from the café has thousands of likes and people commenting that they didn't even know the place existed, which is really good and makes me feel like a real influencer. Last week, I reviewed a new Italian restaurant in town after being invited there. Two courses and a bottle of wine for free in exchange for a review.

I'm really excited that just recently restaurant freebies are starting to come my way as I enjoy dining out.

There's a new cocktail bar opening in town next month, and I would love to get my hands on an invitation for the opening night. Especially as it's rumoured that a hot dancer from a well-known Saturday evening show who has recently become single will be doing the opening. He's not currently on the dance show, but is now carving out a career as a presenter and frequently pops up on reality shows.

I'm putting the finishing touches to my packing, when Lulu calls.

'Hi, honey, just wondering do you have any mosquito spray?' she asks. 'I've been in work this morning and don't have time to nip out and get any now as I want to give the house a good going over. I think I might need a mask and a hazmat suit to enter Tom's bedroom though.'

'I have indeed,' I reassure her. 'And don't you think Tom is getting a bit old for the slobbish teenager routine?' I can't help asking as he is almost twenty years old.

'I know, but he's been a bit stressed lately. Not only has his girlfriend recently dumped him, but he isn't really enjoying his uni course.' She sighs.

I resist saying that I hope he tidied his bedroom before his girlfriend came around, also that he needs to grow up a bit and treat his mum with a bit of respect.

'Anyway, it will make me feel better if the place is all clean before I go away. Clean sheets on the bed ready to flop into after I return from a late flight.' She laughs.

'I agree with you about the clean bedding,' I tell her, thinking of how I like to do the same thing.

'Right I had better get on,' says Lulu. 'See you Friday, text me when you get to Santorini on Thursday.'

'Will do. It can't come quick enough,' I tell my friend, hoping that she can switch off and enjoy a well-earned break from everything. No one deserves it more.

SIX

Sipping a caramel latte at a Starbucks in the airport, I feel a tinge of excitement at the thought of soon being on the most photographed island in Greece. I can hardly wait to share it all with my followers.

Lulu is joining me tomorrow, so I'm travelling alone, although I am so looking forward to seeing her when she arrives and we can stretch out on a sunbed and really catch up before the wedding.

Checking through my socials, I see a guy has told me to 'sort my eyebrows out' which is unusual for a bloke to make such a comment. Not that any of that bothers me. I learned early on that if you want to make a career out of social media, then you must learn to ignore such remarks and grow a thick skin. If you can't, then as unfair as it is, you are maybe not cut out for it. We seem to live in a world where some people like to drag others down. At least from behind a keyboard.

Interestingly, there is no photo of the guy, who I politely thank for his comment and tell him I hope his inner trauma heals. (BTW my eyebrows are just fine. Not too thick and perfectly tinted. At least I think so. My gran would certainly have told me otherwise.)

'If you put yourself out there, then you are going to attract the opinions of a lot of people, some good some bad,' my gran told me the first time someone made a nasty comment. 'But as they are not the ones living your life or paying your bills, well stuff them,' she said, or maybe something a little less polite.

Sage advice indeed.

Checking my flight, I can see that it is on time, and soon enough I am climbing the stairs of the plane, before taking a selfie, wearing a straw fedora and sunglasses, even though it's cloudy and overcast.

I find myself seated next to a couple around my age, who smile, the woman engaging me in chit-chat for a few minutes before we take off. The bloke seems to be staring at me and I smile politely. After a few minutes, he asks me a question.

'Excuse me, but are you Mia from TikTok?'

OMG, am I being recognised?

'Yes.' I smile. Hardly able to believe that someone actually knows who I am.

'I thought it was, I love your travel videos.' He beams. 'Montenegro looks cool, I like the look of that climb up the Ladder of Kotor.'

'Thanks, oh that was fun, but maybe not in the height of summer. The scenery was stunning at the top though,' I tell him, recalling the beautiful forest all around.

His partner is glancing at us both, with what seems to be a forced smile.

'Oh, and the one in Dublin in that club.' He grins. 'You looked like you were having a ball.'

I remember that one too. I was wearing the skimpiest dress ever and was slightly the worse for wear after unlimited free Prosecco. There may even have been a glimpse of underwear when I slid off a bar stool. Definitely not my proudest moment.

That particular video was posted by a so-called friend at the time, and has since been deleted, along with the friendship.

The bloke is given a filthy look by his partner, before she plugs some earbuds in. He gives a little shrug before pulling a book from his bag, and that is the end of the conversation.

I was recognised though, with almost fifty thousand followers. Imagine what it would be like if I had a million followers. Maybe I would have to fight off paparazzi!

Later in the flight, the woman next to me seems to have softened, and offers me a boiled sweet that I politely decline.

We chat for a little while then, and she tells me she isn't really one for the internet and prefers to read books.

'He's always online though.' She nods to her partner, who is now the one wearing earbuds. 'I don't really know what he looks at half the time. Sorry if I was a bit off earlier,' she says sheepishly.

'It's fine, really.' I smile.

'It's just that, well, we have had a couple of trust issues in the past,' she reveals. 'I found out he was messaging someone online. Gosh, sorry you don't want to be hearing this.' She rolls her eyes.

'Honestly, it's fine. And I'm glad you came through it,' I say.

'We did thankfully and we're now coming up to our third anniversary,' she tells me.

Maybe him saying he recognised me from the internet dredged up bad memories for her.

'I think the fact that he recognised you just triggered something in me,' she says, confirming my suspicions. 'But if you can't trust each other, then what's the point? It was only an old school friend he was messaging anyway, and he swears that they were just catching up, and that nothing happened.'

And that is why I am happily single, I think to myself as I take a mirror from my bag and apply a little lipstick, even though my ex never cheated. Or maybe he did. He very quickly hooked up with someone else after things ended between us, as I recall.

Anyway, for now, I am quite happy working on my Insta and TikTok accounts, and maybe reprising my singing career sometime in the future.

Unless, of course, I just happen to meet someone who is meant to be in my life. I truly believe that everything that is meant to be will come along at just the right time. Until then, I am ready to just enjoy the ride and see what life throws at me!

SEVEN

Stepping off the plane is like walking into a hot oven and I squint at the bright sun, before popping my sunglasses on.

This is what it's all about, I think to myself, taking a quick selfie at the bottom of the plane stairs, the brilliant blue sky in the background in complete contrast to the grey sky on the journey out here.

A woman behind me tuts loudly, but I guess I did come to an abrupt stop at the end of the stairs, and she is balancing a baby on her hip, so I mumble an apology. Going on holiday with kids must be so stressful.

Santorini Airport is buzzing with excitement and I join the queue for passport control, along with the other passengers. In a short while though I will be stretched out on a sunlounger, sipping something ice cold, and the thought of it keeps me going as the queue continues at a snail's pace.

The scent of suntan lotion and perfume mingle in the air as I squeeze my way towards the baggage carousel to retrieve my suitcase.

Two women, maybe in their early sixties, are laughing loudly, one of them swirling a hand-held fan in front of her face.

She looks vaguely familiar, but I can't quite place her. Maybe she just has one of those faces.

I find myself wondering what their story is. Are they old or new friends? Are they happily married, or off escaping an unhappy marriage for a week in the sun? Perhaps they have become newly divorced or widowed and are kicking up their heels having the time of their lives?

I have always had a vivid imagination. In fact, my schoolteacher once told me that I had the potential to become an author, but maybe that was down to the creative excuses I would invent for not handing my homework in on time.

Retrieving my suitcase I head outside, where a driver is holding my name up on a board. I climb inside the white taxi and the air con blasts a welcome breeze all over me.

'Is it your first time in Santorini?' asks the amiable middle-aged driver as we head out of the airport.

'Yes, it is. I'm attending a wedding in Fira,' I tell him.

'Ah Fira.' He nods. 'A most beautiful place. Very popular with tourists.'

'I believe so, although if it's as pretty as it looks in the brochures I can understand why.'

We travel the rest of the journey in silence as I take in my surroundings, the quietness punctuated by an occasional comment from the driver, when he points out a place of interest. An olive oil factory here, a winery there and more than one church perched on a hill.

As the taxi driver negotiates bends and we climb higher, I am soon glancing down to a jumble of white buildings dotted with blue domes with the sparkling sea in the distance. As we descend the road and head to the village of Perissa, I can feel the excitement build in the pit of my stomach.

I had already paid for the taxi in advance, but I tip the driver when he unloads my hefty suitcase from the boot, and he thanks me warmly.

Standing outside the block of apartments that is literally across the road from a black sand beach, as most of the beaches are it being a volcanic island, I stand for a second and take in the view before I head inside.

Tasha and Owen will be staying in the hotel in Fira where the wedding is taking place, before heading off to a secluded island for a few days. I'm hoping I can take a few photos of the hotel that will look amazing on my social media platforms.

After being given the keys to my apartment, a white-painted room with pine furniture, I shower and change, then head out to a nearby bar and order myself a long, freezing cold beer and some halloumi fries. It's late afternoon, but I want to save my appetite for a delicious dinner later at one of the many restaurants that line the road.

I give Mum a quick call to tell her I have arrived, before I ring Lulu. Gran was shouting in the background that I must remember to use a high sun factor, what with my fair skin, and I promised her I will.

'I can't wait for you to get here tomorrow,' I tell Lulu, video calling and panning the phone around to show her my surroundings.

'Oh wow, me neither. I'm finishing at midday on Friday, but my flight won't land until about eight Greek time,' says Lulu.

'That's fine. We can have dinner and a glass of wine and watch the sun go down.'

'That sounds perfect.' She sighs with pleasure. 'Just the one glass though, we have a wedding to attend the following morning remember,' she says.

'Okay, Mum,' I tease.

'Gosh, sorry what am I like?' She laughs. 'I definitely need to get out more in the evening, I sound like an old-aged pensioner.'

'Saying that though, some of the pensioners who order stuff

from the catalogue are right party animals,' I remind her and she agrees.

I've lost count of the number of black dresses and sparkly jackets that were ordered on the phone line. They would tell me about their nights out, or forthcoming cruises, some of them in their eighties.

'Maybe I've become boring. Working and looking after a family tends to do that,' says Lulu. 'And my trips to the gym are hardly what you call exciting. I do the same exercises and chat to the same people. It's all a bit samey.'

'Then we need to something about that,' I tell her. 'And perhaps we could do something fun when you are here.'

'Sounds good.'

I am determined that Lulu will have a great time. She could probably have men queueing up to take her out if she gave out the right signals, but she does not give any hint that she is interested in a relationship, her confidence having taken a battering when her ex left.

'You're probably right. I am going to let my hair down. I might even chuck my mobile phone in my suitcase, and only check it in the evening,' she says.

'That's more like it,' I tell her, although I admit to finding that a bit unlikely. I guess it can be hard to step off a treadmill that you have been on for a long time, but if you can't relax on a Greek island, then you would struggle to do it anywhere.

As I arrive back at my apartment, a large group of people are checking in at reception and I wonder if any of them are wedding guests?

As I am about to head upstairs, I notice the two women from the airport sitting in the bar area sipping a drink. It finally dawns on me who the lady with the fan is, so I head over to say hello.

'Excuse me, but are you Tasha's aunt?' I ask her. She looks at me for a second, before recognition dawns.

'Oh, my goodness, it's Mia, isn't it? I haven't seen you in years,' she exclaims.

She places her fan on the table, before she stands and pulls me in for a hug.

Irene, Tasha's aunt, was a regular visitor to her house when we were growing up. I remember her when I was a teenager, slipping us a cheeky drink at family parties. She was always such fun.

'I'm surprised you recognised me as I've changed a bit,' she says. 'I've piled on the pounds, but I blame the menopause.' She chuckles. 'I was never able to lose the weight after that,' she tells me.

She introduces me to her cousin, Patsy, dark haired and thin, who looks around a similar age, so they are both part of Tasha's family, although I don't recall her at any of Tasha's family parties.

'So, who are you here with?' she asks, glancing around.

'I'm on my own for now, but my friend is joining me tomorrow, so will be here for the wedding,' I explain.

'How lovely.' She smiles. 'Oh, Mia, it is so nice to see you. Will you join us for a drink?'

'Of course I will.' I smile.

'I need something ice cold, although maybe not another beer or I will fall asleep. I'm sweating so much, my chins are like Niagara Falls,' she says and her cousin bursts out laughing.

'Chins? Oh, for goodness' sake, Irene.' Patsy rolls her eyes. 'We all put on a bit of weight at our time of life.'

'You haven't,' retorts Irene.

'No, but my bladder must have shrunk to the size of a peanut, given all the trips I make to the loo. Talking of which.'

She excuses herself before popping to the toilet.

Looking at Irene it's clear her appearance is a little different to the lady I last met over ten years ago, although she still has the most twinkling blue eyes that always had a look of mischief about them. She was married back then, and I wonder if she still is? No doubt I will find out during our time here.

Her cousin Patsy, just like Irene, is chatty and engaging and when she returns from the bathroom, the three of us chat away on an outdoor terrace like old friends.

Finishing our cooling drinks, we all agree on a siesta after the early morning flight, and arrange to meet in the hotel lobby at seven thirty and head out somewhere for dinner together.

I'm lying on the bed, where I quickly upload the photo of me at the foot of the plane steps with the sun in the background, to my socials. I then text Tasha to tell her I am here, when a second later she calls.

'Tasha, hi! How are the nerves holding up?' I ask my friend.

'Not bad, thanks, although I haven't been able to eat a thing,' she admits. 'How are the apartments?'

'Oh, really comfortable. And my room has a sea view, I'm thrilled, thank you so much,' I say gratefully.

I had taken a selfie of me, a strip of sea in the background and the black sand beach, earlier from my balcony, so I send it to her.

'Amazing! I'm so pleased it's okay.'

'It's more than okay, thank you. Oh, and I've just bumped into Irene in the reception area.'

'Oh great, I'm going to give Irene a call after I've spoken to you.'

'It was so lovely to meet her after all these years. I met Patsy too. We had a drink together and are meeting for dinner tonight,' I tell her. 'It brought back so many memories of us as teenagers, when we chatted,' I say, a smile crossing my face.

'Ah how nice. I love Irene, and Patsy too. I'm so glad Irene could make it as she hasn't been too well lately,' Tasha reveals.

'I'm sorry to hear that,' I say. 'Although she looked really well, if struggling a bit in this heat.'

'She never did like it being too warm, which makes it so special that she has come out here for the wedding.'

'Anyway, you had better call her soon as she said something about a siesta before we go out for dinner,' I advise her.

'That sounds lovely. I wish I was coming with you.' She sighs. 'But I have a meeting with the photographer later.'

'Don't worry, we will have lots of time to catch up as you prepare for the wedding. Oh, it's all going to be wonderful. Santorini is just the most perfect place to get married.' I sigh.

'I know. Right, I'd better make that call to Irene. See you tomorrow.'

'Bye, Tash, see you tomorrow.'

'I think we are pretty spoilt for choice here,' I say as Irene, Patsy and I stroll along the main street.

It's just after eight, and the beachfront is full of people out for the evening. Shops displaying all manner of gifts, including the traditional blue and white colours of Greece, sit alongside restaurants offering mouth-watering food, including lamb kleftiko and fresh fish dishes.

We eventually settle on the Acropolis restaurant overlooking a quiet stretch of beach.

'I'll sleep well tonight,' says Irene as we flop down onto some comfy chairs, the restaurant being a good walk away from the apartments.

'You will be fine, you had a siesta,' Patsy reminds her as a waiter appears with a menu.

'So tell me what you have been up to all these years?' Irene asks as we order a drink and Patsy lights up a vape.

'Filthy habit,' she apologises, 'but it's got me off the real thing.'

'Not an awful lot to tell really,' I admit. 'I lived with

someone for a while, but am currently single and living with my parents. Oh, and I have recently been made redundant.'

I might as well get it all out there now.

'Oh, never mind, love, you're young,' says Irene positively. 'Something will turn up soon, I'm sure.'

I tell her a little about my social media, but as I speak I realise how uncertain the future seems. My father's words pop into my head once more, asking me why I don't concentrate on my singing, which of course I will do, eventually. I just really want to make a go of my social media. If other people can succeed, why can't I? I do feel a little guilty over the sacrifices my parents made to pay for my singing lessons, but it is definitely something I will return to.

'Things will work out,' says Patsy as she puts her vape away. 'I had no clue about what I wanted to do when I was young. I eventually became a dressmaker,' she reveals. 'Anyway, let's get something to eat, I'm starved.'

We opt for a shared meze and dine on the most delicious selection of food, that includes lamb skewers, meatballs, some assorted dips and pitta bread. The lamb is melt-in-the-mouth tender, the bread soft and the salad crunchy and delicious.

Overlooking the black sand beach, we watch the sun slowly begin to drop as the sky turns darker.

'It's so lovely here, isn't it?' I sigh, sipping some chilled white wine and glancing around. The gentle sound of the rolling sea can be heard from across the road and I feel myself begin to relax.

A waiter catches my eye as he walks past, and gives me a lingering glance before smiling. I congratulate myself then on having made a bit of an effort this evening.

'Oh, it is. So romantic too. Not that I am interested in that sort of thing anymore,' says Irene firmly.

I am about to ask her if she is still married, when the waiter returns with a shot of ouzo for us all.

'Cheers, everyone,' says Patsy, raising her tiny glass.

I'm not the biggest fan of ouzo, but raise my glass too.

'Cheers,' I say, before knocking back the aniseed-tasting liquid and grimacing slightly.

I think about Irene's comment before we call it a night, and how she said that something will turn up for me soon on the job front. I hope so to, but for now, I am going to enjoy every second of my time here in Greece.

EIGHT

The following morning there are hugs and squeals all round, as Owen and Tasha arrive in the village to have breakfast with their other wedding guests and make sure they are happy with their accommodation. As Owen chats to someone, Irene mentions a hen party to Tasha.

'Surely you must have thought about it?'

We are sitting at tables in the Sea Breeze restaurant across the road, filling up several tables as waiters dash around.

'Oh, Irene, I did think about it, but never really got around to arranging one,' says Tasha.

'I don't mean anything fancy, and definitely no strippers.' Irene chuckles. 'I was thinking the four of us could go for a nice meal this evening?'

'Maybe I ought to have arranged something,' I say. 'Sorry for being the most rubbish maid of honour.'

'Don't be silly. You being here for the wedding is more than enough, believe me,' says Tasha kindly. 'I don't want to risk a hangover with the wedding being tomorrow, but perhaps we could have an early dinner,' she muses. 'In fact, yes that would be really lovely.'

'We could have a nice meal and a mocktail or two?' suggests Irene.

'Then how can I refuse,' Tasha replies with a wide smile. 'I kind of did have one back home, but I would love to spend the evening before my wedding with my favourite aunts and my oldest friend,' she says fondly.

'Then it's settled,' says Irene. 'An early meal, and a little drink. We must toast your future.'

'Brilliant,' says Tasha. 'I look forward to it, although we did book a couples massage in the hotel, so I hope Owen won't mind,' she says a little uncertainly.

'I'm sure he will understand. And traditionally you are not really supposed to see the groom the night before the wedding,' says Irene.

'I know, but as we are sharing a room, that isn't likely to happen,' she reminds her. 'And as we have lived together for several years, I'm not sure tradition really applies. I'm hardly going to be the blushing bride,' she says, with a peal of laughter.

'But it's bad luck. If you see your groom the night before the wedding you will have ugly children,' says Irene, and I burst out laughing.

'Irene. You can't say that,' says a shocked Patsy, shaking her head. 'And I'm pretty sure you made that one up.'

'Well, I might have.' She chuckles. 'Although, I swear I read it somewhere.' She frowns in thought.

'Luckily, I don't hold with all that superstition then,' says Tasha good-naturedly.

When Irene takes Owen to one side to ask if he minds if we steal Tasha this evening, I overhear him confess to her that he is not really fond of massages, but went along with it for Tasha.

'And don't worry, we will make sure we are all fit for tomorrow, including Tasha,' Irene reassures him.

A taxi has been ordered to take the four of us to Tasha and Owen's hotel tomorrow morning at eleven. One or two guests, including Tasha's dad and his new girlfriend, are staying at the wedding hotel too.

Tasha did give people the option to stay at the hotel under their own expense, but was generous enough to book the apartments free of charge, which many guests have taken her up on. Last night, Irene confessed she didn't think she could have afforded the prices at the 'posh' hotel, and was grateful for the offer of the apartment stay.

'I had to cut my hours down at work,' she had confessed as we sipped ice-cold beer at the restaurant on the black beach the previous evening. 'I've got a dodgy back and recently been told I am heading for type 2 diabetes,' she tells me, and I recall Tasha saying that she hadn't been well lately.

'Oh, I'm sorry to hear that. Has the doctor given you any advice?' I had asked.

'My doctor just told me to lose weight, which is easier said than done.' She had sighed. 'But after this wedding, I'm going to try hard to do something about it. Being here in this heat has made me realise that.' She had said told me with conviction.

'Ooh we will have to make sure we keep hydrated. Says Patsy as we finish our breakfast and she consults her weather app, 'There is meant to be a heatwave starting tomorrow. It might be reaching forty degrees, but at least everywhere indoor has air conditioning, thank goodness.'

'A heatwave? Dear Lord, as if it isn't hot enough,' moans Irene. 'Even my eyelids are sweating.'

'You'll be fine 'I assure her. 'As long as you always have a bottle of water with you, as we all will,'

I had taken a picture of our delicious breakfast that included fruits, yoghurts, pastries and granola, along with a photo of the black sand beach, its blue and white umbrellas flapping gently in the breeze and quickly posted it to my socials.

It's so beautiful here. I think of how fortunate I am to be at my childhood friend's wedding. I fleetingly wonder if I will ever marry and, if I do, would it be in a place like this? Or maybe an English country mansion, with grounds sloping down to a river.

Gran doesn't think it matters where you marry, and maybe she has a point. Her and Grandad married in a registry office, and were happily wed for over forty years before he passed. She thinks huge weddings are all for show, and has been to known to say, 'The bigger the wedding, the quicker the divorce.' Which is probably a bit unfair, although several people I know who have had the fancy nuptials are, in fact, now separated.

An hour later the groups disperse and head off to enjoy their day. I give Tasha a hug and tell her I will see her this evening.

It seems many of the guests are staying here for a week to enjoy a holiday before and after the wedding, thanks to Owen and Tasha footing the bill for the apartments.

'So tell us about your social media stuff,' says Irene as we stay at the café and order another coffee. 'Is there any money to be made from that?' she asks, before resisting a croissant on a nearby plate.

I tell her a little bit about it, before a waiter appears and asks if we have finished with our food.

'Take it,' says Irene, pushing the remains of breakfast away. 'Or I'll eat the lot.' She laughs.

After settling the bill, Irene and Patsy opt to read on the beach beneath an umbrella, so I take myself for a little walk around the village before the sun reaches its height.

Heading towards the edge of the main street, I spot a car hire place that is offering incredibly cheap hire rates, and I negotiate a great deal for a car, before calling Lulu and telling her I will collect her from the airport in the morning rather than her take a taxi. She had messaged me earlier, apologising that she was taking a later flight than the planned two p.m. one after an incident at home – which she said she would fill me in on later – and wouldn't now be arriving until early tomorrow morning. I didn't mind, though it's just a shame she will miss Tasha's impromptu hen evening.

'What? Are you absolutely sure you don't mind picking me up?'

'Positive.'

'Then, thanks. Have you ever driven abroad though?' she asks me doubtfully.

'Actually, yes,' I tell her, recalling a holiday with my boyfriend, who had one too many drinks one evening, and I drove us home in the darkness. It was a mountain village in Spain, and I was terrified. I don't tell her that though. Besides, it will be broad daylight by the time I collect her.

I drive slowly along the beach road, getting accustomed to the car, and stopping here and there to take a photo of a boat, or a pretty stretch of beach where I take a selfie.

Driving to the far end of the road, I park up and walk to the white church with the rugged mountains in the background. The door is locked, but I take a photo of the exterior.

The church is so tiny I imagine you would not be able to fit many guests inside. I can see myself getting married somewhere like that, if I did marry, as I don't have a large family, or an awful lot of friends. Not that my social media following would give any clue to that, I think to myself.

I climb into my hire car and drive the short distance to the apartments, where I park the car at the rear of the building. I take a shower and upload some more photos to my social media, before I get myself ready for the evening.

'Welcome, ladies,' says the elderly Greek man who guides us to our table inside the stylish restaurant set with white-cotton tablecloths. Despite the smart interior, the food prices are reasonable, if the menu on the board outside is anything to go by. I reserved a table earlier in case it got busy, and as we step inside I am enticed by the tantalising smell coming from the kitchen.

We enjoy a delicious meal of creamy moussaka for Irene and Patsy, while Tasha and I opt for a slow-cooked casserole, bursting with chunks of tasty chicken and peppers and topped with feta cheese. We also enjoy a couple of delicious fruity mocktails, although we do have one glass of wine with our meal.

Our meal is finished off with some tasty baklava as we sit around chatting, enjoying the spectacular sea view.

'Oh, Tasha, you really couldn't have picked a nicer place to get married,' I tell my friend, taking in our surroundings. 'I am in love with Santorini already, and I haven't even seen half of it yet.'

'I thought it would be somewhere most people would enjoy.' She smiles. 'Not to mention it being a little closer than Australia! Greece is a very popular destination and I'm thrilled that so many people have made the journey here for the wedding,' she says gratefully.

We have a wonderful evening, laughing and sharing memories, and all too soon it's time to head off as Owen arrives to collect Tasha.

'Owen!' she says in surprise. 'What are you doing here? I was about to call a taxi.'

'I didn't have anything to drink, so thought I would come and collect you. I sent Irene a text earlier to keep you here until I arrived.' He smiles.

'Good job she wasn't covering a stripper in whipped cream then,' Irene says with a wink and Owen roars with laughter.

'Hmm. It seems a little tame around here for that sort of thing,' he says, glancing about.

'And it's a good job you are not superstitious, seeing the bride before the wedding,' says Irene. 'Or you might risk having—'

'Oh, shut up, Irene,' says Patsy, cutting her off and I can't help but laugh.

On the way back to the apartments, after saying goodnight to Owen and Tasha, I decide to take a few photos on the beach.

'You two go on ahead if you like,' I tell Patsy and Irene.

'As if we would leave you,' says Irene. 'Come on, I'll take your photos if you like as I don't suppose you would want me in them.'

'Or me,' adds Patsy. 'You don't want us oldies ruining your image.' She laughs.

'Don't be silly.' I smile, although truthfully, I probably wouldn't add a family photo onto my TikTok account. I would store that in my personal photo album and maybe share it on Facebook.

There is a huge, flat rock near the water's edge and I perch myself on it, my hair blowing in a gentle breeze as Irene snaps away.

A couple walk past holding hands, before stopping to kiss, clearly enjoying the romantic setting. The moon is out now, bathing the tips of the rolling waves in a silvery white glow. I suddenly feel a little bit foolish sitting here alone having my photo taken in the semi-darkness.

'Thanks, ladies. I will walk back with you now,' I say, sliding off the rock.

'If you're sure. I hope your photos are okay, love. I'm no David Bailey,' says Irene.

'Who's he?' I ask and Patsy rolls her eyes and laughs.

'Gosh, I feel ancient now,' she says. 'Although saying that, he was at his height in the nineteen eighties. I met him once, you know.'

'You never did,' gasps Irene.

'I did. I went to London on a weekend with college. He was

in a bar with two blokes. I asked him for his autograph and he was very polite as I recall,' she says wistfully.

'Do people still ask for autographs these days? Or do they ask for a selfie, and, if so, I wonder how often is it declined?' muses Irene.

'Goodness knows,' Patsy says with a grin. 'I can hardly believe that London trip was over forty years ago.'

'Good Lord, was it really?' gasps Irene. 'I think I need another drink.'

'I think you've had enough for one night,' says Patsy, linking arms with her.

'Don't be a party pooper, the night is young,' protests Irene, giggling.

'Which we most certainly are not,' says Patsy, which earns her a gentle shove on the arm. 'Okay, maybe we will have a nightcap at the hotel bar.'

They chuckle all the way back to the hotel, Irene giggling away and I get the feeling this holiday is going to be a whole lot of fun.

NINE

'Lulu!'

I squeeze my friend in a hug at the airport, just after seven thirty the following morning.

I'm so glad I didn't overindulge last night, as I feel fresh this morning, and ready for some breakfast.

'How are you?' I say, when we pull apart.

'Apart from shattered, I'm fine,' she says. 'I did manage a few hours' sleep on the plane, thankfully, but I still feel a bit rough. I bet I look a right sight.' She pulls a face.

Lulu with her curly hair, sunhat, and long white-linen dress looks as fresh as a daisy.

'You look great. Anyway, come on, let's get to the apartment, freshen up and I'll take you for breakfast before the car collects us to go to the hotel for the wedding. Ooh I can't wait,' I squeal excitedly.

'Lead the way,' says Lulu as we leave the airport terminal and head into the brilliant sunshine outside, even at this early hour.

'Oh wow, that's a bit different to back home,' says Lulu,

squinting up at the brilliant blue sky, before she puts on her sunglasses.

'Just a bit. In fact, it's even hotter than usual, a bit of a heatwave I'm told. Actually, let's have a selfie.'

We pose outside the hire car, and I will post to my followers later saying something about heading off in a car to explore the island.

Pulling away from the airport, we are soon on a road flanked by pastel-coloured hotels and villas, some with huge ferns and palms in the front gardens. We drive past early morning joggers, dog walkers and older couples enjoying a leisurely stroll before the sun really gets up.

I couldn't help noticing that one couple, maybe in their eighties, were holding hands as they strolled, and marvel at how people can find that kind of enduring love. Or maybe they have recently met on Tinder. Perhaps they are each other's first love who have hooked up again, following the death of their spouses. There goes that imagination of mine again!

'So what happened that you needed to get a later flight?' I ask Lulu as we drive.

She sighs. 'Phil gave me the afternoon off, so I was set for an earlier flight as you know, then Tom called me in a panic.'

'Oh no what happened?' I frown.

'He'd had an accident at work. A concrete slab fell on his hand,' she tells me.

'Ouch, sounds painful. Is he alright though?' I ask. Tom works part time around his university course, as a labourer on a building site, and despite health and safety regulations can be a bit accident prone.

'Oh fine, but I went to meet him in A and E and you know how long the wait can be these days.' She sighs. 'I decided to stay with him and take him home. Turns out his finger was broken, which is what he suspected. No nerve damage thankfully, which was what he was initially worried about as he couldn't feel anything in his fingers,' she tells me.

'Well that's a relief, I suppose.'

I hope Tom realises how lucky he is to have a caring mum like Lulu.

'I'm pleased he's okay.' I smile. 'And now you know that is the case, I hope you can relax and enjoy your time here.'

'Oh, I will do,' she assures me. 'This break is exactly what I need.'

Back at the apartment, while Lulu takes a quick shower, I text Patsy and ask if she and Irene are okay.

She texts me back saying they are downstairs and about to have a Bloody Mary as a 'hair of the dog'.

I suggest meeting in the lobby in half an hour, so we can all go out for breakfast together and she sends me a thumbs up emoji, alongside an angry face, which I am pretty sure she has sent in error. Surely, I am not such unpleasant company?

When Lulu is out of the shower, she fishes her phone from her bag that has been ringing, and begins chatting to Chloe. I can see a crease form in her forehead as she talks.

'I thought you were going to keep that in your bag,' I remind her.

'Oh, I know, and I will now.' She smiles.

'Is everything okay?' I ask.

'Oh yes, it was just Chloe asking me where something was at home.'

Give me strength.

'Anyway, maybe you ought to do the same. With your phone, I mean.' She laughs.

'Well, I would, but I need to take photos for my social media pages, you know that. I certainly won't be on it all the time though,' I reassure her, feeling a little stung by her remark.

'Me neither.' She smiles.

Surely taking a photo here and there is hardly the same as having grown-up children pestering you when you are meant to be having a well-earned break, is it? Although I refrain from saying this out loud.

Talk of phones soon disappears as we enjoy a breakfast at the Sea Breeze restaurant across the road that overlooks the sparkling sea, the morning sun gently dusting the water.

Greek yoghurts, honey, and an assortment of fruit and pastries jostle for space on the table, alongside jugs of fresh orange juice. Patsy and Irene are having a Bloody Mary with a celery stick poking out.

'A virgin one for me,' says Irene, raising her glass of tomato juice. 'I shouldn't have had that large ouzo as a nightcap last night,' she continues with a groan. 'I have the faintest of headaches this morning.'

'No one was forcing you,' Patsy reminds her. 'Although mine has no alcohol in it either. I'm saving myself for a glass of champagne at the wedding.'

'I will be fine,' says Irene, slathering a hunk of seeded brown bread with butter and honey. 'A bit of breakfast will sort me out.'

I ask a waiter to take a group photo of us, and I send it to Tasha before giving her a video call.

'Good morning, how are we?' I ask.

Tasha is having a coffee on the balcony. Owen has gone for a swim in the indoor pool, before having a Turkish shave, she tells me.

'I feel nervous, happy. Oh, I can't wait to see you all!' she says excitedly. 'And thank you for last night, it was just wonderful, and thanks to me abstaining from alcohol, I feel as fresh as a daisy,' she says.

I tell her we will be there before she knows it, and we all wave and I introduce her to Lulu before I end the call.

Irene is dabbing at her face with a tissue, as at nine o'clock the sun can already be felt.

'This must be the beginning of the bloomin' heatwave,' she says, pouring herself a glass of water. 'I'll have to make sure I have my fan with me, although I can't really have it whirring around during the marriage vows, can I?' She sighs.

'No, you can't,' says Patsy. 'There's a shop across the road that I'm sure sells some traditional fans, you will have to make do with one of those.'

'I guess so. Anyway, it's better having a wedding here than back home where you can't rely on the weather,' she says. 'It rained on my wedding day.'

'Isn't that mean to be good luck?' asks Lulu, helping herself to some yoghurt and fruit.

'So, they say,' agrees Irene. 'And I suppose we were happy together for almost forty years, even though, thinking about it, we never really had that much in common,' she muses.

'They do say opposites attract though,' says Patsy.

'I used to think about our old age, going on holidays, that sort of thing,' Irene continues. 'Malcolm didn't enjoy driving, so we thought we might do a couple of coach holidays, maybe even a cruise, but it wasn't to be,' she says, her eyes misting over. 'Malcolm died two years ago.'

'I'm so sorry,' says Lulu sheepishly. 'I didn't mean to dredge up memories for you.'

'Don't you worry.' She smiles. 'These things happen, don't they?' says Irene, a widow for over two years. 'And we did do a lot together during his lifetime, I'm sure he would have no regrets'.

'You're okay though, aren't you?' says Patsy. 'And we do enjoy our days out and weekends away, don't we?' she says, gently placing her hand over Irene's.

'That we do,' agrees Irene. 'I can spend as long as I want mooching around markets, something Malcolm hated. And watching soaps on television without him complaining or talking all the way through them,' she says, hiding her hurt with her usual humour.

'Who needs men, eh?' Patsy says laughing, just as two gorgeous-looking men in shorts and tight T-shirts walk past, and cast a glance our way and smile.

'Oh, I don't know,' I say, nudging Lulu as I watch them disappear out of sight along the strip of restaurants.

'Ah to be young again.' Irene sighs theatrically as she fires up her handheld fan, the air blowing her shoulder-length ash blonde bob. 'If I had my time over again, I would do things a little differently.'

'Would you?'

'I would have travelled abroad more,' she reflects as she sips her orange juice. 'Malcolm preferred to stay in England, as he wasn't a lover of the sun, although neither am I these days.' She laughs.

We settle the bill, and head to a gift shop across the road, where Irene purchases a cotton fan displaying the sights of Santorini to use later at the wedding.

As we walk, I take in the rugged mountains in the background, and the tip of the blue-domed church at the end of the main street. It's certainly pretty enough to have a wedding here, but I guess Fira just tops it for vista when it comes to stunning wedding photos. The far-reaching sea with the view, taking in the volcanic island known as the caldera in the middle, and the jumble of white buildings with steps leading down to the port, will all make for the most perfect wedding album.

Inside, we freshen up and change into our wedding outfits, and before we know it, a taxi has arrived to take us into Fira to see Tasha as she prepares for her wedding. The other guests will be arriving in a coach laid on later for the ceremony at two p.m., that will continue into the evening at the luxurious hotel.

'You look stunning,' says Lulu kindly, appraising my knee-length pale-green silk dress I bought in a sale from John Lewis. I have accessorised it with a silver necklace and I have a white blazer for this evening in case it turns a little cooler.

'So do you,' I tell Lulu, who looks effortlessly stylish in a pale-blue trouser suit.

Irene and Patsy are wearing pretty summer dresses, and Irene has a white, wide-brimmed hat, while Patsy's dark hair is clipped up into a stylish bun.

As the taxi winds along the roads, we once more take in the glorious scenery against the backdrop of a cloudless blue sky. The roar of a motorbike as it overtakes has Irene flinching, then smiling as she recalls riding pillion on a bike as a young woman with her first boyfriend.

'Oh, I thought I was the bee's knees, even though it was only a Kawasaki moped,' she tells us laughing. 'Still, the boy in question was the first person to get one in our street, so I was the envy of the local girls,' she recalls.

We drive through the village, with its throng of bars and restaurants, set against a rugged mountain landscape devoid of any greenery.

Restaurants, car hire places and shops – one with a full-sized straw donkey outside – line the roads before we head out onto the highway, where the rugged landscape is interspersed with sightings of white villas with pink bougainvillea climbing the walls.

Fields of grapevines stretch out ahead of us, the vines growing on the ground like a bush and Irene comments on this.

'They are wound around in crowns to secure them, due to the island being so windy,' I tell her knowledgably, a fact I learned from a Santorini travel guide I found in a charity shop.

Passing one of the iconic blue-domed churches makes me think of Tasha. Her and Owen originally thought of marrying in a church, but as neither of them are religious they opted for the hotel instead, which I guess is more genuine than wanting a church purely for the photographs.

I wonder how her nerves are holding up, although I imagine she will be doing just fine. As a child, Tasha was always the calm one, sensible even. She followed a career path to become an interior designer, certain from a young age that was what she wanted to do.

Even then she had an eye for design and would sit in our lounge flicking through magazines, commenting on the home interior pages, rather than the fashion and make-up as I did, so I guess it was always going to be her destiny.

Me? I flitted in and out of jobs, although really I wanted to be one of the celebrities on the glossy pages, envying the women having their hair and make-up done, and posing for photographs. I guess not much has changed really, other than my photos are for my own social media profile, rather than some high-end magazine. But who knows what the future holds?

TEN

We pull up outside the hotel that is slightly elevated and looks magnificent, even from the outside, with its flight of white steps and olive trees either side of the glass-door entrance.

The interior of the hotel lobby is just as impressive, with marble floors, and floor-to-ceiling windows. Stone-coloured sofas adorn the vast space, a sparkling chandelier at the centre of the ceiling. The whole place feels sumptuous, yet welcoming.

'Wow, this place is really something,' says Patsy, taking in the elegant surroundings. 'Pity we are not staying here, although it might have made a bit of a dent in my savings,' she admits.

'I like our little place,' says Irene. 'And I like our local across the road,' she says, referring to the Sea Breeze restaurant.

As we enter the lift, a tall Greek man of possibly around my age, or a few years older, steps inside and asks us which floor we are heading to, before pressing the correct button. I feel oddly self-conscious standing next to him, taking in his cologne which smells very expensive.

'Thanks,' I tell him as I step out of the lift followed by the others, and he mutters, 'My pleasure,' before delivering the most charming smile.

'Whew, he was a bit of a hottie,' says Irene. 'I nearly whipped my fan out.' She chuckles and we all laugh. Although she is absolutely right. A Greek Adonis, if ever there was one.

We tap on Tasha's door, and she lets out a little squeal when she opens it, before welcoming us inside.

The room is huge with two dusky-pink sofas, a table and chair in a seating area, and the hugest bed you have ever seen, adorned with an assortment of velour cushions.

'The honeymoon suite, not bad hey?' says Tasha, waving her arm around the room.

We stand at the window open-mouthed, taking in the view, as Tasha takes a bottle of champagne from the fridge, and cracks it open.

'It might even persuade me to get married again, if I could stay in a place like this,' says Patsy as she takes in the scenery, and Irene rolls her eyes.

Patsy was married for several years in the nineties, but divorced after deciding that she wasn't suited to marriage, she told me over dinner the other evening.

I must admit, it's the kind of place I hoped I might have got married in too. Especially during the early months of my relationship with my ex. I could never have imagined how things would turn sour between us, after that first flush of love. Maybe next time I will take things a little more slowly.

A few minutes later, a young woman called Eve arrives, who is Tasha's best friend since she has lived in Australia, and we hit it off immediately. Soon enough, the hair and make-up lady has arrived and we are all ensconced in the vast room, sipping champagne and swapping stories about Tasha.

'I'm glad girl friends don't have to give speeches like a best man does.' Tasha grimaces when I recount a particular drunken evening when she took a desperate wee in what she thought was a field, just as the security lights came on from a house. A dog came bounding towards us as she had her knickers around her ankles.

'Oh my gosh don't!' she says, her face reddening. 'And who has that much land, for goodness' sake, we weren't to know it was someone's actual garden.'

'I know.' I laugh. 'As I recall, the bloke was quite nice about it, amused even, it was his wife who was a bit frosty, which was hardly surprising. Especially when you fell over and your boob fell out of your dress and he copped an eyeful.'

'Stop!' She covers her ears with her hands as we all dissolve into fits of giggles.

'Right,' says Tasha, sounding serious. 'Two glasses of champagne are more than enough, I think, we need to crack on,' she says firmly, and the make-up lady agrees as she opens her vast toolbox of make-up.

We sip our drinks slowly, chatting and watching the transformation as Tasha, who is already pretty, is transformed into something stunning. After her make-up has been carefully applied, the make-up artist artfully sculpts her hair into a bun with soft curls, a few blonde tendrils framing her face, and I have to hold back a tear.

'Oh my,' says Irene, sniffing. 'You really are the most beautiful bride. Your mum would be so proud.' She stifles a sob as she crushes her in an embrace.

Half an hour later, we all refresh our own make-up and head downstairs to the hotel bar for a soft drink. As we were leaving, Tasha's dad entered the room, and after hellos and hugs all round, we left them to have their father and daughter time before the wedding. He had been in a dark place for a while following his wife's death, but has recently started dating.

'This place is something else. isn't it?' says Patsy, taking in the sumptuous décor in the bar area. White walls display tasteful art and the lounge areas have expensive-looking sofas draped around the room. One or two Greek gods even make an appearance, in the form of marble sculptures.

'It is. Everywhere you look there is something stunning to admire,' I agree.

Right on cue, the guy from the lift walks past with a young woman, and makes eye contact with me, before flashing that smile. He is wearing a cream jacket now, over the top of the dark shirt he was wearing earlier, and I can't help thinking that he is a bit full of himself, smiling at me like that when he is with his other half.

'You can say that again,' says Patsy, eyeing the undeniably attractive bloke and Irene tells her she ought to stop taking the HRT as it's making her sex mad.

'You must be joking,' protests Patsy. 'And chance would be a fine thing. I am merely admiring a young man's good looks,' she says. 'Besides, I don't think I would have the energy to get out of bed in the morning if I gave up my HRT,' she says, making me dread the eventual arrival of the menopause.

Owen is obviously ensconced somewhere with his male friends, as I haven't come across him yet. When I nip to the loo a few minutes later though, snapping photos of the gorgeous lobby en route, there he is striding towards me.

'Mia,' he says, greeting me with a kiss on both cheeks. 'How are you?' he asks with a beaming smile.

'I'm good, thanks, and so excited to be here. Hope you didn't mind us stealing Tasha away last night.'

'Not at all. We ended up having a bit of a boys' night, although I never had a real drink until I had collected Tasha. It ended up being a bit of a late one, although I was sensible.'

He introduces me to his friend Bryn, a tall, fair-haired bloke who shakes me warmly by the hand.

'So how are the nerves holding up?' I ask Owen.

'Good, good.' He grins. 'I think I feel more excited than

anything, although I am a bit worried about fluffing my vows.' He pulls a face. 'Sometimes I think we should have just eloped.'

'I bet everyone worries about that,' I reassure him. 'I'm sure you will be just fine.'

'As long as he doesn't cry,' says Bryn. 'You are a bit of a crier, aren't you?' He laughs, and Owen looks mortified.

'Not really, well, yes, maybe sometimes.' He laughs it off good-naturedly.

'Sometimes?' his pal carries on regardless. 'I have known you to cry at TV ads, episodes of *Ambulance*, you name it,' he says in his Australian accent that has a Welsh undertone.

'Once,' says Owen, raising a finger. 'I shed a tear once during *Ambulance*, and that was when the old bloke lost his wife, and looked so lost,' he reasons.

'I get that, I do that too.' I touch him gently on the arm. I'm not sure I like this pal of his. 'Anyway, Owen, you look great, and just wait until you see Tasha. She looks sensational. See you at the wedding shortly.'

'See you later.' Bryn winks at me, and I think to myself, not if I see you first.

A short while later, a hotel worker appears and asks us all to make our way outside to the large, covered stone balcony where the wedding will take place.

The terrace has been beautifully decorated, and a stunning white drape overhead keeps the glare of the sun at bay. There are striking displays of flowers in huge urns and the chairs are covered in an ivory-coloured fabric, with a pretty bow.

On a table at the end of the terrace is a register, and a bottle of something chilling in ice. A registrar in a navy suit and white shirt stands patiently waiting for the happy couple to emerge.

The stone railing of the terrace has small posies of flowers intermittently threaded through it, in colours of those matching Tasha's bouquet. The huge terrace gives a wonderful view of the three bells of Fira, an iconic church landmark. It looks absolutely picture perfect.

I take a seat on a row next to Tasha's aunts and Lulu as the rest of the guests begin to file in from the hotel reception area. I furtively take some pics before Tasha arrives, unable to resist the stunning vista, but of course I won't post any pics of the wedding until the official ones have been released.

'Are you okay?' I glance at Lulu, who seems to be miles away as she stares out across the gorgeous view.

'Fine,' she replies quietly. 'It's just being at a wedding makes me think of my own,' she admits.

'Gosh, I never thought about that,' I tell her.

'It's fine. I can't go avoiding weddings for the rest of my days, can I? And to be fair, our wedding day was really something.' She manages a smile.

I squeeze her hand, as just then all eyes are on Tasha as she makes her way down the aisle with her father. There are audible gasps as guests take in the sight of her looking resplendent in her cream dress that has a sweetheart neckline, the bodice encrusted with crystals. Her hair and make-up are flawless, her peach lipstick matching the shade of the flowers in her hand-tied bouquet.

Owen is standing at the front waiting for her, tapping his thigh with his fingers, I notice. When she arrives beside him, he looks like the happiest man in the world.

The gentle chatter from the assembled guests ceases then when the registrar clears her voice and begins to speak.

Irene and Patsy dab at their eyes with a tissue as Owen and Tasha exchange vows and I am filled with joy for my oldest friend, even though I can't see myself ever getting married. At least not for a long time.

Soon enough, they are declared husband and wife, and a wedding song plays as the newlyweds walk back down the small aisle, beaming with happiness, beneath a shower of confetti.

'Gosh they look so happy, don't they?' Patsy says, with a smile on her face and I must agree.

'They do.' I nod. 'I truly hope they live happily ever after.'

We take it in turns squeezing and congratulating them both, before we file into the reception area, where lines of staff and residents burst into applause and shouts of congratulations, to the delight of the happy couple.

As we make our way to the hotel restaurant, I spot the handsome hotel worker we met in the lift, who appears to be walking towards me.

'I hope you enjoyed the wedding ceremony,' he says. 'And by the way, you look beautiful,' he whispers, and annoyingly the hairs on my arms stand on end.

'Does your girlfriend know you like to pay compliments to random women?' I ask him, flattered but slightly irritated. The cheek of the man.

'My girlfriend?' He raises an eyebrow. A very attractive eyebrow, I might add.

'The woman I saw you with earlier.'

'Ah, not my girlfriend at all.' He smiles. 'I was simply showing her around the hotel as she is considering it for her wedding,' he explains.

'Oh, I see.'

'Anyway, I will see you at the wedding meal,' he says.

'You are a guest?' I ask, surprised.

I'd noticed him during the wedding ceremony, of course, but assumed him to be merely a member of staff making sure everything ran smoothly. Not unless Owen and Tasha have really pushed the boat out, and invited some of the hotel staff.

'Yes, I am a friend of Owen. He helped with the building of this very hotel. My father owns this place,' he reveals.

'Wow, well it's very beautiful,' I tell him, slightly taken aback.

'Thank you, I think so too. See you shortly.' He touches me gently on the arm once more, before he disappears.

I grab a glass of ice-cold champagne from a tray a passing waitress is carrying and gulp it down, as I suddenly feel a little flushed.

'Take it easy there. We don't want to be picking you up off the floor later,' says Irene with a giggle.

'What? No, I'm fine. I promise you won't need to do that.' I smile as I try to regulate my heartbeat.

As we file into the breakfast room, Lulu takes her phone from her bag and answers a call. She covers her ear with her other hand before apologising, and sloping off outside.

'Everything okay?' I ask when she returns, just as waiters are pouring wine into glasses.

'Fine, it was only Chloe,' she tells me. 'She was asking me for a bit of a loan,' she divulges, even though I never asked.

Chloe has at least two jobs and wastes money, if past conversations with Lulu are anything to go by, including a penchant for eating out and constantly buying takeaway coffees.

'Oh right, what for?' I ask casually.

'Does it matter?' she asks, a tad frostily.

'No, of course not,' I say, wishing I had never asked. 'Gosh, sorry if that was a little nosey.'

'Oh, I'm sorry, Mia.' She sighs. 'And I think I really will leave my phone in my suitcase after today, I promise.'

'That might actually be a good idea,' I say gently. 'You work so hard; you really deserve to chill and enjoy your time here.'

'I know, and I will. I am going to mute it until I get to the room later,' she says, stuffing it back into her bag.

There is no more talk of kids or phones, as we raise our glasses and toast the happy couple, before Tasha's dad does an emotional wedding speech and Tasha and Owen say a few adorable words to each other, and thank us all for being here.

Bryn steps into his best man role then and tells a couple of cringey stories that clearly embarrass Owen and do little to change my opinion of Bryn.

He is about to launch into another story about a weekend in Amsterdam, when Owen's dad tactfully takes the microphone from him and thanks everyone for coming.

'It's been so wonderful seeing so many of our friends here from the UK, and typically thoughtful of Owen and my new daughter-in-law Tasha to hold a wedding a little closer than Australia,' he says. When he finishes speaking, everyone breaks into a round of applause.

Goodness knows what Owen sees in Bryn, or what he was about to say about the weekend in Amsterdam, but then I guess we never know how people's relationships work, but safe to say, they just do. Bryn must surely have some redeeming features as Owen surely can't be that bad a judge of character. Especially as he has chosen someone as wonderful as Tasha to be his wife.

Speeches over, we dine on the most delicious meal of a sea bream starter, followed by lamb in a red wine jus with lemony Greek potatoes and roasted vegetables. We finish off with a pavlova bursting with juicy berries.

'Oh, my goodness, I don't think I will ever eat again,' I say, throwing my napkin down onto the table as coffee is served. Platters of cheese and cubes of baklava are being placed along the tables, as if we haven't had enough to eat already. I have taken photographs of every course, and can't wait to show my followers.

'Me neither,' says Irene. 'Although that probably isn't true.' She laughs. 'Gosh, I really will need this slimming club when I get home.'

'This is wonderful,' Lulu says wistfully, glancing out across the water. Patio doors have been opened in the large restaurant, bringing a much-needed gentle sea breeze wafting through the room. 'And you're right, maybe I do need a break. I never seem to stop back home.'

'Perhaps you could step away a bit from doing everything at home. Maybe draw up a rota to share some tasks with the kids,' I suggest, even though they are hardly kids.

'I know I probably should, but I enjoy doing things for them,' she admits. 'It makes me feel needed, which is pathetic, right?' She takes a long glug of her red wine. 'And maybe even a little selfish. They really ought to stand on their own two feet a little more, if they are to navigate this world.'

'It's not pathetic at all. I won't lie though, I think they take advantage of you at times,' I say honestly. 'You are allowed a life of your own, you know,' I remind her gently.

I resist adding that because when they do finally decide to leave home and do their own thing, Lulu certainly won't be their priority, which will be a difficult pill to swallow. I have seen it too many times.

'I know, and if I was to psychoanalyse myself it's probably a feeling of being needed, you know, after Carl left,' she admits. 'I think all my confidence went out of the door with him,' she says as she sips her wine.

'Well, he was an absolute fool.' I reach for her hand. 'Don't ever let him make you feel like you weren't good enough. Typical mid-lifer trying to turn back the clock. He will come to his senses, when it's too late, trust me.'

I do hope Lulu is strong enough to tell him where to go, should he ever try to come home. I saw him with his new girlfriend in town last week, wearing a tight shirt and dark jeans that would look better on a man half his age. His much younger girlfriend was sporting a skimpy dress and inflated lips. I'm pretty sure he will get fed up soon enough. He didn't look like a happy man to me, as he sat on a bench outside a fashion shop, scrolling through his phone and yawning, as his young partner headed inside.

'I'm not that daft.' She smiles and I really hope she means it.

'Have you thought about going to your dance classes again?' I suggest.

Lulu was once really keen on her salsa dancing classes, which seemed to tail off for no reason.

'Do you know, I have actually been considering doing just that,' she agrees. 'Maybe those offspring of mine ought to fend for themselves a bit more, but it's more than that, it is something for me,' she admits. 'I just seem to go to work, nip to the gym, then crash in front of the TV these days.'

'Then you should definitely take up your dance classes again. And I might join you one day on a trip to Cuba for the real thing,' I say dreamily. 'Can you imagine the Insta photos?'

'I might just hold you to that,' she says, raising her glass.

People swap seats and chat as the wedding meal is leisurely and not rushed, just as I expected it to be in Greece. Even more dessert is placed on tables, in the form of some sweet almond biscuits and more cheeses.

As we sip our coffee, the hotel hottie – who introduces himself as Christos – asks for our attention and informs us that some Greek dancers will be appearing shortly for a floor show.

He stands tall and confident, the kind of man who addresses a crowd with ease.

'Do you fancy a bit of that?' Irene asks Patsy as she listens.

'A bit of what?' asks Patsy.

'Greek dancing, what did you think I meant?'

Patsy rolls her eyes and laughs. 'I wonder if there will be any plate smashing?'

'I doubt it, not in this day and age. Times are hard for everyone,' Irene reminds her.

'Not for the owners of this hotel, judging by the décor, although I suppose it is a bit wasteful smashing plates,' Patsy concedes.

I recall Christos telling me that his father owns this place.

I have just finished chatting to Tasha, taking a few selfies of us, when Christos slides into the seat she has just vacated as she chats to another guest.

'Are you having a good time?' he asks, fixing me with those dark-brown eyes. He has taken off his jacket, and has rolled the sleeves up on his shirt. He seems to be sitting awfully close. Has he pulled his chair nearer to me? I wonder.

'Wonderful.' I sigh. 'The hotel really has done Owen and Tasha proud.'

'We aim to please,' he says, taking a grape from a plate and popping it into his mouth. 'Actually, I was wondering if you are free tomorrow evening?' he asks, taking me by surprise.

Lulu, Patsy and Irene are deep in conversation, and out of the corner of my eye I notice Patsy nudge Lulu and nod her head towards me.

'What? I'm not sure, we haven't really made any plans yet,' I say, my heart hammering as I try to sound casual. Is he about to ask me out on a date?

'Maybe you would like to come to my nightclub. I promise a free cocktail, for you and your friends, of course.' He smiles.

'You own a nightclub?' I try not to let my mouth fall open.

'It's a strand of the family business.' He shrugs. 'My father owns many businesses in Santorini: hotels, shops, bars. I manage the biggest nightclub in Fira,' he says proudly.

Handsome and from a seriously rich family? This wedding just gets better and better.

'We might pop in, if I can persuade them,' I say casually.

'Good.' He winks, before departing and leaving a Tom Ford scent I recognise hanging in the air.

'He seems to have taken quite a shine to you,' says Patsy after he leaves. 'Although I can't say I blame him, you look absolutely gorgeous,' she says kindly.

'Thanks, although I'm sure he was just being friendly.' I

shrug, yet feeling thrilled inside. 'He actually invited us to the nightclub he runs, with the offer of a free cocktail.'

'Us?' says Irene.

'Sure. He said bring your friends along.'

'Nightclubs aren't really my thing at my age,' says Patsy. 'A nice bar with some background music will do it for me these days. And an early night,' she says, and Irene agrees.

'Do you fancy it, Lu?' I ask my friend.

'Sure, sounds fun.' She smiles. 'And I'm all about trying to have some of that, remember?' She winks.

'Great,' I say, feeling thrilled to have a look at the nightclub.

ELEVEN

I'm already thinking about what I can wear tomorrow evening. The biggest nightclub in Fira? I can hardly wait. I wonder if there will be any famous people there.

I put all thoughts of tomorrow aside, as the Greek dancers file onto a small stage dressed in traditional costume, and a familiar Greek dance tune strikes up.

We are clapping and foot tapping along to the music, watching the dancers intently, a flick of the leg here, arms linked around each other's shoulders. An 'Opa,' every now and then.

I am watching every move because, as I suspected, I am soon taken by the hand to join in with the dancing. Soon, a dozen or so people have joined in, throwing their heads back and dancing, including Owen and Tasha, who has removed her veil and looks as though she might burst with happiness.

I'm high kicking my legs, when Bryn slides in and puts his arm around my shoulders, asking me if I fancy meeting him later, a lecherous grin on his face. As we dance, his hand moves down the side of my body, before he snakes his arm around my waist setting my skin on edge. It's all I can do to stop myself from slapping him but I don't want a scene at my friend's wedding, so I gently remove his arm instead.

Thankfully, just then Christos appears, apologising to Bryn and cutting in, placing his arm around my shoulders, before seamlessly and very expertly joining in with the dancing. The feel of his arm around me is so different to that of Bryn's, and I can feel my face flush, hoping he doesn't notice when he gives a sideways smile.

'Are you having fun?' he whispers in my ear, almost making me go wrong-footed.

'I am actually, now that I have mastered the steps.' I am really enjoying myself, I think to myself.

'You certainly have the moves,' he says approvingly.

'Thanks,' I mutter. 'Although I have watched Greek dancing many times,' I explain just as someone approaches and calls him away. I feel disappointed that he must leave, so excuse myself and head back to my table, before Bryn can rejoin the dancing.

After the dancing, everyone is sitting around chatting once more, and soon enough Owen and Tasha have reappeared from getting changed into casual wear, before saying goodbye to us all.

This evening, they are taking a private catamaran to a secluded island where they will spend a few nights at a private villa, which is apparently the only one for miles around. Tasha tells me they will spend the day snorkelling and swimming in the clear blue water.

Once the guests have finally drifted off, and we have all said our goodbyes to the happy couple, some heading to another bar in the hotel, others out on the town, Lulu and I sit in the hotel bar chatting, before ordering a taxi back to our village.

When we arrive at the apartment just after nine o'clock, a

message pings through on Lulu's phone and a smile spreads across her face.

'It's Phil from work, asking if I am having a good time, before you ask,' she tells me.

'Oh, yes.' I raise an eyebrow. 'I told you he liked you, didn't I?'

'Just a friendly enquiry.' She bats away the suggestion. 'He says to say hi to you too.'

'Ah, that's nice. He's a good bloke.'

'He is.' She smiles. 'Anyway, I don't think he sees me in a romantic way, he's nice to everyone.'

'What would you do if he did? Like you, I mean?' I ask.

'Not sure.' She kicks off her shoes before lying on her bed, and lacing her hands behind her head. 'He's kind and handsome, I guess, but I think I'm a bit out of practice.'

'Maybe it's time you started to get back in the game then,' I suggest.

'Hmm, maybe.' She fluffs up her pillow and turns onto her side.

While Lulu has a little snooze, I flick through some photos and upload them to my social media.

Some of the church photos look incredible, as do the sunset and sea views from the restaurant in Perissa. I idly wonder whether I might soon be uploading photos of myself and a certain good-looking Greek, before I head out onto the balcony and take some more shots of the white buildings that snake down the hillside as the light begins to fade.

I snap away with my camera phone watching a boat gently drift across the horizon, as lights begin to come to life in the harbour.

Taking a seat on a balcony chair and closing my eyes, I feel my eyes become heavy after the excitement of the day. I grab a nearby throw from a chair and wrap it around me, feeling happy and relaxed. Maybe I will just close my eyes for a minute.

As I drift off, I wonder whether I ought to have asked Christos for a photo with him at the wedding, although that might have seemed a bit strange as we had only just met, even though it would look good on my Instagram.

TWELVE

I wake with a stiff neck, wishing I had climbed into bed for half an hour like Lulu, instead of on a balcony chair.

'I should have had a snooze on the bed like you,' I tell Lulu, who is awake and looking at her phone. 'I might grab a quick shower, maybe it will loosen the knots in this neck,' I say, rubbing at it. 'Do you fancy going for a nightcap to a bar across the road?' I ask.

'I don't mind,' she says, putting her phone down and frowning.

'What's up?' I ask.

'Oh nothing, it's just Chloe.' She sighs. 'She says she isn't feeling well, and is missing me.'

'Ah well, I guess we all want our mum when we're ill. What's wrong with her?' I ask.

'She thinks she might have tonsillitis, she sounded really awful.' She chews her lip anxiously.

'Ooh, poor girl. Has she managed to see a doctor?'

'Hard to get an appointment but she has a high temperature and everything.'

'Give her a video call, if it puts your mind at rest,' I suggest, while grabbing a towel from my bed, ready to take a quick shower.

'I think I will.' She nods.

As the warm water cascades over me, I rub at my neck and feel the knots begin to loosen.

It's so beautiful here, I really think I could get used to it. I still have over a week to explore the island, so I might drive off up into the hills, and explore some remote villages and see how the locals live. Or maybe Christos could show me around, I think idly. We could stop at mountain restaurants eating food and sipping ouzo and watching the sun go down together.

Back in the bedroom, Lulu has finished her call.

'Is Chloe okay?' I ask gently as I get ready.

'Yes, fine.' She smiles. 'She managed to see someone at a walk-in centre where she called me from. They think it is a virus rather than tonsillitis.'

'That's a relief then,' I tell her. 'Rest and painkillers and hopefully she will be as right as rain.'

'I know, kids, hey? They still worry you whatever their age.' She sighs.

'I get that.' I smile.

I do understand, of course I do. I just hope Lulu doesn't worry too much. She does the lion's share of the parenting, since her ex shacked up with his new girlfriend, and really deserves this break.

'Actually, Mia, do you mind if I don't go out for a drink?' Lulu asks. 'I'm a bit pooped after the wedding, which was wonderful, but it's been a long day.' She stifles a yawn, despite having had a little siesta.

I can't lie, I'm a little disappointed, as I thought we might have a cocktail at one of the many bars to round off the day, and maybe even find one with some live music. But I guess there is always tomorrow.

Thinking of music makes me realise it's ages since I've sung in a bar which is a shame really. I used to love covering well-known songs, that always received rapturous applause. I even recall doing a duet with my brother Lewis, a Kylie and Jason number at a caravan park that had people on their feet. Maybe we ought to have got the whole family involved, as Mum and Dad can hold a tune too. Gran admits to being tone deaf, so I'm not sure where the singing talent comes from. Perhaps she could join our band and bang a tambourine or something!

My mind flits to the nightclub tomorrow evening that I imagine will be a sleek club with a chilled vibe and moody lighting, not to mention a gorgeous manager, who I realise I can hardly wait to see again. The photos are going to be insane.

'Sure, that's fine.' I smile. 'I guess it has been a long day,' I tell Lulu.

'But you have got yourself ready now,' says Lulu.

'It's fine really. And if you change your mind, we can go for a drink later. The night is still young here.'

'Sorry I am being a party pooper,' she decides, sliding off the bed. 'It's only ten o'clock, so go out with Patsy and Irene if you like. Really, I'm happy hanging around here, and getting an early night,' she insists.

Right on cue, Patsy knocks on the bedroom door and asks if we are heading out.

'Come in.' I smile at the sight of Irene and Patsy, who have changed outfits and are raring to go.

'I spotted karaoke tonight at a bar along the front,' says Patsy, glancing at her watch. 'I think it starts shortly.' She touches her lipstick up in a compact with a mirror. 'I might get up myself. I used to do quite a good rendition of Tina Turner's "Nutbush City Limits",' she reveals.

'Now that I simply have to see.' I laugh.

'Maybe you ought to lower your expectations,' whispers Irene. 'Although, I do recall you and Tash singing in her bedroom as little girls, dreaming of being in Girls Aloud,' she says. 'So, you should be the one on the karaoke. As I recall, you had a very good singing voice.'

'Thank you. I do still sing occasionally,' I tell her, realising it's been a while. I still remember my first paid gig at a local working men's club when I was eighteen. It went down a storm, especially with the older people who adored my covers of a couple of country songs.

When Lulu tells them she won't be joining us, Patsy does her best to persuade her, but she isn't budging.

'Then at least come and have one cocktail at the Sea Breeze bar over the road,' she suggests. 'We will leave you alone after, that I promise.'

'Hmm. Oh, go on then, one drink won't hurt.' She smiles and I couldn't be happier. I'm glad she is joining us or she will only sit worrying about her daughter if she stays here alone.

While Lulu does a quick change, we arrange to meet the ladies at the Sea Breeze, when my phone rings.

It's my gran asking me how the holiday is going.

'Hi, Gran. Oh it's great. Look.'

I walk outside onto the balcony and show her the view all around, of twinkling lights around the village, gently illuminating the rapidly darkening sky.

'That looks amazing. If only I was twenty years younger, I'd be there with bells on.' She laughs. 'I bet there are some fit men there.'

'Gran!' I can't help but laugh. Especially as she would be in her sixties even twenty years ago.

'So how was the wedding?' she asks.

'Oh, it was wonderful,' I tell her, recalling the event that was just about perfect. 'Tasha and Owen looked fabulous, so happy.'

'I look forward to seeing your pics on that Instantgram,' she says.

'Instagram, Gran,' I correct her, laughing once more.

'Well, whatever. I'm sure your followers will love it. Santorini is very popular, I believe.'

'It is. And thanks, Gran. I'll post some pics tomorrow, just not the wedding ones until the official ones are out there,' I tell her. 'But I can send you one of Tash and Owen that I took myself. Just don't post it anywhere.'

'Don't worry about that, love. I wouldn't know how.' She chuckles.

Just then, Mum comes into view, depositing some tea and biscuits down in front of Gran and we have a little chat.

'Perhaps we could do a little family holiday to Greece next year.' She smiles.

'I'd love that, Mum.'

It would be lovely for Gran to come too, but she is so unsteady on her feet these days. Still, you never know.

'Okay, well enjoy the rest of your holiday and give my congratulations to Tasha and Owen,' says Mum, before she ends the call.

Half an hour later, we are across the road at the Sea Breeze, where Patsy and Irene are enjoying a cocktail and I wonder where this pair get their energy from.

'Ooh here you are,' says Irene with a beaming smile. 'I highly recommend this,' she says, lifting her drink. 'It's an ouzo-based cocktail,' she informs us.

'Oh nooo, not for me,' I say, recalling a bad experience with too much ouzo at a Greek restaurant back home that I have no desire to repeat.

'So what are you ladies up to tomorrow?' asks Patsy. 'We thought we might have a lazy morning, then head up to Oia later in the day for the sunset views. There's a trip going from the hotel, leaving at around four, including a light dinner. The restaurant balcony is a prime location for the sunset apparently.'

'That does sound lovely, but I kind of fancied a day exploring the streets of Fira tomorrow. What do you fancy doing?' I turn to Lulu.

'Actually, yes, I like the sound of exploring Fira, I believe there are lots of little shops and galleries there,' she agrees.

'Okay, just thought we'd ask.' Irene smiles. 'Maybe see you back for a nightcap when we return.' She winks.

Diners all around are enjoying delicious-looking food, and the tantalising smell makes my stomach rumble a little. It's been hours since we ate at the wedding, so we decide to order some food.

We have the most relaxed evening tucking into calamari, drizzled with lemon and parsley and a huge Greek salad dotted with olives and salty feta to share. Warm pittas and dips jostle for space on the table, and we tuck in hungrily.

'I don't know why I'm so hungry, perhaps it's the sea air,' Irene says as she polishes off some complimentary honey cake at the end of the meal.

'Well, it was hours ago since we ate at the wedding,' I remind her.

'You're too kind.' She smiles. 'I just can't seem to stop eating. I've tried to lose weight, of course, it's no good carrying extra weight in this heat.' She admits. 'I think it all started after Malcolm died, even though I was still angry with him.' She sighs. 'Some people drown their sorrows; I ate my way out of grief. I still am, truth be told.'

'As long as you're happy,' ventures Lulu.

'And are you?' I ask honestly.

'That's the thing though, no, I'm not.' She says honestly. 'But I just sort of give up, as it's like climbing a mountain. I make a little progress, then slip back,' she admits.

'I know someone who could help you with that, if you like. Are you on Instagram?' I ask.

'What, no I'm only just on Facebook.' She laughs. 'And even that I hardly bother with. Why do you ask?'

'There is someone on there who busts the myths about weight loss. Lots of people are like you, they give up after the first hurdle.'

'What kind of myths?'

'Well, it's about the calories you consume. For example, did you know you would need to eat around eighteen Mars bars to gain a single pound. It's all about calorie deficit, which I am sure you already know.'

'I do. I just seem to make the wrong choices,' she says as she pushes her plate away from her. 'But you know, I think it is time I joined a slimming club again. I need the support of other people,' she admits. 'And I know a lot of overweight people are fit, happy even, and that's absolutely fine if that is the case,' she says. 'But I'm not. Trudging about in this heat has made me realise I need to do something.' She sighs.

'People can only make changes when they are ready to. I think joining a slimming club is a great idea though,' I tell her. 'Lots of people need the support of a group.'

'I am definitely one of those people,' says Irene. 'I have been watching reruns of *Fat Friends* on Netflix, and it reminded me of how being part of a group really can motivate you, in any situation.'

'I'll come with you, if you like,' offers Patsy supportively. 'At least for the first few sessions.'

'As if you need to.' Irene laughs, rolling her eyes. 'Although it's kind of you to support me.'

'Ah, but you would be surprised. I have got a right old tummy on me. I just dress to disguise it,' says Patsy.

'Thank you,' says Irene softly, reaching for her cousin's hand, and I feel almost emotional witnessing the strength of their friendship.

'But for now, as we are still on holiday, let's enjoy these cocktails,' says Patsy as she raises her glass.

'I wonder how Tash and Owen are enjoying the secluded island?' I ask no one in particular, imagining them sharing drinks on the terrace of a villa overlooking the beach, and watching a sky studded with stars.

I sip my delicious pina colada when it arrives and try not to imagine sharing such a romantic location with a certain Greek guy who I can't seem to stop thinking about.

'I bet they will be having the most wonderful time,' says Lulu. 'They just seem so happy together. It was a beautiful wedding, and thanks for inviting me as your plus-one,' she says to me.

'I wouldn't have wanted anyone else.' I smile, thankful that she appears to be enjoying herself.

Having decided to head to the karaoke bar at the end of the beach road, I ask the waiter to take a picture of us all together and he takes my phone.

The photograph shows us all happy and beaming, and it makes me think that whoever said the camera never lies wasn't maybe quite telling the whole truth. We all look great on the surface, don't we? Especially on social media, yet no one's life is perfect, despite the image they might present. Not many people post about their boring days, me included. All the world's a stage, as Shakespeare once said. And it really is true.

THIRTEEN

'Well, fancy meeting you here.'

Bryn has sidled up to me as I am choosing my song at the karaoke bar and I find myself wishing that it was Christos. He's with a rather good-looking bloke, who I recognise from the wedding earlier, who introduces himself as Ash.

Following me back to the table where the others are sitting, Bryn asks if he can buy us all a drink, lazily looping his arm around my shoulder as I take a seat. I try not to show my irritation as I gently remove his arm.

'No thanks, love, we've just got them in,' says Patsy, lifting her cocktail. 'You can join us if you like though?' she offers, gesturing to the two empty seats on our table with six chairs.

'If that's okay?' says Ash, probably noting my lack of enthusiasm.

'Sure, why not,' I say breezily and Lulu looks pleased as handsome Ash flashes her a big smile. She returns his smile, and I wonder if she fancies him. It's great to see a little spark between them either way, and I really hope Lulu can start noticing attractive men, and maybe practise a little flirting.

'Are you ladies having fun then?' asks Bryn when he returns from the bar with drinks for him and Ash.

'We are. It's so beautiful here, who wouldn't,' says Lulu.

'And the wedding, oh it was just magical,' says Irene. 'Owen and Tash make such a beautiful couple.'

'Oh, they do, but you would never catch me getting married.' Bryn pulls a face. 'Footloose and fancy free I am, and I intend to stay that way.'

His leg brushes against mine then, and I swiftly move it away.

'Have you and Owen been friends for long?' asks Patsy as she takes a puff of her vape and blasts a scent of watermelon in the air.

'At least ten years,' says Bryn as he sips his drink. 'I used to work for him,' he reveals. 'That was before I made it big myself in the property business. Oh yes, he has competition now.' He laughs. 'I have a portfolio of hundreds of houses now, best in the business, I am. I—'

'And what do you do, Ash?' asks Irene, cutting him off in mid-flow.

'I'm a musician,' he tells us. 'I used to be in a band, but I sing solo now, write songs and the like. In between gigs, I work in a theatre bar.'

'Which is still being involved in the industry, I guess,' says Lulu.

'Exactly, and we get discounted tickets to watch the shows.' He grins.

'Talking of performers,' Lulu tells Ash. 'Mia here has a great singing voice. In fact, we are here to watch her sing on the karaoke shortly.'

'Really, well I will look forward to hearing you sing,' says Ash.

We chat for a while, and I chastise myself for taking an instant dislike to Bryn. I have never been one to judge a person too quickly, as none of us are perfect. I remind myself that he must be okay deep down, or surely Owen wouldn't be friends with him, would he?

The conversation continues until the first karaoke singer of the evening steps up to the stage at the front of the restaurant, and does a pretty decent rendition of 'Pretty Woman' that has everyone clapping and singing along.

'That song reminds me of a someone I once went out with,' says Bryn. 'Now she was a *real* pretty woman.' He grins. 'She was a nutter though. Never did trust me if I went out alone, and I wouldn't mind but I only cheated on her the once when I was drunk as a skunk on a stag do.' He laughs. 'Which doesn't really count in my book.' He shrugs.

Ash raises his eyebrow as I sit with my mouth open. It seems I am constantly re-assessing my opinion of this guy.

I don't have time to respond as my name is called up and it is my turn on the karaoke. For some reason, I feel a little nervous as I haven't sung in public for a while. Maybe Dad's right, I ought to do it more often or I will become out of practice at facing an audience. Use it or lose it.

The bar seems to have filled up in the last half hour, and my friends whoop and cheer in anticipation as I reach for the microphone.

As is usually the case, once I start to sing, the nerves disappear and I can't see a single person in the room. The uplifting ballad seems to have people mesmerised, conversations stalling, as they give me their full attention. And then comes the bit that thrills me the most as the song concludes.

I thank the audience as I soak up the rapturous applause, the whistles, the confirmation that my voice is as good as I believe it to be. And it feels wonderful.

Bryn is on his feet shouting, 'You go, girl, that was bloody magical.'

Maybe he isn't so bad after all.

Walking back to the table, I pass tables of people clapping and telling me how much they enjoyed it.

'You really are very good,' says Ash kindly. 'Maybe I should write a song for you.'

'I'm very flattered.' I smile, feeling pleased by his comment.

'Amazing,' Lulu says as she squeezes me in a hug.

'Well, well. You have come a long way since the days of singing in the bedroom,' Irene comments with a smile. 'That was bloomin' fantastic. Girls Aloud would be lucky to have you now.'

'I don't think they are together anymore, Irene. They must be in their forties, surely,' Patsy says, laughing.

I am on a high as I say take a seat, and the sound of another song fills the bar.

'Good job he's not a bad singer,' says Patsy. 'Imagine having to follow you.' She gives me a nudge.

Just then, I hear the deep thrust of an engine outside the bar, and glance over at a silver Porsche. There's a bloke in sunglasses in the driver's seat, with the roof down, and I notice a few women cast a glance his way. I recognise Christos immediately as he lifts his sunglasses and waves over.

At that precise moment, Bryn congratulates me again, before pulling me in for a hug, and kissing me squarely on the lips. I am so shocked it takes me a second or two to push him off.

The sound of the throaty engine can be heard once more, as I watch Christos make his way along the street.

We have another drink, and I find myself wondering if Christos might have come into the bar when he saw me? Who am I kidding though? He was obviously off somewhere, and was just waving over when he spotted us all.

Even so, it was the wrong moment for Bryn to have moved

in for a kiss, I think frustratedly, and I find myself hoping that Christos doesn't think we are a thing.

Patsy has recorded me singing, so I decide to forget about Bryn's kiss, which thinking about it was just celebratory, and I even manage to see the funny side.

'Upload it to TikTok,' says Bryn enthusiastically and I freeze.

'No! Honestly, I would rather you didn't,' I say and the others look on in surprise.

'Why ever not?' says Irene, looking puzzled. 'You never know who might be watching, maybe even Simon Cowell.'

'Unlikely, as we don't follow each other,' I explain.

'Even so, your followers would love to hear you sing, surely?' reasons Patsy. 'I would be shouting it from the rooftops, if I could sing like that.'

'I know, it's just that, oh I don't know, I'm not as confident with showing people my singing, as with other things,' I let slip.

'Well, I think you're mad,' says Bryn. 'Never hide your light under a bushel, that's what I say.'

'I'm sure that's not something you have ever been accused of,' I find myself saying, but with a smile on my face. 'But I will do it in my own time.'

'Sure thing. Whatever you want,' Irene says with a shrug. 'I have to say I think Patsy is right though. I would be sharing it with all and sundry, if I had such a beautiful voice.'

'And you know how I feel,' adds Lulu. 'I am always telling you to share your singing with your followers.'

Long after we have said our goodnights, and the evening is over, I lie in bed and think about everyone's comments. I like to show my followers the places I have been to, the best places to shop and eat. Recommendations for all kinds of things. I want the big time, the money and the status, don't I? So why do I find it so difficult to show people who I really am? Who is that girl on the screen reviewing the latest cocktail bar in town? Maybe that's something I can figure out being over here. At least I hope so.

FOURTEEN

Tasha video calls us the following day from the deck of a boat.

'Oh wow. Just look at you,' I say, glimpsing the mountains in the background of the small yacht that is gently swaying in the sparkling water.

Owen appears then and hands Tasha a glass of champagne, and I think of how Instagram worthy that shot of them would be. I let out a little sigh as I allow my mind to daydream about hanging around with a certain Greek bloke in such a setting.

Tasha and Owen will be heading back here in a few days to spend an evening with us all, before they fly back to Australia.

'So how's it going?' I ask as I relax on the balcony with my morning coffee. 'I'm not jealous at all.'

Ash called Lulu earlier and asked her out for a drink, and I am thrilled that she has accepted. I'm quite happy to have a quiet day as we are off to Fira this evening to have a meal and visit the nightclub, the thought of which gives me a tingle of excitement.

'It's bliss,' says Tasha, looking tanned and relaxed.

'It sure is,' says Owen, leaning over and giving her a kiss.

'We have a chef too, who is just amazing. He comes to the

villa to cook our evening meal, so we barely have to leave the villa at all,' she tells me. 'Although the surroundings are pretty irresistible.'

'I see what you mean, who wouldn't want to be out on the water with those wonderful views all around,' I say.

'I know.' Tasha sighs contentedly. 'We spend our days swimming and sunbathing, occasionally taking a taxi boat across to a different beach, it's dreamy.'

After saying goodbye, and with Lulu out for the afternoon, I spend some time uploading photographs to my social media accounts.

As I upload my photos, I wonder again why I am so reluctant to post myself singing at the karaoke evening, especially as the reactions were so positive. Maybe it's because I was trolled once, when a video of me singing was posted online. I was only a teenager at the time and just mucking about, and in fact the footage was not even posted by me. Even so, it kind of left me reluctant to share anything else, even after all these years, which is silly I know.

Within minutes, my phone is pinging with likes and comments on my photos, people adoring the black sand beach as the sun goes down, and the delicious plates of Greek food. I can't wait to share some wedding photos, with the stunning backdrop that looks out over the sea.

Lulu pings a text to me saying she will be back early evening, as she and Ash are going to take in a winery tour, and I send her some love heart emojis. I'm considering going for a walk, when Patsy sends me a message asking if I fancy taking a taxi boat across to Kamari for a few hours, and I tell her that sounds like a lovely idea. It might stop my nerves from churning at the thought of seeing Christos this evening.

'There might be a nice breeze on that water in the taxi boat,' says, Irene, whirring her trusty fan in front of her face when we meet in reception. 'At least I hope so. I'm not sure I can take much more of this heat,' she complains.

'I'm pretty sure it will be cooler,' I reassure her. 'There is always a nice breeze out at sea.'

Patsy glances at her watch, and tells us we had better get a move on if we want to catch the next taxi boat. So we take the short walk to the pick-up point at the beach.

'The boat looks a bit small,' says Irene doubtfully, as we stand in line ready to board. 'I hope it can take my weight.'

'Of course it will, you're not that big,' says Patsy, which is actually true.

'See,' says Patsy as we settle into our seats. 'The boat man would have said something or at least asked you to sit in a certain place, but, not a thing.' She winks. 'So just relax and enjoy yourself.'

'I will do,' Irene replies with nod. Then, 'Oh, look.' She points out a shoal of fish in the clear blue water. 'I wish I had a little bread,' she says, recording the silvery fish on her phone as they swim around in circles.

As the boat moves along the sun-dappled water, a grey-haired bloke sitting opposite Irene smiles at her.

'Nice day for it,' he comments.

'Oh, it is. A bit too hot at times, though. For me at least.' She returns his smile.

'I know what you mean,' he agrees. 'I thought it might be a bit cooler out on the water.'

'I thought so too,' she tells him.

As they continue their conversation, Patsy gives me a knowing look.

'I think she's in there,' she whispers.

I study Irene's pretty face, her startling blue eyes framed by soft, slightly curly hair. She has such a magnetic personality too; it's not surprising the bloke has taken an interest in her. I wonder how many other people out there have worries and insecurities about the way they look that are completely unfounded.

We settle into our short trip across the water, and we reach Kamari in no time. The boat docks several metres from the black sand beach and I notice Irene looks a little panicked.

'I didn't realise we would have to get into the water,' she says, looking a little flustered.

'It's only a few feet,' says Irene's new friend as she flushes bright red.

'But I'm wearing a long dress,' she protests.

'Hitch it up around your knees, you'll be fine,' Patsy tells her.

'I most certainly will not,' replies Irene, her usual humour deserting her.

'Maybe I try to get the boat a little closer,' the elderly Greek boat man says, noting her obvious embarrassment.

He glides as close to the sand as possible, without actually mooring on the gravel beach, and Irene thanks him. It takes her a little time to descend the rope ladder of the boat, as she carefully places one foot in front of the other.

'Thank you.' She smiles to the boat man, who takes her hand for the last few steps.

'No problem,' he says kindly, even though he will have to push his boat back into the water. 'I hope you have a nice afternoon.' He smiles warmly.

Once in Kamari, we head to a bar and Irene knocks back an ouzo.

'Are you okay?' I ask her.

'Oh yes, fine, much better now.' She musters a smile. 'I just got myself into a bit of a tizz and that ladder felt a bit flimsy, I was holding on for dear life.'

'Well, we're here now, so let's enjoy it,' says Patsy. 'And I have to say, that bloke on the boat was quite taken with you, wasn't he?' She raises an eyebrow. 'Can't take you anywhere.' She laughs.

'What do you mean?' Irene looks bemused.

'He definitely fancied you,' says Patsy.

'Nonsense, he was just a friendly bloke, making conversation. How could you even think that?' She seems shocked by the very suggestion.

'You wouldn't have noticed, but when you were gazing out to sea, he could hardly take his eyes off you,' insists Patsy.

'If you say so. Anyway, come on, let's have a little stroll,' says Irene, unconvinced.

An abundance of restaurants line the cobbled beach road, along with fashion shops and tour operators offering trips to ancient Fira and Oia to watch the sunset. Souvenir shops offer up the usual Greek gifts, such as ouzo and Greek herbs, for tourists to take home.

'This is gorgeous, isn't it?' says Irene, taking in the palm trees dotted along the promenade that overlooks the long stretch of black beach, set against the backdrop of the mountains.

'Everything I have seen so far is beautiful.' I sigh.

'Including Christos?' she teases.

'He's undeniably good-looking, but I wasn't thinking about him.' I roll my eyes, even though truthfully, I have thought of him rather a lot.

'If you say so.' She grins.

I take a photo of us at the small, bustling harbour and shortly afterwards, the grey-haired gent from the boat appears again, as we peruse garments on rails outside a clothes shop. 'I'd say that suits your colouring,' says the bloke, who Patsy said is a dead ringer for an older actor on *Emmerdale*.

'Do you think so?' Irene visibly blushes as her fingers run over the blue and cream coloured scarf.

'Definitely.' He smiles. 'What time will you be heading back?' he asks, glancing at his watch.

'We will be catching the boat in a couple of hours, I suppose,' I suggest, and the others agree.

'The four o'clock one?'

'Probably, yes,' says Irene.

'Oh, me too,' he says, before asking her where we are staying in Perissa.

I glance at Irene, who looks a little uncertain about telling him.

'Look, I'm very flattered, but I will be spending time with my friends, we only have a few days left here,' she tells him, with a polite smile.

'I understand. I suppose I could be anyone.' He laughs. 'Although I promise you, I'm not an axe murderer. Not with all these crowds,' he jokes. 'Well anyway, it was a pleasure to meet you. Maybe I will see you around.'

'Perhaps. Bye then.'

'I wouldn't mind you know, if you decide to spend a bit of time with a bloke,' says Patsy as we walk along the harbour front. 'It might remind you that you are not past it.' She laughs.

'Past it?' Irene says indignantly, standing tall. 'I'm sixty-two, that's all, and isn't sixty meant to be the new fifty? Maybe I just didn't like him.'

'Fine, whatever,' says Patsy, fishing a vape from her bag and taking a quick drag.

An hour later, we have stopped to look at a menu outside a restaurant, with a view of fishing boats bobbing in the glistening water, when a friendly waiter ushers us inside. I grab a selfie with the colourful boats in the background, while Patsy studies the drinks menu.

'And by the way, I don't doubt the guy on the boat seemed like a nice bloke,' says Irene, obviously mulling things over as we await our drinks. 'But I've told you, I'm sure he was just being friendly,' she says. 'And nothing more.'

'Why wouldn't he be interested in you romantically?' Patsy asks.

'Well, I am hardly Kate Moss, am I?' Irene says with a laugh.

'Oh, give over, and he was hardly George Clooney. Honestly, Irene, are you ever going to loosen up and have a little fun? You're a bit overweight, big deal.' She takes another a drag of her vape. 'Does that mean you stop yourself from ever meeting someone? That guy was obviously interested in you, and you gave him the cold shoulder,' she tells her cousin.

'Do you think so?' asks Irene doubtfully, as she digests Patsy's words.

'You know he was. So, either give up on men, which as I recall you always rather liked.'

Irene opens her mouth to protest.

'Or get on with it,' continues Patsy. 'Next option? Join that slimming club if it will make you feel better about yourself,' she says, rather bluntly I feel. 'Or stop living your life.'

'Well, I'm hardly doing that. I'm here in Greece, aren't I?' she retorts. 'And I have been considering the slimming club, you know that,' says Irene, seemingly unoffended by Patsy's remarks. 'I just never seem to get around to it.'

I am quickly learning that this honest back and forth chat is something the pair exchange quite easily without upsetting each other.

'I do get that,' concedes Patsy. 'I'm still having to puff on my vapes until I can quit the evil weed, so I know making changes isn't easy. I just want you to be happy, that's all.'

'I know you do.' Irene gives Patsy a squeeze on the arm.

We order our food and make short work of tasty bowls of creamy moussaka all round, and make appreciative noises as we eat, along with a generous bowl of hand-cut fries that we share.

'Anyway, getting back to that bloke, I think you are rather missing the point,' says Patsy as she finishes her food.

'Oh, not this again, can we give it a rest?' Irene sighs.

'I promise, no more talk of it, but I just want you to realise that that man liked you just the way you are,' she says more gently. 'He would hardly be wanting to spend time alone with you otherwise, would he? Anyway, I fancy a mojito. Anyone else?' she asks, closing the conversation down for the last time.

I guess that's all anyone wants, isn't it? To be loved for who they truly are. Maybe one day I will sing along to songs on the radio that will have my partner smiling, rather than rolling their eyes, or even going into another room, as my ex sometimes did.

'Mojitos all round.' I smile as Irene fumbles in her bag for a tissue. 'It's blinking hot here, isn't it?' she says, dabbing at her eyes.

FIFTEEN

There is no more talk of Irene's admirer on the return journey and back at the apartments, my stomach churns a little at the thought of seeing Christos later this evening. But then I wonder if he will even remember me? I'm pretty sure he sees thousands of women in the hotel and the nightclub. The club that will undoubtedly be filled with leggy model types I realise, as I stress over what I should wear, before grabbing yet another outfit from my wardrobe to try on.

Lulu has been back for an hour, and is sitting on her bed scrolling through her phone as I consider what I should wear.

'Everything okay?' I ask.

'Oh yes, just Chloe telling me she is feeling a lot better,' she tells me.

'Glad to hear it.'

'In fact, she is off to Newcastle on a hen do next weekend and was wondering if I could lend her some money.' She stares at her phone and chews her lip.

'Is it a last-minute thing?' I ask, wondering why Chloe hasn't saved some of the money herself, but I keep that thought to myself.

'Not sure.' She sighs. 'The thing is, I don't have a lot spare with being on holiday myself. I don't think she was too impressed when I said I couldn't help though.'

'Try not to feel bad, you are entitled to have a holiday,' I tell her gently, as I finally decide on a white jumpsuit that will look good against my auburn hair and lightly tanned skin, courtesy of the spray tan I had before I came here to help it along.

'I know that. I just wish I could give them whatever they want. But you're right, as usual.' She smiles. 'And, of course, she is earning her own money. She could have saved up herself for next weekend.'

Once more one of her offspring has managed to ruin the mood of her holiday. It seriously makes me think twice about having kids, but as I don't even have a boyfriend that stuff seems like a million miles away.

'Exactly. And you do an awful lot for both her and Tom, which obviously, as a mother, I get that, but they really are very lucky,' I tell her, reminding her of the number of times she has been a taxi to them both. They don't seem to ask their father for anything either, which I think unfair, but then I guess I don't really understand their relationship with their dad, which Lulu tells me is complicated at best.

'Anyway, I have said I can't help her, so that's that,' says Lulu, putting her phone away. 'Now let's go out and hit that nightclub.' She smiles.

I take a quick glance at my phone after it pinged to see that the Santorini pictures have been very popular. The view of the caldera in the sunset already has over half a million views! I can't wait to go into Fira this evening and try and grab some cool pictures of the nightclub that I know my followers will go wild for.

'Anyway, how was your afternoon with Ash?' I ask. 'You didn't really say much when I asked you earlier,' I comment as I spray some perfume onto my wrists.

'It was a really pleasant day,' she says, but without much excitement in her voice. 'Ash knew of this small winery and we sampled a couple of local wines,' she tells me. 'I bought a bottle to take home for Phil, you know, as a thank you for giving me the extra time off work.'

'That's a nice gesture. I know that Phil enjoys a good glass of wine.'

'He does.' She smiles.

'Buying wine for another man while you were on a date though?' I raise an eyebrow. 'So the date really was nothing more than a pleasant outing?'

'I'm afraid so. Don't get me wrong, Ash was very attentive, but I don't think there was any chemistry between us,' she admits. 'By the end of the date, I think he realised that too.' She shrugs. 'But it was a lovely day, all the same.'

'I'm glad you had fun, although it's a shame you never really connected,' I tell my friend, feeling pleased she is at least dipping her toe into the dating world again.

'It's fine.' She smiles. 'He and Bryn are back off to Australia anyway in a few days, so I don't think it was ever going to go anywhere.'

'That's true, although maybe it's also because you have someone else on your mind,' I suggest, thinking of Phil, and she laughs but doesn't protest.

'Come on, let's go,' she says, looping her bag over her shoulder. 'Before you let that fertile imagination of yours run away with you.'

We are perched on bar stools, marvelling at our surroundings and the mesmerising ball of sun in the sky. We were lucky to get a seat at the elevated bar that gives such great views, having arrived just as a couple had vacated their seats.

At nine thirty, it's a little early to head to the nightspot so we chat easily, slowly sipping our soft drinks, having decided to save ourselves for a couple of cocktails later in the club. I can hardly wait.

Down on the streets below, crowds of tourists dressed casually in shorts and T-shirts are milling around, taking photos and weaving their way along footpaths. Others are dressed to impress and clearly out to dine at fine restaurants for the evening. I love watching the mixture of people, all out to enjoy themselves.

Earlier, we had passed a long queue of people patiently waiting to enter a very popular eatery, that is so well known it doesn't take bookings.

'Do you reckon that's a genuine Gucci bag?' Lulu points to a woman weaving her way along a crazy-paved footpath, dressed immaculately, with a partner who looks equally well turned out.

'Probably. But then the fakes are so good who can really tell?' I reply, thinking of my little blue-leather dupe bag that I bought from the shopping mall back home. 'Although, yes, I would say it is probably genuine. Those highlights look as though they have been administered by a stylist at a premium salon,' I say, admiring her butter-soft streaked hair.

It's so wonderful here, just people watching and making up little scenarios about the people that pass, something I also like to do back home. We never really know what is truly going on in someone's life though, despite outward appearances. I marvel at how the human spirit has most of us still managing to put one foot in front of the other each day and getting out there.

'It's lovely here, but I'm kind of glad we are staying in Perissa,' says Lulu, sipping her drink.

'Really?' I say, a little surprised. 'But it's absolutely stunning here.'

'Yeah, I mean it's beautiful, sure, but does it have any heart?' she muses. 'It's almost too picture perfect.'

'Hence the crowds and their cameras.' I nod to a tourist clicking away, and really think I ought to consider investing in a decent camera.

'Not to mention the poseurs.' Lulu laughs and for some reason a picture of Christos pops into my mind. Still, I imagine a guy like him knows how to treat a girl on a date. Imagine being collected in his Porsche and whisked off somewhere exciting. I can only dream.

'Oh, I don't know, I would love to live here.' I sigh as I glance around. 'Although I can't imagine nipping out to the corner shop for a pint of milk in a pair of old leggings.' I laugh. 'I mean, do people actually live here, and do such things, I wonder?'

'They must do,' says Lulu. 'Maybe it's very different in the winter months.'

I think of Christos and his family home once more, which is surely like something from a glossy magazine, as didn't he tell me his father owned many businesses here in Santorini? I idly wonder whether I will ever get to see a glimpse of his home. Or maybe Christos has his own apartment somewhere. Gosh what am I thinking?

I cast my eyes around the bar, observing the stylish couples, some men with expensive hair transplants. Well, possibly, as some of them look well into their fifties. I guess it's hard to tell these days, what with so many cosmetic procedures so readily available.

'Talking of cameras though, we simply have to have a photo of that backdrop,' I say, turning my camera onto us both, with the startling sky behind that is beginning to turn indigo, the sun quickly disappearing. They sky is so clear, a million twinkling stars will appear later in a navy night sky.

'May I?'

A passing waiter offers to take our photo, so we give our best pout as he snaps away with my camera phone. I thank him, then quickly upload the photo to TikTok.

An hour later, having had a gentle stroll along the winding, cobbled streets, we hear the gentle thrum of music as we approach the cool-looking nightclub that has a cave-like entrance. My stomach rolls a little at the thought of seeing Christos again, but I remind myself that he was probably just being courteous when he offered us a free cocktail. Even so, I reapply some lip gloss and spray on some more perfume before we enter the club.

Inside, the space is cavernous, dimly lit and extremely stylish.

A long bar displaying every kind of drink against a mirrored backdrop has several people sitting on bar stools, sipping drinks.

As we explore further, we pass booths with red-leather banquettes and in the middle of the room is a DJ playing club tunes from an elevated platform.

'Wow, this place is seriously cool,' says Lulu. 'I feel ancient though.'

'As if.' I laugh.

'I'll be forty soon,' she says.

'Which is no age these days,' I remind her.

'Maybe so, but what the heck, I'm up for enjoying myself,' she says, as she glances around.

As we make our way to the bar to order a drink, Christos appears out of nowhere and my stomach does a little flip. He looks smart in a dark shirt and a pair of cream-coloured trousers, an expensive-looking watch on his wrist. As he draws closer, I can see it is a Rolex.

'So you made it.' He leans in and gives me a kiss on the cheek, and I smell the Tom Ford scent once more.

He greets Lulu with a kiss on the cheek too, as we take our seats on bar stools.

'So, what is the cocktail of your choice? Spyros here can

make anything,' he says to the handsome but slightly serious-looking barman, or perhaps the correct term is mixologist.

'Really? In that case, you can surprise me,' I say. 'Anything vodka based.'

'I'll have whatever my friend is having,' says Lulu.

'Coming up,' says Spyros.

'I'm so pleased you came,' Christos whispers in my ear, as the bartender makes a theatrical display with the cocktail shaker. 'You look sensational,' he says, and I feel my heart rate go through the roof. Seriously what is wrong with me? This guy might as well have playboy stamped across his forehead.

'Thanks,' I manage to mutter.

Soon enough, a pink-looking liquid garnished with lime is poured into two cocktail glasses and pushed towards us.

'Oh my goodness, this is incredible,' Lulu says after taking a sip. 'What's it called?' she asks our bartender.

'The house cocktail. I call it a Spyros special.' He smiles, and it transforms his face. 'A little raspberry vodka, lime, ouzo and soda.'

'Wow, I agree it's delicious,' I say, although it feels a little potent.

Christos chats for a short while, talking about the wedding, and asking how long I have known Tasha. He is courteous and includes Lulu in the conversation, asking about her kids when she tells him she is a mother of teenagers.

'That must be hard work,' he says, sipping his iced water. 'I can't ever imagine having kids.'

For some reason, his comment gives me a twinge of disappointment and I tell myself to get a grip.

A while later the club begins to slowly fill up as the DJ ramps up the volume and plays some familiar club tunes.

A man around his own age approaches Christos, and he makes his excuses and disappears somewhere with him, telling us he will chat later.

'Bye.' I smile brightly, and then he is gone.

We take a seat in a booth, and listen to some music as I snap away with my camera phone. The selfies are amazing, and I cannot wait to upload them later.

'Fancy a dance?' I say half an hour later, having had another cocktail and raring to go. When I had produced my bank card at the bar Christos appeared out of nowhere once more and told us that they were on the house.

'Two cocktails.' Lulu had nudged me. 'He definitely fancies you.'

I brushed off her comment, but feeling secretly thrilled.

The floor is graced by impossibly glamorous types, some going for it and showing off their dance skills, others barely moving their feet and sipping drinks through straws.

'Go on then,' she says. 'Let's have a dance, another step towards really letting my hair down.' She winks.

As we approach the floor, the music switches to a well-known nineties club classic and Lulu and I really get into it, waving our arms and singing, as a bunch of women who have just entered the club join us.

Some of the too-cool-for-school types have drifted off to booths; others including Christos are watching the dancers from a balcony that surrounds the dance floor. Am I imagining it or can I feel his eyes on me?

An hour or so later, after a few more boogies, and a refreshing soft drink, Lulu and I decide to make a move. We have thoroughly enjoyed our evening here, but have planned a day out shopping in Fira tomorrow.

Even though Christos was watching from a balcony, I haven't spoken to him since earlier in the evening, when he generously paid for a second cocktail. In fact, I feel a little foolish for thinking that I might have been someone he was interested in.

We scan the room before we leave, hoping to say goodbye, but he is nowhere to be seen.

'Never mind, let's just slip out,' I suggest. 'He is obviously busy somewhere.'

Just then, I spot him in a dark corner of the huge bar, sitting on a bar stool and leaning in close as he chats to a beautiful blonde.

'He's over there,' says Lulu, pointing him out, and I kind of wish she hadn't so we could have just left unnoticed.

'And very busy by the looks of things. Maybe we should just leave him to it,' I say, striding towards the exit.

'It might be a bit rude if we don't say goodnight though,' she says. 'He did invite us here,' she reminds me, and I reluctantly agree.

'Maybe I just don't want to acknowledge the fact that actually this invitation was nothing special,' I say to Lulu. 'Perhaps he offers a free cocktail to everyone in an attempt to boost the numbers of clubgoers. It's probably nothing more than a bit of PR.'

'I'm not convinced. I have seen the way he looks at you, I think he really likes you,' she insists.

As we make our way towards him, our eyes meet, and Christos jumps to his feet.

'Mia, Lulu, are you leaving already?' He frowns.

'Yes, we have a busy day tomorrow, we were just coming over to say goodnight. Thanks for the drinks.' I smile.

'It was my pleasure. And actually, I realise I do not have your number.' He locks eyes with me.

'Oh right, and why would you want that?'

I nod towards the woman on the bar stool.

'She is a regular visitor here, I talk to everyone as you can imagine, as the manager of the club,' he tells me. 'I have to keep the customers happy, she is no one special.' He smiles that winning smile, and I tell myself that this guy is trouble. Even so, I find myself putting my number into his phone.

We stop for a couple of selfies on the way home, and Lulu takes one of me alone standing against an olive tree covered with twinkling fairy lights.

'So, what time do you fancy leaving tomorrow?' I ask Lulu as we sit chatting to each other in our adjacent beds.

'Not too early,' she jokes. 'I'm really relishing having a lie-in, and not having to set an alarm clock for work.'

Once more I am reminded that back home I currently have no such routine, which is something I would rather not think about, at least while I am here in Santorini.

'In that case, let's just head out when we are ready,' I say as I apply my nightly moisturiser.

'Okay. I'm really looking forward to exploring Fira in the daylight, and doing a little shopping. Some of those boutiques and gift shops look really cute.'

'I agree. I already have my eye on a couple of things I spotted tonight in a window.'

I wonder whether we might bump into Christos while there, but decide that is a selfish thought, as it's my day with Lulu.

'Maybe we could take the bus, rather than the car in case we want to have a drink,' she suggests. 'The buses are every hour, so maybe we could take a late morning one.'

'Sounds like a plan,' I reply as I stifle a yawn.

Later, before I drift off to sleep, I relive the evening at the club and the delicious scent of Christos as he stood close. He has such an effect on me, and I realise it's been a while since I have felt really attracted to anyone. He has bad boy written all over him, and yet I gave him my phone number. Oh well, if he is interested in giving me a call, then maybe I ought to loosen up a bit. Surely a little holiday romance can't hurt. Can it?

SIXTEEN

I go over the events of the previous evening as I get ready, wondering if I will ever hear from Christos again. He did take my number though, although perhaps that is what he does, then when there is not much happening, he scrolls through his phone and calls someone, his contacts like a little black book.

I finish brushing my teeth, before applying a slick of clear lip gloss and heading downstairs with Lulu.

'Are you having breakfast this morning?' asks Irene as we approach them.

We are booked in on a room-only basis, but have taken breakfast at Sea Breeze across the road most mornings.

'They do a continental breakfast here, you know,' Patsy reminds us. 'If anyone fancies some cold cuts and cheeses.'

'I probably shouldn't be spending so much, but the omelettes at the Sea Breeze are the best,' I say.

'And we did save a little money on drinks last night, due to the gratis cocktails, after all,' Lulu reminds me.

'Sea Breeze sounds good, mind if we join you?' asks Patsy.

'You don't need to ask, of course you can join us,' I say as Irene folds her newspaper and places it on a coffee table.

We take a seat at our favourite table overlooking the sparkling water, and Irene asks us about our evening at the nightclub.

'It was something else, really cool,' I tell her, recalling my reaction as I walked through the door. 'Expensive though. I'm glad Christos bought us those drinks,' I say dreamily, as I think of him once more. I can't seem to erase the image of him, that chiselled jaw, those dark eyes and that easy smile that makes my heart skip a beat. I tell myself to get a grip and stop acting like a love-struck teenager.

'Oh, to be young again,' Irene says. 'I bet the club was full of handsome young men.' She sighs deeply, and Patsy tells her to behave.

'Anyway, those young studs wouldn't give me a second glance, although I have read that some men like an older woman. Cougars they are called.' She winks and I can't help but laugh out loud.

'Nobody calls men studs anymore, Irene, now you really are showing your age,' Patsy tells her as she sips her coffee.

I describe the interior of the club, then imagine what it might be like to share a booth with Christos, sipping a cocktail before dancing together to a slow number, his arms wrapped around me. Afterwards, he would take me back to his place. I wonder if his bedroom is huge like the ones featured on the Abbey Clancy programme.

'Earth to Mia, I said do you want any water?' asks Patsy again, pulling me out of my delicious daydream.

'Sorry, yes, sure. So what did you two get up to?' I ask Irene as the already warm sun bathes my arms.

'We had some food, then we went for a bit of a walk along the beach. I'm starting my fitness and weight loss programme right here, trying to achieve a certain number of steps every day,' Irene informs me. 'I have installed an app my phone.'

'That's brilliant, well done you,' I tell her.

'Yes, and as we were walking, I stumbled upon something,' she says, reaching into her bag. 'I found this.'

She pulls out the most beautiful gold necklace with a sizeable emerald.

'Oh wow, that is stunning,' I say, looking at the jewel that glints in the sun.

'Someone must be missing that. Are you going to hand it in to the police?' asks Lulu.

'Yes, of course,' says Irene. 'But I just thought I would first ask around this morning at the breakfast restaurants to see if anyone has lost a necklace. It was directly opposite a café further down the road.'

'Don't describe it though,' says Patsy. 'Just ask if anyone has lost any jewellery.'

'Well I'm not that daft,' says Irene, rolling her eyes.

An hour later we say our goodbyes as we head off in different directions.

'Bye, I hope you find the rightful owner of the necklace,' I say to Irene.

'Me too. Catch up with you soon. Enjoy your shopping,' she says.

Window shopping more than anything, I think to myself, as I need to rein in my spending a little. It will be a great place for photo opportunities though, and I can't wait to explore the back streets and all the boutiques. One thing I will be spending a little money on is a gift for my parents and my gran. I don't know what I would do without either of them in my life.

As the bus rumbles along the road away from Perissa, we take in the grapevines and rugged volcanic scenery once more, before we finally pull into Fira. The road is lined with several coaches, carefully inching their way towards a car park, the area around bustling with pedestrians.

Alighting from the bus, the first thing we do is grab some bottled water from a nearby kiosk.

'That was an experience,' Lulu says, laughing and straightening her sunhat. 'The bloke standing in the aisle was practically sitting on my knee it was so crowded.'

'At least he was good-looking though,' I say, as once again an image of Christos pops into my head.

'True enough.' She laughs.

We head to the harbour, and watch a huge cruise ship making its way across the water. No doubt the empty restaurants, their tables set with cutlery, will soon have an influx of tourists descending on them.

'Fancy a beer before we do our shopping?' I ask Lulu. The bus was very hot, and the bottled water barely touched the sides.

'Sure, why not?'

We take a seat at a table with a blue-and-white checked tablecloth and a waiter hands us a drinks menu.

Sitting with our ice-cold beers and a gratis bowl of olives, we both peer out across the water to the caldera.

'You can take a boat trip out there,' says Lulu, popping an olive into her mouth as she glances at the island in the middle of the sparkling sea.

'What's there?' I ask.

'Not much really. It's the crater of the volcano, which although dormant still has volcanic activity below the surface. It hasn't actually erupted since nineteen fifty though,' she informs me. 'I read all about it.'

'I'm impressed with your knowledge, but you wouldn't catch me there, if there's a chance it could still explode.' I pull a face.

'Erupt,' she corrects me. 'Although I guess it's the same thing when you think about it.'

'Well, I prefer to admire it from a distance,' I say, before grabbing a selfie of us with the huge cruise ship in the background. 'It looks pretty though.'

'It really does. Do you fancy taking the cable car to the upper level when we finish our drinks?' Lulu asks. 'I mean, I don't mind walking up, but it might be fun. I've never been on a cable car before.'

A footpath can also be taken up to the main tourist area that has all the shops and restaurants, as well as some pretty churches.

'Although there is always the option of taking a donkey ride up,' I suggest, gesturing to some forlorn-looking donkeys at the foot of a path that heads upwards. 'Then again, no, that's a little cruel.' I quickly reconsider the idea.

We begin our ascent, walking for a few minutes, stopping to admire the view, and passing an abandoned white building with a blue wooden door hanging off its hinges. The walls are covered in graffiti of the evil eye, a Greek symbol said to protect people. As I stand staring at the house, wondering who might have once lived there, a lizard darts across my path and has me almost stumbling down the steps.

'You do know there are almost six hundred steps to the top?' says Lulu as the heat begins to pick up.

'Never!' I gasp.

'Yep, although I suppose it is a pretty good workout.'

'Maybe not in this weather though. Shall we go up in the cable car after all?' I suggest, thinking that maybe now is the time to cure my fear of heights. I might then fulfil my ambition of taking a trip on the London Eye to take in the views of the city.

'Sure.' She smiles. 'And you're right, that sun is pretty hot already.'

We make our way to the cable car departure point and join a queue, where I suddenly feel a little nervous. Maybe now isn't the time to be brave after all. Perhaps we ought to have just taken the steps very slowly. Too late now though, as the queue moves quickly and we are suddenly next in line.

As the cable car chugs along slowly, I close my eyes, when I feel it swing and we are momentarily suspended mid-air. Now is definitely not the time to tell Lulu that I am afraid of heights. She is chattering on about the sight of the caldera, and the rocky mountains either side that I imagine crashing into as I keep my eyes firmly closed. I barely have time to worry though, as in no time at all we have stopped.

'That was fun, and the views were stunning as we climbed, weren't they?' she says cheerfully.

'If you say so,' I tell her as we climb out of the car, before making our way towards the exit. I can feel my heart racing a little, although I am proud that I did it.

Stepping out of the cable car station into the dazzling sunshine, we eye the restaurants and the blue dome of a church with pretty stained-glass windows.

'Right, let's find these shops,' says Lulu, striding off towards a busy street. 'I have enough money left to treat myself to something nice, a reminder of being here,' she says.

'I'm not walking around with you if you buy a top saying "I love Santorini".' I giggle, although I am pleased that she has decided to treat herself.

'I doubt they would sell stuff like that,' she says, glancing at a dress in a shop window with a price tag of two hundred euros. 'At least not in this particular shop.'

'Anyway, you ought to get yourself something nice, you work hard and deserve it,' I remind her.

'I do, don't I?' She stops walking and faces me. 'And you're right, if I had given a handout to Chloe that wouldn't be the case. She has her jobs, she ought to save for the things she wants. Maybe she has learned a lesson, me saying no,' she reflects. 'I think it's time to close the bank of Mum and Dad for a while. Well, Mum mainly.' She rolls her eyes. 'Although I would never see either her or her brother in a fix.'

'Of course you wouldn't.' I smile. 'You are a good mother.'

'Thanks, although I do let them walk all over me a bit. You made realise that,' she admits. 'I do like being needed, but I know they ought to be a little more independent. Besides, they won't be living with me forever, so I'd better get started on making a life for myself.'

'That's the spirit.' I link my arm through hers. 'Let's start with some shopping.'

Weaving our way along the crowded, narrow paths, we pass dozens of white buildings selling all manner of things and jostling for space. Juice bars and cafés rub shoulders with fashionable boutiques and jewellery stores, some with their wares displayed outside on small wooden tables. A couple are peering at rings through the window of a jewellery store, their hands entwined.

As we descend some flat steps, we come across a shop with baskets outside containing traditional holiday souvenirs such as straw donkeys and fridge magnets. There are even T-shirts bearing the logo 'I love Santorini' with a little red heart at the centre and we both laugh. I spot tea towels and ships in bottles, when a snow globe catches my eye.

'My gran loves a snow globe,' I tell Lulu as I retrieve one from the basket and head inside. 'In fact, so does Mum.' I backtrack and grab another one. I buy Dad a wooden backscratcher with the word 'Santorini' painted across and with a shoehorn on the other end. Given all the huffing and puffing Dad does when he puts his shoes on, I'm sure it will come in handy.

We shop until we drop, although mainly window shopping, me taking photos here and there and loving every second of my day out with Lulu.

'I'll just nip in here and grab us some more water,' says Lulu, so I tell her I will pop to a shop next door for a sunhat. I stupidly forgot to bring mine with me, and I can already feel the effects of the burning sun on the top of my head.

After browsing in the shop, I select a plain straw hat and head to the till to pay.

'I think I will need this in these temperatures,' I say cheerfully to the guy behind the counter. 'Especially in this heatwave.'

'It is always very hot in July,' he tells me. 'Although it is a little hotter than usual. Probably due to climate change,' he says as I pay for the hat and my receipt chugs out of a card machine.

'Do you think so?' I ask. There have been many discussions about this in my household back home.

'I am sure of it,' he insists. 'Although it is hardly surprising with all the planes, and ships full of diesel making their way across the globe. Speaking of which' – he glances at his watch – 'a cruise ship will be descending on the island shortly.'

I would be quite happy to continue the conversation with the handsome shopkeeper, but a small queue has formed behind me, so I say goodbye.

Strolling along, I stop intermittently to take photos of my surroundings.

'Imagine staying there.' I point out a house to Lulu as she hands me a bottle of water.

We both glance down at a white, super cool house that looks a bit like a cave. 'They have their own private swimming pool too,' I say.

'Not that private though, is it?' reasons Lulu as we spy a couple below, stretched out on sunbeds next to their pool.

'I still wouldn't say no.' I eye the luxury accommodation enviously, although I take her point.

'I won't be a sec, I just need to nip in here,' says Lulu, indicating a nearby pharmacy.

I wait outside and the view is so stunning below, I perch myself, somewhat precariously, on a wall, and pout in preparation for a selfie. The camera wobbles a little, so I place one hand firmly on the wall to steady myself.

Just then, I notice a good-looking guy striding towards me.

'Would you like me to take the photo?' says the Greek guy from the shop earlier. 'It is quite a long way down.'

'Um, sure, if you don't mind,' I say, handing him my phone. 'And I guess you are right, it is a bit of a drop.' I smile.

'Although maybe you would have had a soft landing,' he says, a smile on his face as he glances down at the path below.

I take a peek and see that I was sitting on a wall directly above a load of donkey dung.

Lulu returns then, and raises an eyebrow at me when she notices me chatting.

'Maybe your friend would like to be in the picture too?' He turns to Lulu.

'Let's take a few of Mia alone, for her Instagram page, then, sure, I will get in one,' she tells him.

'So, are you a social media influencer?' asks the guy from the shop.

'I guess I am.' I grin. 'Although not as big as some I know. My followers are definitely growing though, so I'm happy.'

'And do you want to be rich and famous?' he asks me candidly.

'Erm, maybe I do,' I answer just as honestly. 'Isn't that what most people want, deep down?'

'Not necessarily,' he disagrees. 'Being rich is not a guarantee of happiness, which is far more important, I think.'

'Said no poor person ever,' I retort and he shrugs.

I give my best pose as he takes several photos before he takes some of Lulu and I together, before handing me back my phone.

'Thank you.' I smile.

'No problem,' he says, returning the smile before he disappears.

I watch him walk off, dressed casually in chinos and a rumpled blue-linen shirt, displaying the kind of look that says understated money. Maybe he isn't still living with his parents, unable to afford a deposit for a mortgage, then he might think twice about money not bringing happiness, or at least some sort of independence.

He has a vaguely familiar look about him but maybe he just looks similar to a lot of Greek men I have encountered, with his dark-brown eyes and well-trimmed beard.

I am staring after him, thinking how handsome he is, when he glances back and smiles, so I busy myself with my phone.

'All sorted?' I ask Lulu. 'Actually, are you okay, what did you need from the pharmacy?'

'Yes, fine, don't worry, I just needed some painkillers. Of all the times to get monthly cramps.' She pulls a face.

'Oh no. I hope it doesn't spoil your day, we can head back to the apartment if you like?' I suggest.

'No, I'm not going to let something like this ruin my holiday, I only have a few days left here.' She pops two tablets from a blister pack and swallows them down with a glug of water.

'Right, let's explore one more street, then we can find somewhere nice to rest and have some lunch.'

'Now I like the idea of that,' she says, linking arms with me.

We walk full circle and end up outside the gift shop I nipped in earlier for my hat.

Outside, wind chimes crafted from wood and seashells flutter gently in the wind. Tiny windmills made from metal and wood are displayed alongside glass sea horses on wooden shelves inside an old boat standing upright, making a unique display case.

'Let's make this our last stop, shall we? I barely had time to look around earlier,' I tell Lulu, who agrees and follows me inside.

A treasure trove of jewellery and gifts greets us, many in the colours of the sea, and there behind the counter is the bloke who took my photographs.

'We meet again.' He grins. 'The woman I saved from certain death.'

'That's a little overdramatic, don't you think?' I say, although I can't help laughing.

'She was about to disappear over a high wall before you arrived,' he explains to Lulu, who had a puzzled look on her face.

I tell her about me almost losing my balance on the wall, and how he came to the rescue.

'And yet I don't even know your name,' I tell him.

He introduces himself as Andreas.

'Hi, Andreas, I'm Mia and this is my friend Lulu,' I say cheerfully.

'Nice to meet you too, formally that is. Anyway, welcome once more and take a good look around. I am sure you will find something that takes your fancy,' he says, meeting my gaze.

'I'm sure I will.'

'Were you two flirting?' asks Lulu as we peruse some tasteful-looking blue wine glasses.

'No. At least I don't think so.' I laugh.

'He seems nice though,' she says, before sliding her fingers over a silk scarf, artfully draped over a piece of driftwood.

'He does. He's quite funny, too, which I like,' I find myself saying.

'Hmm. You haven't forgotten about Christos already, have you?' she teases. 'It's like speed dating, although you are probably too young to even remember that.'

'Oi, I know what speed dating is.' I nudge her playfully. 'I'm just saying he seems nice, that's all.'

'If you say so.' She raises an eyebrow.

'I do. Besides, he was probably just being friendly in the hope that we will buy something from his shop.'

'You're probably right, some of the stuff in here is gorgeous though,' she says, glancing around and taking it all in.

Lulu buys some silver earrings as a gift for her daughter and a shirt for her son, after asking a fashionable-looking guy around her son's age if he would wear the shirt and he confirmed that he would.

I select a honey drizzler made from olive wood, as I love to have honey and Greek yoghurt when I am back home. As Lulu looks at some more jewellery, I admire a few wooden sculptures. One is the face of a man who is stroking his face with his hand.

'Do you like that?' Andreas appears at my shoulder.

'I do, yes, it's quite eye-catching.' I stand and admire the sculpture, while Lulu is eyeing up some candles.

'Thank you. I actually made that myself,' he tells me proudly.

'You did? Wow, it's amazing,' I tell him honestly and he thanks me again.

'I love a wooden sculpture. I bought one for my friend as a wedding present,' I tell him, thinking about the gift I brought for Tasha. 'Is it the face of someone you know?' I can't help asking.

'Actually, yes, it is my father,' he reveals. 'Even though he doesn't see my art as proper work, but merely a hobby.' He shrugs.

'Really? Well, I think it's wonderful. You obviously have a real talent,' I tell him sincerely.

'Thank you,' he replies.

'I'm afraid I can't resist,' says Lulu, approaching us with a scarf and a chunky blue candle containing sea salt and sage that I spotted earlier. 'It is a gift to myself,' she says as she plonks it down on the glass counter.

'Good to see you treating yourself,' I tell her.

'I second that,' says Andreas as he takes Lulu's payment. 'In fact, feel free to treat yourself as much as you like,' he says with a cheeky grin.

Just then, the tinkle of the doorbell can be heard as a steady stream of customers file into the shop.

'Please excuse me,' says Andreas as he hands Lulu her bag of shopping. 'These people will be from the cruise ship. I may be very busy now.'

So you don't like the pollution from the cruise ships, but you don't mind the ringing of the tills? I think to myself, but for some reason, I stop myself from saying anything.

As we are about to leave, a young woman arrives and joins him behind the counter. They chat to each other in Greek, as the throng of day trippers make their way around the shop, searching for gifts.

'Can we get that lunch now, I'm starving,' I ask as we leave the shop with our gifts.

'Yep, let's go,' says Lulu.

'Thanks again,' I say, but Andreas is busy serving someone else and barely glances up as we leave. It was nice to chat to him and he seems happy creating sculptures and selling some in his lovely shop. Maybe there's something to following your passions and having a simple life?

SEVENTEEN

We manage to find a seat at a place down a side street that looks smart but casual, and without the eye-watering prices of some of the other restaurants in prime locations.

Sitting and relaxing in the sun, surrounded by plants on a pretty stone patio, I find myself thinking about Andreas and his talent. I also wonder why his father does not encourage it. Maybe he is like my father, who doesn't think being a social media influencer is a 'proper' job either. Although he does have a point, unless you can earn a living from it, I guess. Even then, it can be short-lived.

We both choose a tasty chicken dish, cooked in a tomato and ouzo sauce, that comes with salad and fries that we will wash down with ice-cold lemonade. I have just finished taking a quick photo, when my phone pings. It's a text from Christos asking me if I am free tomorrow.

'Everything okay?' asks Lulu, noticing me quietly staring at my phone.

'It's Christos, asking if I am free tomorrow.'

Much as I would love to see him again, I don't want Lulu to be left on her own. I did invite her here with me after all.

'I will tell him I have plans.'

'No, you go for it,' she insists as our food arrives. 'I might take things easy tomorrow anyway, after all the walking today. And with it being the time of the month.' She grimaces.

'Are you sure?' I feel excited by the prospect of a day out with Christos, but only if my friend doesn't mind.

'Absolutely,' she assures me. 'I would love nothing more than a beach day. Really, you go out and have some fun.'

'In that case, I will tell him I am free.' I feel a surge of excitement as I tap out a reply, telling him I am available, and he tells me he will collect me from my apartment at ten in the morning.

'Gosh, I wonder where he is going to take you,' says Lulu as she sips her drink. 'Somewhere smart, I'd say.'

'Do you think so? Oh my goodness, I don't know what to wear now,' I panic. 'What if it's somewhere *really* smart?'

'You look great in anything,' she says kindly. 'And you have lots of lovely clothes with you. Maybe a nice dress, and those white sparkly trainers, just in case it involves walking, an outfit like that could take you anywhere.'

'Sounds good. Can I hire you as my personal stylist?' I say, popping a chunk of salty feta from a Greek salad into my mouth.

'I don't think you need me.' She laughs. 'Not if all your followers are anything to go by, they love your style.'

When the bill arrives, Lulu insists on getting it, despite my protestations.

'No, really I want to,' she says firmly. 'It isn't the most expensive restaurant around here, and it's the least I can do after you inviting me to be your plus-one. I only paid for my flight and spends,' she reminds me.

'Thanks, Lulu, and I hope you are enjoying yourself,' I say as I finish the delicious meal.

'I really am.' She smiles. 'It's exactly what I needed, yet I didn't realise it,' she tells me as she wipes her mouth with a napkin. 'It was a harsh reality to hear that I run around after my children a bit too much, yet I knew it deep down,' she admits. 'Do you know, Chloe would never take a bus anywhere, and I indulged her, giving her lifts at the drop of a hat. My parents would never have done that for me, especially during daylight hours.'

'I understand you wanting to help, but they have to learn to stand on their own two feet. Maybe you could start by refusing to be a taxi during daylight hours when there is plenty of public transport,' I suggest.

'I know, and she seems to be able to do just that, when she is with her friends. Do you know, whenever I text her she doesn't reply for hours on end as she's doing her own thing, ditto Tom,' she says with a sigh of resignation. 'It makes me realise that I don't want to be one of those mothers who lives their life through their children,' she says firmly. 'I need to get one of my own.'

'Exactly.' I reach over and gently squeeze her hand. 'And I know a certain bloke who would be happy to help you do just that.'

'Who knows?' She shrugs. 'Maybe I would be open to that. If Phil likes me as much as you seem to think he does.'

'I'm pretty sure of it.'

She picks up her glass and clinks it against mine. 'Here's to the future,' she says.

Heading home tired out after our day shopping, we are approaching a roundabout, when a car with the roof down cuts into our lane and our taxi driver beeps his horn and shouts something in Greek as the car disappears in a cloud of dust.

Although I can't be certain, I thought the driver of the car was Christos. There was a woman sitting beside him, a headscarf tied around her head and wearing sunglasses, and looking very chic. I tell myself I must be mistaken. There are many men who drive sports cars and I never actually got close enough to see the driver properly.

Surely it could not have been Christos, I tell myself, the incident clearly playing on my mind, as we pull up into our village and pay the taxi driver. It was barely an hour since he asked me out on a date. Surely he would not have the cheek to do such a thing while out with another woman. Would he?

Arriving back in Perissa, we meet Irene and Patsy sipping tea at the Sea Breeze and they call us over.

'I hope you had a good day shopping,' says Irene. 'And you will never guess where we have been today,' she says excitedly.

'Ooh do tell,' I say, plonking down on a seat next to her, my mind still distracted by the bloke I thought was Christos.

'Well, I found the owner of the necklace,' she tells me.

'It was me actually, but never mind,' Patsy corrects her.

'Whatever. We found the owner,' Irene corrects herself.

'Oh, that is wonderful news. I bet they were thrilled.'

'You can say that again,' Irene continues. 'The necklace belonged to a lady whose husband had bought it for their wedding anniversary.'

'Yes, and he was so grateful, he invited us to their home for lunch in the afternoon, although it was more like a palace really, wasn't it?' Patsy turns to Irene. 'It had this huge marble balcony, overlooking a swimming pool.'

'Oh, it was not far from here actually,' Irene says, pointing along the road. 'Uphill slightly and directly overlooking the beach. Lunch was like a feast, served by their own staff, can you imagine? We had champagne too.' She smiles. 'We had to go for a little siesta afterwards, didn't we, Patsy?' She giggles.

'We did. They offered a reward too,' Patsy says, picking up the story. 'But Irene wouldn't hear of it.'

'Are you saying you would have taken it?' asks Irene in surprise.

'I might have,' says Patsy, fishing her vape from her bag and taking a puff. 'They weren't exactly short of money, and that necklace was worth a bob or two,' she muses.

'You never encouraged me to take it,' Irene replies with a frown. 'But perhaps I should have.' She ponders this for a moment before deciding that lunch was more than enough, and that it wouldn't have felt right accepting a reward for doing a good deed.

Later that evening, Lulu and I have some snacks on the balcony, before watching a subtitled romcom in the apartment bedroom. Lulu snoozes gently in the bed nearby before the ending of the film, and having decided to relax and put the incident at the roundabout out of my mind once and for all, I switch off my bedside light and drift off too.

EIGHTEEN

I am awake early the following morning buzzing with excitement, wondering what Christos has in mind for our day out.

After showering, I change and take Lulu's advice as I don a bright-green cotton dress and my white sparkly trainers.

'Oh my gosh, it seems we are going swimming,' I tell Lulu, who is sipping coffee outside on the balcony.

'Really? Are you going to the beach then? Or maybe a private club with a pool?' she suggests.

'I'm not sure but he has told me to bring a swimsuit,' I tell her as put a bikini on under my dress and stuff a towel into a beach bag. I'm feeling a bit rushed as he also said that he will meet me downstairs in five minutes.

'Sounds like it might be fun.' She grins. 'But only do what you are comfortable with.'

'I will,' I tell her, suddenly feeling a bit nervous. What does he have planned? I wonder. Maybe it is a private beach club? Or perhaps we are going to his house? I imagine that would have a swimming pool.

I don't have long to wait for the answer as downstairs, after

Christos has greeted me with a kiss on the cheek, I am being whisked along the seafront in his Porsche.

'Are we heading back to Fira?' I ask as we pass the familiar landscape.

'Yes, to the harbour.' He turns to me and grins. 'We are going to take my boat out.'

'Your boat?'

'Well, it belongs to my father really, but I like to think of it as the family yacht. And I guess it will be mine one day,' he says.

Did he just say yacht?

I take glances at him as we drive, sunglasses perched on his head, dark hair blowing ever so slightly in the wind, loving every minute of his life. Greek music is booming out from a car radio. I am pretty sure this guy would disagree with the bloke from the shop, who seems to think that money cannot buy happiness.

A family yacht though! I don't really know what I was expecting, but certainly not the sleek, long vessel that awaits us at the harbour. A waiter welcomes our arrival on board with a glass of chilled champagne.

'Please.' Christos gestures to the inside, panelled with walnut and decked out with cream leather seats.

'This is amazing,' I say, glancing around as I clutch my champagne. I almost feel as though I am in a scene of a James Bond movie.

'I'm glad you like it.' He moves closer to me. 'I love it. But then, I like all beautiful things,' he says, holding my gaze.

His cheesy line should have me rolling my eyes, yet something stirs in me.

'Come, let me show you to the sunbathing deck.' He takes me by the hand and my heart gives a little flutter.

He leads me to the top deck, where two sunbeds are waiting, along with the rest of the champagne bottle in an ice bucket and a bowl of strawberries.

'So how are you enjoying being here in Santorini?' he asks as the boat begins to move away from the marina and out into the open water.

'It's wonderful.' I sigh. 'Everything is just so picture perfect.'

'I'm glad you are enjoying it. Holidays should be about relaxing and having fun.' He smiles. 'Did you bring your bikini?' he asks. 'I thought we might anchor in a little while and enjoy a swim.'

'I have,' I tell him as I peel off my short dress to reveal my white bikini, a flattering, lacy number I bought in a sale back home. I notice Christos's eyes flick over my body as I place my dress down beside me.

He attempts to refill my glass, but I place my hand over it.

'Maybe later, but I'm not sure it's a good idea to go swimming after a couple of glasses of champagne.'

'Sure.' He shrugs. 'Whatever you think.'

We chat as the yacht sails, and he tells me all about his work at the club. I tell him a little about my social media, although he never really asked, but rather is keen to tell me about his own life.

'I spend a lot of time at the club,' he informs me as he sips his drink. 'And not just in the evening, I am involved in the staff recruitment, hiring DJs from around the world, arranging drinks promotions. Some might say I am a bit of a workaholic, but I love it.'

'Do any of your siblings work at the club?' I ask. I thought Spyros the barman bore a slight resemblance to him, but he tells me no.

'They have no interest in it,' he tells me. 'Besides, I don't think my siblings could do the job as well as I do.'

Modest then.

We sail across the striking blue waters, Christos spending some time on his phone I notice, only telling me about the surroundings when I ask him a particular question. When I enquire what the island is like in the winter, he pulls a face.

'Quiet. Too quiet, for me at least,' he reveals. 'Many people like it that way, especially the old people who say they have reclaimed their home.'

'Surely tourism is good for the economy though?' I ask.

'Undoubtedly. But the islanders don't think they really benefit. Unless they are business owners, of course.' He sips some water from a bottle of Evian.

Business owners like his own family, who must surely benefit?

'I can't imagine what it must be like to live here when the crowds leave,' I say as I lean on a rail and feel the wind blowing through my hair. The striking shades of emerald and navy give way seamlessly to swathes of blue that match the sky above as we move through the water.

'As I say, it suits those islanders who are glad to see the back of the tourists.' He shrugs. 'But I often take off for Ibiza when the season ends here,' he reveals.

'Ibiza?' I'm a little surprised as surely the tourist season is similar to here.

'Sometimes I spot up-and-coming DJs in the smaller clubs that still operate in the cooler months,' he says, answering my question. 'Then I might invite them here to work at the club the following summer.'

'Oh, I see. Gosh, you truly never are off duty, are you?'

'I told you the club is my life. I always make time for a little relaxation though. I believe the phrase is "work hard, play hard".'

He gazes at me in such a way that I can feel those tingles again. 'Are you ready for that swim now?' he asks.

'Sure,' I say, thinking that cooling off in the water is exactly what I need to do.

He calls out in Greek to the captain on the upper deck, and

a few minutes later we have anchored in the crystal-clear water. Christos pulls the white T-shirt he is wearing over his head, to reveal a most impressive six-pack.

He produces some goggles and snorkels from a storage trunk and hands me some.

'It is the best way to see what lies beneath the water,' he explains.

Lowering myself into the water from a ladder, I can feel his eyes on me. As I reach the water, I am surprised to find the water a little warmer than I anticipated, and enjoy the feeling as it washes over my skin.

Christos is standing on the deck of the boat, and he does a perfect dive into the water and soon appears at my side.

'Impressive dive,' I tell him. 'Do you practise?'

'Who wouldn't living here?' He glances around. 'And yes, I practised a lot to perfect my dive. I like to strive for perfection in everything I do,' he says proudly.

We explore the blue-green water, my breath taken away by the sight of the colourful sea life as I swim below the surface.

I'm thrilled to spot a baby octopus swim by and I tell Christos, who takes my hand in his and guides me to a spot where dozens of rainbow-coloured fish are crowded around a rock. It's all so magical. I could easily see myself living like this, spending days on the water and sipping champagne. I'm not sure how anyone could ever tire of this lifestyle.

After exploring the nearby waters we remove our goggles and snorkels, and Christos throws them up onto the deck, before we swim and lounge around in the glorious sea. I dream of having this life and can hardly believe that I go home to continue my job search in a few days' time.

I flip onto my back, and stare up at the warm sun, never wanting this afternoon to end, as Christos playfully flicks water over me.

He disappears from sight for a second and I squeal as he

reappears and I am suddenly hoisted up onto his shoulders from beneath the water.

We laugh, and swim some more, before we find ourselves drying off in the sunshine back on the deck of the yacht.

'That was wonderful.' I sigh, stretching out on my sunlounger, feeling the heat of the sun massage me all over. 'What a wonderful way to spend the afternoon.' I can hardly believe that someone like me could be experiencing this type of luxury. 'Thank you for bringing me here today.'

'It is my pleasure.' He smiles. 'Are you ready for that refill now?' he says, reaching for the bottle, and I gratefully accept another glass. Just then a waiter appears with a mixed meze of dips and bread, along with a platter of melon and grapes.

'This looks amazing,' I say, hungrily, tucking into the tasty buffet.

I ask him some more questions about his life, but he seems more interested in topping up my glass.

When the yacht eventually docks back at the harbour, Christos dismisses the staff and I feel wonderfully relaxed. Especially when below deck, he wraps his arms around my waist and draws me to him. When he kisses me, it feels like a thousand fireworks are going off all around the harbour.

'There is more to see on the yacht,' he says breathlessly, before he takes me by the hand and leads me to a room and pushes the door open. I glimpse the room that has a huge bed at its centre.

I am captivated by Christos and the seductive surroundings, but something brings me to my senses.

'Christos, I have had a wonderful day, but I really think I ought to be going,' I say, realising the champagne has gone to my head slightly. Thank goodness I had no more than a couple of glasses.

'Are you sure?' He kisses me gently on the neck, and my resolve almost disappears.

'Yes, I'm sure,' I say, feeling in a quandary. Part of me thinks, where is the harm in spending the afternoon with him here?

'Of course,' he says, with a smile that doesn't quite reach his eyes. 'Whatever you want.'

'I've had a truly wonderful time,' I tell him, when he drops me back at the apartments later. 'Thank you for everything.' But with the change in his demeanour, I wonder if I would have just been another conquest to him? The number of women he comes across at that nightclub certainly gives him plenty of opportunity for casual encounters.

'The pleasure has been all mine,' he insists, before he gives me a perfunctory kiss on the cheek. 'I will call you,' he says, before climbing back into his car, and roaring off.

Did he really think I was going to sleep with him in exchange for an afternoon on his fancy yacht? Then again, perhaps he really does like me. I hope he doesn't see me as an immature teenager, running off like that. I remember Lulu's words then, advising me to only do what I felt comfortable with, and feel happy that I trusted my instincts.

I bump into Irene and Patsy walking out of the apartments and they tell me they are heading over to the Sea Breeze, and ask if I would like to join them for a coffee.

'Sure,' I say, falling into step with them. Maybe a distraction from Christos is exactly what I need right now.

'So have you had a nice time?' asks Irene as we take a seat at our usual table.

I tell them all about my afternoon on the yacht as we order a latte.

'Oh, that sounds wonderful,' says Patsy, having a puff on her vape, and blowing it out to sea. 'Although I do get a little seasick on large vessels.'

'When have you ever been on a yacht?' asks Irene.

'The summer of nineteen seventy-eight. A college friend and I met two blokes in the South of France when I accompanied her there to meet a pen pal,' Patsy replies.

'A pen pal?' I ask.

'Oh stop, you're making me feel ancient again.' She laughs. 'A pen pal was someone you wrote letters to. There was no texting in those days, remember,' she says. 'Anyway, yes, these two blokes worked on this yacht and kind of smuggled us on for drinks and stuff,' she says, a faraway look in her eyes.

'Stuff?' teases Irene, with a raised eyebrow.

'Yes, we played music and danced. Get your mind out of the gutter. Anyway, the ship's owner arrived earlier than planned, who it turned out was really nice and let us have a little sail. I was as sick as a dog later, after those secret drinks though,' she admits, laughing.

'What did the pen pal do, while you were cavorting on the yacht?' I ask, now invested in the story.

'Oh, he had a chess competition as I recall. In fact, he played chess every day. It was the longest week of my life.' She shakes her head, and Irene and I laugh. 'And I wouldn't mind, but a heatwave had started back home, so I needn't have gone to France until the autumn. Anyway, I am more interested in hearing about how your day went.'

I tell them all about the swimming and snorkelling, the delicious platter of food and the cold champagne.

'Oh, that all sounds wonderful. Anything else to tell?' Irene asks with a wink.

'Nope. And even if there was, I'm not the type to kiss and tell,' I tell her.

I can't help reliving that glorious kiss though. And it would have been easy to have spent the afternoon with him in that huge bed. Too easy. Maybe I should have done.

'Oh, now you're just teasing,' says Irene. 'Did you even kiss?

I'm living my romantic life vicariously through others.' She sighs. 'I can just imagine a pair of strong Greek arms wrapped around me. That's all I can do though, is imagine.' She chuckles.

'Irene! Give over,' Patsy says. 'Are you sure you aren't the one on the HRT?' she continues, and Irene chuckles.

'We did kiss, actually,' I find myself saying. 'And yes, it was nice, but I don't think anything can happen between us as I'm going home in a few days,' I remind them.

'Never heard of a holiday romance?' asks Patsy.

'Yes, but they are not really my thing.'

Maybe I am just an old romantic, thinking Christos might fall madly in love with me, but something tells me he is most definitely not ready to settle down. Especially with someone who lives hundreds of miles away.

Spying Lulu on a sunbed a little further along the beach, I finish my latte and head over to her.

'How are you feeling?' I ask as I plonk myself on an empty bed next to her.

'Oh hi, Mia, I'm okay, thanks. I think chilling here today has done me the world of good.' She smiles. 'So how was your date?' she asks as she sits up.

I recount the story I have just told to Irene and Patsy as she takes a sip of her water.

'Are you going to see him again?'

'I'm not sure,' I tell her truthfully. 'There is no doubt he knows how to give a girl a good time, but I'm not sure he will contact me again.' I shrug. 'He has my number, though, so I guess it's up to him.'

'Why do you think he won't contact you if you had such a good day?' she asks, puzzled.

'Because he wanted to sleep with me,' I tell Lulu. 'It was as if he had carefully planned a seduction,' I tell her honestly.

'And obviously you weren't comfortable with that?'

'I guess I wasn't. And, as I recall, you did tell me to only do what I was comfortable with,' I remind her.

She reaches across from her sunlounger and takes my hand in hers.

'No one would blame you for having a little fun on holiday, but I think you should always follow your instincts,' she says wisely.

'Most definitely,' I agree. 'And I would rather not have my heart broken.'

I wonder whether men like Christos can ever be truly happy with one woman? And if they do settle down, are they constantly tempted? The thoughts swirl around in my head, yet despite everything I know that if he asked me out again I would probably say yes.

Lulu walks back to the apartment with me half an hour later, and that evening we take a stroll into a nearby village and eat at a small restaurant overlooking the sea. The outline of mountains dotted with a church and a cluster of villas close to the beach, their lights shining on the sea beyond, make for a pretty backdrop.

'Oh, I forgot to tell you that I bumped into Bryn and Ash on the beach earlier. They tried to persuade me to go paragliding,' Lulu tells me with an eye roll.

'Really? Oh my goodness.' I laugh.

'Bryn's alright really you know, he was going on about what a great voice you have,' she tells me as she squeezes lemon juice over some calamari.

'I know, I guess he's harmless, if a little touchy-feely,' I concede. 'I just thought he embarrassed Owen with the wedding speech, but maybe that's what blokes call banter.'

'It's funny how men insult each other and call it banter, isn't it?' says Lulu, before she takes a bite of her food. 'If a woman insulted another woman, she would be called a right bitch.'

'That is so true.'

'Anyway, talking of you singing, there is another karaoke evening at a bar tomorrow evening a short taxi ride away from the apartments,' Lulu tells me. 'Bryn was telling me all about it earlier. Apparently, it's a great evening, and often frequented by bar and club owners looking for decent singers.'

'Here in Greece? Maybe I won't go home then,' I say jokingly. 'Assuming someone thought I was good enough to offer me work that is.'

'They would be mad not to,' she says kindly. 'So do you fancy it then?'

'Sure, why not? I enjoyed singing the other night, maybe I ought to get a little more practice in.'

'Great.' She smiles.

I tuck into my delicious sea bass, with capers and herby Greek potatoes, and take a sip of chilled white wine. As we sit listening to the crashing of the waves on the nearby beach, despite everything, I imagine sitting here with Christos, when my phone rings. It's him.

'Do you mind if I get this?' I ask Lulu.

'Of course not.' She smiles.

Christos asks me if I am free to go on a winery tour tomorrow, to a small select vineyard.

'It is my day off, so I am all yours,' he says, and my heart rate increases. I had wondered if not agreeing to go to bed with him on the yacht had made him lose interest. But maybe I was wrong about him. 'There is a pretty wonderful hotel next door, although I guess I would say that, as it belongs to my family,' he informs me.

'Sounds delightful, although I thought you hardly ever took days off?' I tell him.

'Even workaholics need to take a break.' He laughs. 'I have been training a deputy manager, who is keen to take charge in my absence. Let's just say, I am making the most of it.'

I only have two days left with Lulu though, so I explain this and tell him I will message him to confirm. When I return to the table to finish my meal, I feel torn.

'So, has he asked you out again?' she asks.

'He has. Tomorrow though, which I don't think I want to do. You go home the day after tomorrow, and I want to spend time with you.'

'But you really like him,' she protests.

'And if he really likes me, he will arrange another time,' I tell her firmly. 'There is no way I am ruining your last full day,' I say and she thanks me. 'Besides, I love spending time with you.'

'Ditto.' She smiles.

'So what do you fancy doing?' I ask her. 'There's a Jeep safari into the mountains if you like the idea?' I suggest. 'I mean, I could get a map and take the car, but I think the Jeeps go off-road a little.'

'Actually, that does sound like a lot of fun. Sure, let's do it,' agrees Lulu. 'Let's book the Jeep safari though as we don't want to risk destroying the hire car.'

'Probably a good idea.'

We tap our glasses together and I message Christos and let him down gently. I also wonder why he mentioned the hotel next to the winery?

I am determined Lulu will enjoy the rest of her time here, especially as I am staying on for a few days longer to have a catch-up with Tasha when she returns from the island with Owen, before they head back to Australia. Handsome men come and go, but my friends have been there for me, through thick and thin; even Tasha all the way in Australia has always been at the end of the phone or a Zoom call.

So if Christos really wants to take me out again, then he knows how to contact me.

NINETEEN

We are up early and after a breakfast of fruit and pancakes at the Sea Breeze, we are waiting outside our hotel for a coach to pick us up for the journey that promises 'a mesmerising adventure to Santorini's most photogenic spots'.

It will be just perfect for my social media pages, as well as sounding like a whole lot of fun.

'There is a monastery on this trip,' I say as I look at the itinerary on my phone. 'I love a monastery visit.'

I'm not sure why that is as I'm not from a particularly religious family, but I just find them fascinating, the way they take pride of place sitting high in the mountains like a watchtower over the villages below. Plus, they tend to be beautiful inside, with stained-glass windows and ancient stone floors.

'We visit Red Beach too,' says Lulu, consulting the itinerary on her own phone.

'What's that?' I ask.

'I'd say it's a beach with red sand.' She laughs. 'But I guess we will find out more on our trip. We will then head to Akrotiri Lighthouse and have a wander around. Apparently, it is very picturesque.'

A few minutes later, we excitedly climb into our white Jeep that has arrived with a loud toot of the horn.

Our smiling driver, who is wearing a grey baseball cap, greets us warmly and tells us to buckle up and prepare to have a great time. Another couple are already seated inside the Jeep, and I recognise them at once as the couple from the plane on my outward journey.

'Hello again, how is your holiday going?' I ask brightly.

'Hi, fancy meeting you here!' says the bloke from the plane who had recognised me from my Instagram page. 'Oh, we're having a great time, aren't we?' He turns to his partner.

'Oh, we are.' She smiles. 'It's so gorgeous here it would be hard not to. How is your holiday going?'

'Loving it,' I tell her. 'There is so much beauty all around.' My thoughts flit to Christos then, and the day out on the open water.

I explain to Lulu about us being seated next to each other on the plane, and introductions are made.

Four more Jeeps arrive then, and we set off in convoy. Soon enough, we are heading away from the main tourist areas, and traversing the windy mountain roads. As our Jeep crawls higher towards the monastery, the views below become more and more breathtaking.

The plane couple, who are called Lisa and Paul, tell us they are considering the area for their future wedding and I tell them all about my friend's wedding a few days earlier. Once more, my mind flits to Christos and how I first encountered him in the lift at the hotel.

'Sounds idyllic, although I'm not sure we could consider anything that expensive,' says Lisa.

'I don't think it needs to be,' I say. 'There are plenty of smaller venues and the sunshine really makes it. Not something you can ever be certain of back home.'

'That's true,' she says. 'I'm dreading leaving this sunshine behind.'

Our driver knowledgably points out places of interest as we travel, including the remains of old villages destroyed in the earthquake, and the names of pretty little white churches set back in the hills.

Eventually, we climb out of the Jeep and I stand in front of the Profitis Ilias that seems to be almost touching the clouds.

Pushing open the heavy wooden door of the church and stepping inside, I feel the sense of thousands of years of history wash over me. There is a faint smell of incense, along with candle wax from candles burning gently in a copper stand. A lady wearing a black-lace veil sits in one of the dark wooden pews, her hands joined in prayer.

'Oh wow this is beautiful,' whispers Lulu as we glance around. A huge stained-glass window behind an altar at the far end of the church casts light into the dark space.

I always feel a sense of peace in such places and take a candle from a box, and light one for my grandad, the funniest man I have ever known, who passed away three years ago.

Outside, I take some photos, including a selfie, standing alongside the Jeep and with a view across a valley.

'I'm sure your social media will go wild when they see your photos from Santorini,' says Lulu as we walk.

'I hope so.'

I think she might be right as the posts I have uploaded up to now have had thousands of views.

'Imagine being able to make a living from your social media?' says Lulu. 'Although I do hope you would still take on some singing jobs. You should never waste your talent,' she tells me as we stand on top of the hill taking in the vista.

'Ideally I could combine the two, but I think I am still a long way from earning any real money through social media, although my followers are growing,' I tell her.

'But you do get recognised.' She nods towards the couple from the plane, who are walking towards us.

'That rarely happens, but yes, I guess so.' I smile.

'And an awful lot of freebies too,' Lulu reminds me, so I guess I am pretty fortunate in that respect. 'But I know you work hard on your content to make that happen,' she acknowledges.

'I do, and all the really highly successful influencers must have worked so hard to get to where they are too. It doesn't come easy,' I tell her, thinking of the hours and hours I have spent making and uploading videos and sharing content, yet I still only have a fraction of the followers they have. The free gifts and invitations are coming though, so I guess I need to just keep going.

Soon enough, we have jumped back in the Jeep and are making our way towards Red Beach, where we will make a quick stop to look at the windmills of Emporio.

Passing peasant houses with goats in the front gardens, and nearby allotments growing vegetables, I idly think of what Christos would make of this environment. The lifestyle of the villagers is a far cry from the flashy nightclubs and luxurious yachts he frequents. And even though I like those things too, there is such a calmness and feeling of authenticity about being here that I can't help but find it completely charming.

Stopping at the windmills that date back to the nineteenth century, some intact, others in ruins, we explore the remnants of the ancient village, and admire the endless sea and mountain views.

Our driver tells us knowledgeably that the windmills were once owned by a wealthy landowner who wanted to produce wheat, the location being perfect to power the mills with its high winds. They became obsolete in the twentieth century, with the onset of modern machinery.

I take a couple of selfies and a few with Lulu in front of the windmills before we move on.

Outside a village house, we spot some home-made olive oil and ouzo for sale, displayed on a wooden stand. We both make a purchase, much to the gratitude of the seller.

'What a way to see the real Santorini,' says Lulu as we climb back in the Jeep and are driven along, sometimes on rocky, single-track roads where we are gently lifted from our seat.

'It's wonderful, isn't it? Although Christos was saying that the locals don't always appreciate the tourists.'

'I think those locals appreciated us,' says Lulu, lifting her bag of organic olive oil and two jars of local honey.

'I think he was referring more to the residents of the congested areas. Andreas in the shop mentioned the ships and how they descend in huge numbers too.'

'Surely it's good for business though?'

'That's what I thought, which I guess it is, but he said he wished people visited more in the spring and autumn rather than descending all at once in the summer months, as it's kinder to the infrastructure.'

'I get that. Although I guess if you have a beautiful island everyone is going to want to admire it in the sunshine,' she reasons, and I think that is probably true.

Stopping for refreshments a short while later, we order ice cold frappes and I think of how little time I have left here in Santorini. It occurs to me then that I don't really have anything to rush home for. I have no job, and I am living with my parents. Then again, my spends have almost run out and I could never have been here without the accommodation being paid for. I quickly check my emails on my phone to see if there is any news about the jobs I have applied for, but there is nothing forthcoming.

We take a trip to Red Beach, which is pretty much as Lulu said, an unusual red beach made by volcanic eruptions. The rocks are rich in iron which gives them the red colour, our guide informs us. After taking a walk around and snapping some photos, we are soon making the journey back to Perissa.

'I loved every minute of that,' says Lulu as we drive along the mountain roads. 'I know it's a tourist trip, but at least you get to see how the locals live in the villages. I'm not sure I could live in a village though,' says Lulu. 'Everybody knows your business.'

'I think there is a strong sense of community though,' I argue. 'And I wouldn't mind having a couple of goats in the garden. Maybe even a bee hive to make my own honey.'

I surprise myself by thinking it would be a genuinely lovely thing to do. I could make my own goat's cheese too. But as I don't even have a place of my own, I probably have more chance of flying to the moon.

TWENTY

By the time we are dropped off in Perissa, the main street is filled with people strolling along or eating in restaurants and the sound of music can be heard gently playing from bars. The lively atmosphere is in complete contrast to the stillness of the mountain villages we have just left.

Back at the apartment, Lulu begins to place some clothes into her suitcase. 'I can't believe I'm heading home tomorrow.' She makes a sad face. 'I would definitely enjoy spending more time here.'

'I'm so glad you came and put yourself first for once,' I tell her. 'And we can really enjoy your last evening here.'

'Thanks, Mia. For one so young, you talk a lot of sense.' She smiles. 'And I'm so looking forward to hearing you sing once more this evening,' she says kindly.

'Thanks, I am looking forward to it.'

Lulu has persuaded me to go along to the Oyster Bar for the karaoke evening tonight, and despite a slight feeling of nerves at the thought of singing in public again, I actually feel quite excited.

'And maybe it's a good thing that I have a later flight home tomorrow so I can enjoy a cocktail this evening,' she adds.

'Sounds good to me.'

Bryn and Ash are coming along too, as are Irene and Patsy. Bryn has struck up a rather charming friendship with Irene, who tells me they have been texting each other, Bryn updating her on his adventures such as paragliding, her telling him what she and Patsy have been up to.

'I'm just nipping to the shop on the corner for some milk,' I tell Lulu, noting the empty carton in the fridge. 'I could murder a cup of tea right now, I will be back in two ticks.'

'Okay. I'm going to do most of my packing now, so I can relax tonight,' she replies.

The local convenience store has its shutters down, so I walk further along the front past the bars and cafés, and take a right turn to another, larger supermarket. I recognise at once a car parked outside.

'Mia, hi. How was your day?' asks Christos as he emerges from the shop carrying a bottle of ouzo. The sight of him sets my pulse racing.

'It was wonderful, and so nice to get a glimpse of the real Santorini.' I tell him briefly about the villages we drove through and the places we visited.

'I'm glad it was worth letting me down for.' He gives a wry smile.

'My friend goes home tomorrow. I wanted us to spend her last day together,' I explain once more.

'I am teasing,' he says as he climbs into his car.

We chat for a few minutes more, and I am slightly disappointed that he doesn't suggest another date. But then, he has had rather a lot of time away from the club of late, despite having a trainee manager.

'You look good,' he says, before glancing at his watch. 'Look,

I have to be somewhere now, but maybe I can see you again before you head home?' he asks, and my heart soars.

'I'd like that.'

'I'll be in touch soon.' He raises a hand and winks before he roars off.

Walking back to the apartment after purchasing the milk, I relive the day we spent together on the yacht.

As I swam in the gorgeous clear water and sipped champagne on deck, it gave me a glimpse of a life I can only dream about. And I am finding it hard to stop thinking about that kiss and how it made me feel, despite telling myself he is not someone you could ever be serious about, not with his lifestyle. I idly wonder where he is off to, with his bottle of ouzo?

I feel flattered that he has taken an interest in me though, Mia Green, twenty-eight-year-old aspiring social media influencer, when he could have his pick of women.

I'm almost back at the apartment, when I spot Irene and Patsy having a natter with Bryn and Ash in a café.

'Fancy a drink?' Irene calls and I lift the carton of milk.

'I've just bought some milk to have a brew on the balcony,' I tell her. 'Although I'm not sure why either of us are drinking tea in this weather.'

'I'm sloshing about in water I've drunk so much of it,' Irene tells me as I approach their table. 'Nothing like a good cup of tea,' she says.

'And this is nothing like a good cup of tea.' Patsy pulls a face. 'I'll bring my own teabags next time I go abroad.'

'Right,' says Bryn as he and Ash stand up. 'I'm off to see if we can win the jackpot at an afternoon quiz in a pub up the road. It's up to two hundred euros. Anyone fancy making up the team with us?' he asks hopefully.

'Sounds like fun. But we've only just returned from a Jeep safari. I'm a bit pooped, so will save my energy for later,' I tell him.

'You disappoint me.' Bryn puts his hand on his heart.

'See you all tonight at the karaoke though?' I ask.

'Oh, I wouldn't miss it.' Bryn smiles. 'I might even get up myself, if you fancy doing a duet,' he jokes, while Ash shakes his head behind his back.

'Not unless you want to ruin your reputation,' Ash warns me.

Back at the apartment, I enjoy a refreshing cup of tea before I take a shower, then upload some more photos for my social media accounts. I have also received an invite to the launch party of a new upmarket furniture store in the town centre at the end of the month that sounds like fun. They are having acrobats and fire-eaters apparently, along with the usual free cocktail and a buffet. I quickly tap out an acceptance to the party, before I select an outfit for this evening.

I notice Lulu smiling at her phone as I am getting ready.

'All okay?' I ask as I apply some mascara.

'Yeah, it was Phil from work asking if I could bring some sunshine back with him, apparently it's pouring down back home.' She pulls a face. 'There have even been floods, but thankfully not where we live.'

'Great. I might stay here for a bit longer then,' I say, only half joking.

'Oh, and Tom messaged me earlier to say he's off next week trekking in the Andes.'

'Is he?'

It's Lulu's fortieth birthday at the end of the month. I know she will be upset that he won't be around, but I decide not to say anything.

'I guess he won't be joining in my birthday celebrations, although I'm sure they will be pretty low-key anyway,' says Lulu, with a resigned shrug.

'Who says so?' I go and place my arms around the shoulders of my friend. 'I'm sure Phil will brief everyone at work and do something nice. And, of course, there is me and Zoe,' I tell her. Zoe being another friend she has from work. 'And your gym friends.'

One thing Lulu does do is look after herself, with regular trips to a local gym and a hairdresser.

'I know, you're right, although I won't be broadcasting it. Forty and single, with rubbish job prospects, is hardly something to shout about.' She manages a laugh.

'Nonsense! And I was actually wondering if you would you like to be my plus-one for a party at the end of the month?' I tell her all about my most recent invitation. 'It's close to your birthday, if you fancy it? It sounds like it could be a great night.'

'Oh, that does sound like fun. Thanks, Mia.' She smiles warmly.

I imagine she feels hurt that her son won't be around to help her celebrate her big day and I wonder how he could be so thoughtless. It's not as if he doesn't know when his mother is turning forty.

I will also message Phil at the catalogue to make sure they have at least a cake, although I'm sure there will be a little collection for her when he finds out it's her fortieth.

TWENTY-ONE

'Right, let's go,' I say, grabbing my bag. 'Apparently karaoke night at the Oyster Bar is very popular, so we will need to bag a seat.'

'Sure. And to get your name down for singing your duet with Bryn,' Lulu teases and I can't help but laugh.

We meet up with Irene and Patsy, and are soon strolling along the front in the balmy evening air, where the gentle buzz from the busy bars and restaurants can be heard.

'Are Bryn and Ash definitely joining us later?' I ask as we walk.

'Hopefully,' says Irene with a slightly worried look. 'Ash texted me earlier to tell me that Bryn had a run-in with a surfboard and whacked his head.' She sighs. 'He's been checked over, but might have to take things easy for a bit,' she explains.

'Oh no, I'm sorry to hear that,' I say with concern.

Bryn it seems has grown on me these past few days.

'What happened to the quiz?' asks Lulu.

'He got the time wrong apparently. It would have been a damn sight safer though,' Irene comments.

'Well, I hope he turns up,' says Lulu. 'Or he won't be able to be Kenny Rogers to your Dolly Parton on the karaoke.'

'Can you imagine.' I laugh. 'All the same, I hope he's okay.'

At the end of the road a bus appears, heading to the next village where the Oyster Bar is, so we decide to jump on rather than take a taxi. Thankfully there are some empty seats, as lots of people have just disembarked here in Perissa.

'What are you going to sing?' asks Lulu as the bus trundles along. Irene and Patsy are sitting behind, laughing at something together.

'I'm not sure. I am torn between a lively crowd-pleaser, or perhaps a more soulful tune.'

'I'd go for the lively crowd-pleaser,' Lulu advises. 'People like that kind of stuff on holiday, me included, if I'm honest. The moody soulful stuff, beautiful as it is, is best suited to a candlelit restaurant or a piano bar.'

'You're probably right.'

My voice is definitely more suited to easy listening type songs, and I also enjoy singing big ballads too but a lively tune is probably the best choice for this evening.

Alighting the bus, we make the short walk to the bar, which is filling up nicely but we manage to secure a table towards the back.

At the front, adjacent to the bar that has foliage hanging down from a shelf above, is a small stage. The dark wooden chairs and tables have vases at the centre containing a single pink flower.

With pink and yellow painted walls and reggae music playing in the background, the bar has an almost Caribbean feel. The whole place has a good vibe and I think the evening will be a lot of fun.

We take our seats, and a waiter wearing a suitably loud-patterned shirt appears and takes our drinks order. I glance around, but there is no sign of Ash or Bryn.

I'm sipping my drink and tapping my foot to an uplifting song that is being played, when I spot a familiar face amongst a small group of blokes. It's Andreas from the gorgeous gift shop in Fira.

'We meet again.' He smiles at me when I walk past him a while later after returning from the ladies.

'Oh, hi, how are you?' I ask. He seems better looking than I remember. And taller.

'I am good, and you?'

'Yes, I'm great thanks. I wasn't sure you would remember me, given the number of tourists that enter your shop,' I say jokingly.

'Ah, but not all of them needed my assistance with a photograph,' he reminds me. 'Or saving from losing their dignity.'

'Ah the donkey droppings.' I laugh and when he smiles in return, his dark-brown eyes crinkle at the corners. 'I suppose I was lucky that you happened to be there.'

'I believe everything happens for a reason.'

Andreas looks good, in a fitted black T-shirt that shows off a toned body, and a pair of smart stone-coloured shorts.

'So, are you here for the karaoke?' he asks as he places several bottles of beer onto a tray.

'I am. I have just put my name down to sing,' I inform him.

'You have? Then I hope I am around long enough to hear you.' He grins. 'We are heading to another bar later. It is a friend's birthday.' He gestures to one of the small group of men who are chatting in a group a little further away.

'I hope so too,' I say, although I feel inexplicably nervous at the thought of him hearing me sing. Gosh why did I tell him I was singing?

'See you later.' He smiles as he goes to rejoin his friends. 'Good luck with the song.'

'Thanks.'

'You don't waste any time, do you?' teases Irene when I return to the table.

'What are you talking about?' I laugh off her remark.

'I saw you chatting up that bloke at the bar. Have you forgotten about the walking Adonis from the nightclub already?'

'What? Don't be silly, it was just a bloke from the shop we visited the other day. It was Andreas,' I tell Lulu.

'Ah the photographer.' She nods. 'He was a nice bloke, as I recall.'

'Photographer?' asks Irene, and I tell her all about him helping me as I tried to take a selfie on the wall.

'Well, he seems quite taken with you. Don't look now, but he keeps glancing over here,' says Patsy.

A few seconds later, I casually glance his way and sure enough he is looking over. When we make eye contact, he raises his beer and smiles.

Unable to decide what to order, we all decide to share a huge mixed meze, and it arrives in next to no time. The table is groaning with an assortment of dips and pitta breads, lamb koftas, chicken skewers and halloumi fries. A huge Greek salad topped with a slab of feta is placed in the centre.

Soon enough, the first person is up to sing.

'They must be professional,' whispers Irene as the beautiful notes of the female singer reach around the room.

Next up is a bloke who does a rousing cover of a Meatloaf song and has the crowd singing and clapping along. I won't be on until later in the evening, having only just put my name down, so I can sit back and relax for now, and just enjoy the show.

During a short break from the karaoke as a DJ plays some tunes, Andreas comes over to say hi to Lulu, and to inform me that he and his friends are moving on.

'Good luck with the song,' he says kindly. 'Although I may

actually be able to hear you sing, as we are only moving to a bar a little way along the road.'

'How will you know it's me singing?' I ask.

'I think I will just know,' he says, which makes me smile. 'Anyway, enjoy the rest of your evening,' he says to everyone, before he departs.

'What a nice bloke,' says Patsy.

'Mia seems to attract them,' says Lulu, with a raise of an eyebrow.

'What can I say? It must be my sparkling personality,' I say modestly, with a smile.

The standard of singers this evening is alarmingly good, which has my tummy feeling a little nervous. It makes me wonder whether it was this feeling that prevented me from pursuing a career as a singer, as the tension and nerves always get to me before a performance. It probably isn't helping that I have so long to wait this evening before it is my turn.

Bryn and Ash arrive then, and soon distract me with stories of surfing and Bryn gives us a detailed account of his accident in the water.

'I thought my number was well and truly up,' he says dramatically. 'I swallowed water, as I went under, it was a dark moment.' He exhales.

'Good job Ash was there then,' says Irene, leaning over for a halloumi fry before stopping herself.

'I think you would have done just fine; we weren't out very far,' says Ash, smiling. 'In fact, I think I could actually stand up in the water.'

'Oh, let me have my moment, will you,' says Bryn. 'My life flashed before my very eyes.'

'If you say so.' Ash takes a sip of his drink, while trying to keep a straight face.

We chat for a little while longer, until my name is called to sing and my friends are on their feet.

I make my way to the front, to the sound of my friends' whoops and cheers, trying to quell the rising nerves. As always though, the second I grab the microphone, my nerves disappear and I feel the rush of adrenaline.

The crowd-pleasing song in the form of a Shania Twain number goes down a storm and has everyone on their feet waving their arms and singing along. By the time the song finishes, I feel exhilarated as I make my way back to my table to the sound of thunderous applause.

'Wonderful,' says Irene, clapping her hands together. 'Just wonderful. Singing is obviously what you were born to do,' she tells me kindly as I sit down.

We listen to some more singers as the evening wears on, many really good, and Irene's comment sticks with me. Maybe this is exactly what I was born to do. So why am I so fixated on pursuing something so completely different?

TWENTY-TWO

Strolling along as the evening draws to a close, we bump into Andreas and his friends queueing at a local taxi rank.

'Mia.' Andreas waves over. 'I am glad I have bumped into you. I think I heard you singing, if you sang the song about feeling like a woman?' He grins. 'Which is just as well, as you are one,' he says, and has me laughing. 'I have to say, you sounded amazing.'

'You are correct, it was me, and thank you,' I say, doing a little bow.

'No, really you were very good.' He nods slowly, looking ever so slightly the worse for wear.

'Thanks again,' I reply.

He stands with his hands in his pockets for a moment as if he is about to say something else. Just then, one his friends calls him over to a waiting taxi.

'Anyway. See you around,' he says as he departs. 'I might see you if you call into the shop again, before you leave.'

'Maybe I will,' I tell him, thinking that I might just do that.

As we walk, Irene spots the headlights of a bus approaching, so we quickly make our way to the bus stop just up ahead.

'That was quite an evening,' says Irene as we flop down into our seats. 'I have so many happy memories here to take home with me.' She sighs contentedly. 'And I can't wait to see Tasha and Owen tomorrow when they return to Fira. It was so wonderful watching them get married.'

'It really was. And I hope you don't mind me asking, but have you seen anything of Tasha's dad, other than at the wedding?'

'Not really.' She shakes her head. 'Although he has been staying at the hotel in Fira. We did have a nice catch-up at the wedding though, and I am glad he has met someone else, it's just...' She pauses for a moment. 'Every time I see him, it reminds me of my sister. I miss her terribly and it seems to open up the wounds,' she tells me honestly. 'Selfish, I know.'

'It isn't selfish,' I say softly. 'And to be honest, if he was all alone, then yes, maybe I could understand you feeling that way. But he has met someone else now, and seems happy.'

I recall him laughing with his partner, as they got up and joined in the Greek dancing.

'I suppose you're right.' Irene smiles. 'He has managed to move on and I am happy for him. And it's not as if I won't keep in touch with him. It's just that it has only been a year, so it's still a little strange, seeing him with someone else, you know?'

'I understand. Some men don't like to be alone. In a way, it's testament to the happy marriage he must have had with your sister, not wanting to face the prospect of being all alone.'

Irene reaches across and grasps my hand. 'You always manage to say the right thing.' She smiles. 'You really are wise beyond your years.'

'Just look at the size of that moon,' says Patsy, gazing out of the bus window at the giant white full moon. 'And those stars against that clear night sky. I'm dreading going home to the cloudy skies and drizzle,' she grumbles.

'Me too,' agrees Irene. 'This island is providing so many memories, it will be a wrench to leave.' She sighs.

'Then maybe we ought to sell up, pool our resources, and buy a place out here,' says Patsy dreamily.

'I'm not sure I could take the long hot summers,' says Irene. 'And I would be broke from constantly having to fork out for batteries for my fan.' She laughs.

'You're probably right,' agrees Patsy. 'Maybe we will just leave Greece for our holidays.'

As we drive in the darkness along the twisty road back to Perissa, I find myself thinking about Andreas, then give my head a little shake. The prospect of one holiday romance is enough, and even that isn't really a certainty. But two? That surely is a bit much for anyone. Besides, telling me I have a good voice, and mentioning that I might see him in the shop is hardly flirtatious behaviour. But then, Patsy did say he was staring over at me in the karaoke bar, so who knows?

I retrieve my phone from my bag and stare at the video Lulu has sent over of me performing on the stage of the bar. It's okay I think, but there is definitely a high note in the middle that is off. I can hear my voice crack a little, although I'm sure no one else noticed. But maybe they will. The song was in a slightly lower register than I am used to at the beginning. For a second I think about posting it to my socials, finger poised over the share button. But something stops me, and I tuck my phone back into my handbag as we continue our journey towards Perissa.

TWENTY-THREE

After a slightly restless night tossing and turning, I am awake early enough to watch the morning sun rise, and I marvel at its beauty. Not many things are certain in this world, but the rise and fall of the sun can always be relied upon.

I am enjoying a coffee, enjoying this peaceful time of the morning, when Lulu appears at the balcony door, arms stretched above her head and yawning.

'You're awake early,' she says sleepily.

'I know, I didn't sleep too well last night,' I tell her. 'Maybe I will have an early night after I have dropped you at the airport later.'

I haven't really driven the hire car too much, having explored on the Jeep safari and taken local buses, but I may take myself off for a drive another time. It also means I can drive myself back to the airport as there is a branch of the car hire place where I can drop it off.

I tell Lulu to grab a cup, then pour her a coffee from the cafetière on the small table in front of me.

'I can't believe I will soon be back at work, taking orders for clothes.' She sighs as she sips her drink. 'Although, I think I am going to sign up for my dance classes again. Being here has given me a lot to think about,' she says thoughtfully.

'It kind of does that when you are away from everything, doesn't it?' I say, thinking that maybe I ought to try and secure a few singing jobs when I get home. Despite the nerves, singing here has made me realise just how much I love it.

'It does. And having a life of my own is right at the top of the list,' says Lulu. 'Do you know, Chloe called earlier asking me when I would be home, which I thought was nice, and would you believe she was only after a lift somewhere.' She shakes her head. 'Unbelievable. I bet her and Tom won't even think to make sure there is some milk in the fridge, and there is me, always fussing about them.'

'You will always be there for them. I guess that's what being a parent is,' I say. 'But if you prioritise your own needs occasionally, it might make them grow up a bit,' I suggest.

'Most definitely.' She smiles. 'Right, I'm off for a shower.'

'Okay. Is there anything you want to do today?' I ask 'We have hours until you need to go to the airport.'

'Fancy a drive up to Ammoudi?' she suggests. 'I've been googling it, and apparently there is a wonderful fish restaurant there. I don't think there is a lot else but it looks like a pretty setting. I thought maybe we could have a late lunch there before I leave?'

'That sounds lovely.'

While Lulu is in the shower, I receive a message from Christos asking if I am free this evening. I hesitate for a moment, despite feeling those familiar butterflies, before deciding why not? I was half not expecting him to reach out after I turned down the winery. I arrange to meet him at eight thirty after I have returned from dropping Lulu at the airport.

I flick through my socials then to find the pictures of Santorini have tens of thousands of views, and my followers are up by two thousand! I also have another invite to a fashion show next month at a smart hotel in a nearby city.

I hold my phone to my chest, and sigh with happiness. If my followers keep on growing like this, I will soon have ads on my page that can earn me an actual living, so at least things are going in the right direction.

Which is just as well really, as no job offers have come through. I hear that these days there are really high numbers of applicants chasing a single job, which is a bit disheartening to say the least.

We linger over a light breakfast of fruit and yoghurt at the Sea Breeze restaurant, before Lulu says her goodbyes to Irene and Patsy as I will be dropping Lulu at the airport on the way back from lunch.

'I'm going to miss this place,' says Lulu, glancing out across the sparkling sea. 'The local café back home doesn't quite have the same appeal.' She sighs.

'I don't suppose anywhere is perfect, although I would rather be having a bad day over here,' says Patsy as she turns her face to the sun.

We sit chatting for a while longer, before we decide to make a move.

'Well, it has been so lovely meeting you,' says Irene, hugging Lulu as does Patsy after they walk us to the hire car.

'Another friend to add to WhatsApp. It feels good to be in touch with lots of people,' Irene says with a wide smile. 'Even if I don't see them often, it makes me feel connected somehow, which is nice.'

'It does,' agrees Patsy. 'And maybe we could all meet up again when we get home?'

'I would love that,' I say, pleased to be reunited with Irene after all these years. Especially as they only live around an hour's drive away.

'Although I will be joining that slimming club when I get

back, so you might not recognise me next time you see me,' Irene tells us with a cheeky wink.

'Please say goodbye to Bryn and Ash for me,' says Lulu, when she suddenly hears a voice behind her.

'You can do that yourself,' says Bryn, who is with Ash.

'I thought you were going on an early boat tour?' says Irene in surprise

'We've booked a later one as I thought we might have breakfast here first.'

'We've already eaten,' says Patsy. 'But I would love another coffee.'

'I'm glad we caught you before you left,' Bryn says kindly to Lulu. 'And if you ever fancy a trip to Australia, you can come and stay in my apartment. Both of you, of course.' He turns to me. 'In fact, all of you, I have three bedrooms. And did I mention it's a penthouse? I have a view of a park and a glimpse of the river,' he tells us and I realise I would quite like that too. Bryn has really grown on me these last few days.

'Thank you,' says Lulu, before we step into the car.

'Gosh, I feel almost emotional,' says Lulu, after waving to our friends until they are out of sight. 'I really have had the best time here.' She sighs contentedly. 'I can't thank you enough for inviting me as your plus-one.'

'It has made it even more special for me, you being here. I'm so glad you came,' I tell my friend.

'I am glad you persuaded me.' She turns to me and smiles.

I'm so looking forward to seeing Tasha tomorrow too, and making the most of my remaining time here in Santorini. As we drive, I tell Lulu that Christos has been in touch and that I am meeting with him later this evening.

'Well, I can definitely see the attraction,' she says as we make our way along the picturesque mountain roads. 'As long as you are in control, which I have no doubt you are. As you said, you don't want to get your heart broken.'

'Don't worry about me,' I say brightly, realising she is right to be cautious. Despite that, a tiny part of me wonders if there's the possibility of him settling down. Could I be the one to persuade him to do just that? We might fall madly in love and I could stay in this paradise forever. We could be the golden couple of Fira, welcoming celebrities into the nightclub. I could work on the social media alongside him and together we could make a great team.

I guess it does no harm to dream.

Arriving in Ammoudi, we descend some white steps from the main street to a small beach area that leads to the restaurant below. We are greeted by the glorious sight of the Aegean Sea almost lapping at the table legs and circled by red-coloured hills in the near distance. A string of octopuses is hanging over a rail near the edge of the water, and several fishing boats can be seen out at sea.

It's pretty busy here, but Lulu rang ahead and luckily managed to reserve us a table.

'I see what you mean about it being pretty here,' I tell her as I glance around.

As we take our seat at our table on the wooden terrace it feels almost like being on the deck of a boat.

'I know, it's quite something here, isn't it?' agrees Lulu. 'I don't think the photos on the website really do it justice.'

Glancing around I spot a cosy wooden-hut style bar tucked away in a corner, and strung with fairy lights, which I imagine would look incredible in the evening.

'It's a shame we never came for the sunset here, it would be incredible,' says Lulu, glancing around.

'There's always next time. If you fancy returning to Santorini, that is,' I say as we pick up a menu.

'Oh, I would love to,' she says enthusiastically. 'I might even consider it for next year. No doubt Tom and Chloe will be off somewhere on their own travels, and I can't say I blame them.'

She shrugs. 'They don't spend long in some of the places they visit, but at least they are seeing more of the world than I ever have.'

'They don't, do they?' I think of the time I went to Rome for a day on a budget flight. But it's nice to stay a while and really savour a place; being here has made me realise that. 'And it's your time now that the kids are older remember, so maybe you could see some of the places you always promised yourself you would visit,' I suggest. 'And I would always be happy to save up and join you,' I tell her.

'I might just hold you to that. I have always fancied Paris actually,' she says.

'Ah, the city of romance. Maybe you could go there with Phil,' I tease.

'What are you like! He hasn't even asked me out.' She is laughing as a waiter arrives and we place our order.

'And would you say yes, if he did?'

'I think I might.' She smiles. 'What do I have to lose?'

As I know for a fact that he likes Lulu, I might give Phil a nudge in the right direction.

We choose the same dish, the catch of the day, and dine on the most delicious red mullet, drizzled with lemon juice and parsley, served with salad and chunky handmade chips. The portions are so generous, we share a dessert of *galaktoboureko*, a custard cake dusted with icing sugar.

'Well, that will keep me going on the flight,' says Lulu, pushing her bowl away, sated.

Although the restaurant is busy, we never feel rushed as our waiter deposits some more bottled water onto the table. Despite it being a tourist area, there is no pressure to leave the table as there is back home, where everything feels hurried. We savour every minute of Lulu's last day here as we sip our iced water and feel the warm sun on our skin.

After our wonderful lunch, we have a wander around the

area passing more bars, a couple of restaurants, and just taking in the view.

'Those steps back up to the car will work some of that lunch off,' says Lulu, as we ascend the steps back to the car park at the top. We pass donkeys on the way up, and a woman offers their services. We politely decline, despite the heat, especially as there not as many steps as there were in Fira.

Back in the car, I switch the car radio on as we head to the airport, and we listen to Greek music as we drive along.

'These songs remind me of the Greek dancing at the wedding,' says Lulu as we drive, and I recall Christos interjecting as I danced with Bryn, and how I felt when he draped his arm around my shoulders.

'They do.' I smile. 'I'm so happy my friend had such a fabulous wedding. I can understand why people choose to marry here in Greece,' I say, batting away an image of myself and Christos standing at an altar in a tiny Greek church.

When we finally arrive at the airport, Lulu takes a small gift wrapped in tissue paper from her handbag, and hands it to me.

'What's this?' I ask in surprise.

'It's for you.' She smiles. 'Open it.'

Inside the tissue paper is the prettiest blue stone at the end of a leather thong necklace.

'It's lapis lazuli,' she explains. 'It's thought to enhance one's intuitive abilities. Not that I think you need to do that.' She smiles. 'I just thought it looked very pretty.'

'Oh, Lulu, it's beautiful, thank you.' I stroke the stone, admiring its beauty, the stone streaked with a blue and green pattern that reminds me of the sea.

'It's so lovely, but there was really no need to buy me anything,' I tell Lulu.

'I just wanted to get you a gift.' She smiles. 'I have had such a wonderful time here and you are a good friend, Mia. You tell me the truth, even when I don't always like it. That's what I call a real friend.'

I embrace my friend in a lingering hug and thank her once more.

'Safe travels,' I say, feeling a little choked up, before she heads off towards check-in.

As I watch her leave, I realise that despite my aspirations to be a singer, and to live my happily ever after with the love of my life, my friendship with Lulu is one of the most important things in my life. I truly hope that never changes.

TWENTY-FOUR

Arriving back at the apartments a little after six, I think about the evening ahead of me with Christos. I wonder if he will take me to the club this evening, so he can keep an eye on things there? I don't mind if he does really; I would like another chance to visit the cool place. Maybe we could have a photo together for my socials.

As I step out of the car, my phone pings with a text from Christos asking me what time he should collect me, so I suggest around an hour from now.

I take a shower then and change into a summery floral dress. Before I know it, Christos is standing outside my apartment carrying a bottle of red wine. He is dressed in black from head to toe, in jeans and black T-shirt looking as hot as hell.

'I thought we could have a drink here before we head out,' he suggests.

'Um, sure,' I say, thankful that I have tidied up the apartment as I lead him outside to the balcony.

I bring two glasses to the table and he pours us each a glass of red wine.

'Oh, this is delicious,' I say. Even though I know nothing about wine, I can tell this is good stuff.

'I thought it would be, a supplier at the club recommended this,' he tells me as he lifts the glass and examines its contents.

After drinking a second glass of the delicious wine, even though Christos is still nursing his first glass, I wonder where we might be heading tonight. It's doubtful we are going to the club though, as he has driven over here in his car.

'I thought I would take you to dinner somewhere not far from here,' he tells me, answering my question. 'There is a very special place I know of, where the sea laps the shore. You can also see the most amazing sunset.'

'That sounds beautiful,' I tell him, delighted that he is taking me to such a romantic-sounding location.

'Just like you,' he says meeting my gaze. His lines are smooth and practised, yet they manage to thrill me all the same.

We head inside, and as I am about to place the wine glasses into the sink, I feel Christos's arms around my waist. He nuzzles my neck and I almost drop them.

I turn to face him then, and he takes my face in his hands, and kisses me on the lips.

'You look wonderful tonight,' he whispers. 'I almost feel like staying here. Maybe we could go somewhere local later.'

I feel light-headed but somehow manage to keep my composure. When he kisses me again, I almost think that perhaps we ought to just stay here after all.

Just then, my stomach does the loudest rumble.

'Although, maybe you are so hungry, we really ought to go and eat.' He laughs, the moment between us passed.

'I think that is probably best.' I smile, thinking perhaps it is sensible to head out for dinner. I'm pretty sure of which way things will go if we stay here, as having drunk the wine on an empty stomach, it has gone to my head a little.

'And perhaps I am being a little selfish. The restaurant we

are going to really is quite something. Are you ready then?' he asks as he picks his car keys up from the coffee table.

'Ready,' I say, following him outside.

There is a comfortable silence between us as Christos drives as the car radio plays some gentle ballads, fitting for a romantic evening out. Around fifteen minutes later, we pull up outside a restaurant, and as we step out of the car the setting takes my breath away.

As we walk along a crazy-paved path illuminated by large candles in storm vases, I take in the white-painted floorboards of the terrace that is dotted with palm trees in huge stone pots. The sea is so close you can almost touch it.

'Wow, this place is something else,' I remark as a waiter leads us to our table, where the sound of the waves can be heard crashing against the shore.

I notice most of the tables are occupied by smartly dressed couples sipping wine and chatting, the whole place giving off an intimate, romantic vibe.

A red-leather menu is handed to us, and as I glance over it, I can see that the food looks eye-wateringly expensive. Christos doesn't flinch as he orders some bottled water and a glass each of champagne.

'I don't want you to think I am trying to get you drunk.' He smiles. 'Although I can get the whole bottle if you like?' he offers.

'A glass is fine,' I tell him. 'Champagne though, what is the occasion?'

'Do we need one?' He shrugs as he sips his water.

'Perhaps not.'

'Besides, what is the point of having a lot of money, and not enjoying it?' he reasons. 'I work hard, and enjoy my downtime.'

With how many women? I find myself thinking.

The waiter arrives with our ice-cold champagne then, and we place our food orders.

'So here is to enjoying life, and making memories.' He clinks his glass against mine, and locks eyes with me.

'I'll drink to that,' I say, glancing around and thinking how lucky I am to be sitting with a handsome man in a place like this. The sky is already beginning to form a purple hue, the white sun tinged with streaks of red and orange as it begins its descent.

A starter arrives in no time, and is arranged like a piece of art on a plate.

'So was your father from a business family?' I ask Christos as I spear some food onto my fork, interested to know if he was born into a wealthy family or self-made.

'He had quite a good start,' he tells me. 'My grandfather owned a fish restaurant, and his father before was a fisherman.'

He slices into a scallop and takes an approving bite.

'My father had a lot of ambition and expanded the restaurant,' he tells me. 'Soon he had a string of restaurants on the island, as well as a few shops.'

'And the nightclub?'

'Yes, of course, although I did a lot of the work developing that,' he says proudly. 'It was nothing more than a quiet bar to begin with.'

'You were given an opportunity though, not like a lot of people,' I can't help saying, and his face changes.

'Maybe.' He shrugs. 'But even with an opportunity, it takes hard work to make a success of things,' he says, barely acknowledging his father's input.

'I don't doubt that.' I feel like adding how much more I admire people who start with nothing, but I don't want to ruin the mood.

Christos clearly doesn't appreciate that he has been lucky to have been given a good start in life, and I think of how many people make a success of life when they have nothing to begin with. I had to work really hard to build a following on social media, spending hours making videos that are only now beginning to reap benefits.

My thoughts are distracted by the food when it arrives which is utterly delicious. The beef in my stifado is beautifully tender, the sauce rich and deep. A plate of warm olive bread sits beside it on a plate, along with a small mound of delicately fragranced rice.

'This is just fantastic,' I say to Christos as I eat my food. 'How is yours?'

'Amazing,' he says as he dives into a delicious-looking veal dish served with a peppery sauce.

'Do you come here a lot?' I ask, noticing how the waiter shook him warmly by the hand when we arrived, and how they laughed and joked together in Greek.

'Maybe not a lot, but regularly,' he reveals. 'The food and location are exceptional; I am sure you would agree?'

'Oh, I do.' I smile, wondering how many other women he has brought here.

Over dessert, Christos seems distracted and glances at his phone several times I notice. After he has settled the bill, he seems keen to leave.

The sky has darkened now, and the sound of the crashing waves entices me towards the beach. I wonder whether Christos would be keen to take a little walk after dinner, but instead he suggests we head back to my apartment.

'Are you sure you wouldn't like to have a little stroll along the beach first?' I press. 'Walk off some of that delicious dinner?'

'It is a pebble beach, I am not sure I have the right footwear,' he says, glancing down at his expensive-looking leather shoes. 'But we can certainly come here again, if you would like that?'

'Sure.' I smile but feel slightly disappointed. I thought a romantic stroll beneath the stars might have finished off the evening nicely.

On the journey home, I realise he never asked me any questions about my life back home, despite me asking him about his father and the family business. And I wonder why he seemed a little preoccupied with his phone over dessert? Not to mention being in such a hurry to leave.

Despite these reservations, as I sit next to him in the car, I can feel the simmering chemistry between us, and almost wish I couldn't. When he momentarily squeezes my hand on a quiet stretch of road, I feel the familiar desire in the pit of my stomach.

Stepping out of the car, Christos hangs back for a moment, waiting for an invite inside. As he stands close and I take in his scent, I open the door with anticipation, as he quietly follows me indoors.

'Would you like another drink?' I offer, about to take some wine from the fridge, when suddenly his lips are on mine, making me catch my breath.

'Only if you want one.' He presses his body against me and my resolve to hold back a little seems to be disappearing by the second, when all of a sudden my phone rings.

My first instinct is to ignore it, but when I see it is from Patsy, I feel compelled to answer.

'Patsy, hi, is everything okay?'

'Oh, Mia, I'm so sorry to call you, but it's Irene.' She sniffs.

'Irene? Is she okay?' I ask anxiously.

'She's having some tests. I am at the hospital with her now. She collapsed in the street, went down without warning.' She talks quickly. 'She's cut her head; gosh she looks awful,' she tells me, her voice catching.

'Do you want me to come to the hospital?' I offer at once.

'Oh no, don't ruin your evening. I'm just so worried about her, I think I just needed someone to talk to, and I didn't want to bother Tasha on the last day of her honeymoon,' she says.

I can tell Patsy is worried, and most definitely needs someone with her right now.

'I'm on my way,' I tell her, before thinking I will grab a taxi on the main street.

'I'm so sorry.' I tell Christos all about Irene.

'I would take you, but I have to be somewhere very early tomorrow morning, and you may be waiting for hours,' he tells me.

'Don't worry, I understand.'

'But at least let me pay for the taxi,' he says, following me outside into the street.

I protest, but he pays the driver in advance as I step into the taxi, one of several in a nearby rank.

As we head off, I wonder whether Christos will bother contacting me again. Perhaps the stars are just not aligning for us to spend the night together, and maybe there is a reason for that.

I put that to the back of my mind as I think of Irene, wondering what I might find when I get there. I hope her injuries are not too serious, although Patsy did sound a little stressed. Poor Irene. It must be frightening spending time in an overseas hospital.

Despite the situation, I try to enjoy the journey, the roads quiet in the evening. We drive past a café at the top of a hill, the outside threaded with lights. A few people are drinking coffee at outside tables, their quad bikes parked up nearby, probably after a day out exploring.

Half an hour later, having driven through the serene, mountainous landscape, we are approaching the town, when I call Patsy and tell her I will be there shortly.

'Oh, Mia, you are an angel. It will be so good to see you,' she tells me gratefully.

I thank the taxi driver, and after enquiring at the hospital reception desk, I locate Patsy sitting at the bedside of Irene, who is sleeping.

'How is she?' I ask Patsy, who stands and gives me a hug.

'We are waiting for the result of an X-ray,' she says anxiously. 'It seems her heart rate was very high, although the doctor did say that may just have been down to the shock of the fall. At least, I think that's what he said.' She frowns. 'He spoke so quickly some of it may have been lost in translation.' She sighs.

'I'll see what I can find out. In the meantime, I will go in search of coffee, you look like you could use one,' I tell her.

'Thank you. I don't think I want to sleep until I know she will be alright, so I might need it to keep me awake.'

After locating a drinks machine, I am striding along a corridor, when I spot a familiar face walking towards me.

'Andreas? What are you doing here?' I ask in surprise.

'I have just driven a friend here. He injured his ankle during a game of football, thankfully it isn't broken.' He pulls a face.

'Gosh, that sounds painful.'

'For the team too, as he is our best striker,' he tells me with a wry smile. 'Actually, I am about to leave, as my friend's partner is here with him now. Will you be needing a lift anywhere?' he offers.

'Thank you, but I think I want to find out how Irene is doing first.'

I tell him about Irene and Patsy being here after Irene's fall.

'Ah, the ladies you were with the other evening.' He nods. 'I am sorry to hear that. Is your friend going to be okay?' he asks sincerely. 'I am in no hurry, so I don't mind waiting, if you need taking home.'

'Actually, if you are in no rush, I wonder if you could ask the doctor exactly what is going on? Patsy seemed a little confused earlier.'

'Of course. I will be glad to be of help.' He smiles.

Back on the ward, a doctor is happy to speak to Andreas on

Patsy's behalf. The pair speak quickly, and I dearly wish I knew a little Greek.

'Well?' Patsy asks anxiously when the doctor leaves.

'It is as you said,' says Andreas. 'The doctor thinks her blood pressure is raised because of her fall. She was a little shocked but thankfully nothing is broken. She will be kept in overnight for observation.'

'Thank you, Andreas, that's the bit I wasn't sure about, although I know he said something about sleeping.' She nods. 'Talking of which, why is she so sleepy, have they sedated her?' Patsy ponders, by which time the doctor has moved on to another patient.

'I am not sure but maybe they have given her something to help her relax. It seems to be working, as her blood pressure appears to be going down,' says Andreas, glancing at the machine she is hooked up to.

'Have you had medical training?' I ask curiously.

'Hmm, not really, although I did once consider becoming a doctor. I helped to look after my grandmother too, and learnt a little basic knowledge, including reading blood pressure,' he tells me. 'That was before I discovered I preferred making sculptures. In preference to being a doctor, I mean, not to looking after my granny,' he jokes.

I think about my own gran then, and how I also like to look out for her.

'What a lovely thing to do,' says Patsy as she sips her coffee. 'Well, it looks like I will be spending the night here too, if Irene is,' she says. 'No sense in going all the way back to the apartment, to be here again at first light. Besides, I wouldn't settle.'

'Then let me ask if there is a guest bed. Or at least a more comfortable chair,' insists Andreas, as he approaches a passing nurse.

'What a lovely young man,' says Patsy. 'And nice thighs,' she says, noting his strong legs clad in football shorts. I can't help but laugh as I think of Irene's comment about the side effects of Patsy's HRT.

I try to imagine what Patsy would do if anything were to happen to Irene, and dearly hope she will make a full recovery. Patsy never had children, and throughout her life Irene has been a close friend as well as a cousin.

'Here we are.' Andreas returns a short while later, carrying a fold-up bed; a nurse behind him has some bedding and pillows. In no time at all, he has set up the bed next to Irene in the spacious room.

'Oh my goodness, I can't thank you enough,' she says to Andreas. 'Here, at least let me buy you a coffee or something.' She peels a ten-euro note from her purse, but he holds his hand up in protest.

'Really, there is no need,' he insists. 'I hope Irene gets well soon. I am sure she will,' he says positively.

Seeing Irene settled, I take Andreas up on a lift back to my apartment.

'Thank you so much for the help,' I tell him once more as we head towards the hospital exit. We soon arrive at his Audi.

'It was no problem. And it has me wondering why we keep running into each other. Perhaps it is written in the stars.'

'What is?'

'I'm not sure.' He cocks his head to one side and regards me as he starts the engine. 'But I think I quite like being in your company.'

'You think?' I laugh, realising that I feel the same way. He is just so funny and easy, and not just on the eye. I feel completely relaxed around him.

'I am sure.' He nods. 'Is that better?'

'Much better, thank you.' I can almost feel the heat rising in my cheeks, and hope it doesn't show.

'So how much longer will you be here in Santorini?' he asks as we make our way out of the hospital grounds.

'For a few more days,' I tell him, having decided when I booked that I would have just over a week here.

'And do you have plans?' he asks me as we join a main road.

'My friend will be returning from her honeymoon tomorrow, so I will spend the day with her catching up.'

'But the day after that? Maybe you are free?' he enquires.

'I could be,' I find myself saying.

'Then perhaps I could take you to the beach where I collect driftwood,' he suggests. 'It is my day off the day after tomorrow. Sometimes I find sea glass too.'

'I like the sound of that,' I tell him, imagining how lovely it would be to go beachcombing with him.

'So you will join me?'

'Yes, why not.'

'Perfect.' He smiles.

It's late as we drive, and I stifle a yawn as I struggle to keep my eyes open, although that may be down to the alcohol I consumed earlier. The roads are quiet at this hour and, in no time at all, Andreas is dropping me outside my apartment.

He takes my phone number, and tells me he will text me. 'Oh, and I will bring a picnic,' he says to my surprise.

I head to my room in a daze. Have I just agreed to go on a date with Andreas? I'm not exactly sure how that happened, yet it felt so natural. And no date of mine has ever prepared a picnic.

I glance at my phone, and notice I have no messages from Christos to enquire about Irene. Or if I even arrived home okay. I then wonder what on earth I would do if he asked me out on another date? Do I really want to be dating two men? I stuff my phone into my bag as I get myself ready for bed in a complete quandary.

TWENTY-FIVE

I climb into bed when Patsy calls and thanks me once more for coming this evening.

'I've just nipped outside for a quick vape, before I settle down for the night,' she says. 'I really must quit.'

'I'm sure you will eventually. Anyway, I will call you in the morning and see what's what,' I tell her. 'I am sure Tasha will also want to know how Irene is doing too.'

'I'm sure she will, although I don't want to worry her, especially as she will be back off home to Australia soon enough.' She frowns.

'She would want to know though,' I assure her. 'Anyway, goodnight, Patsy. Make sure you get some rest.'

'Oh, I will, I'm pretty pooped now, it's all caught up with me,' she says, stifling a yawn. 'Thank you for coming, Mia, I was in a right old state earlier.'

'My pleasure, I don't think I would have settled either, wondering how Irene was doing.'

Before I close my eyes, I think of how the phone call from Patsy caused my evening with Christos to end abruptly. Then I think of the date I have the day after tomorrow with Andreas and my head is filled with confused thoughts. It seems I enjoy the company of both of these men, even though they couldn't be more different. It takes me a little while to get to sleep. What an eventful day this has been.

I'm awakened the next morning by the sound of a shrieking alarm. It takes me a second to realise that a fire alarm is going off in the apartments.

I grab my robe and pull it around me as I head out into the corridor, where a member of staff is leading everyone to a fire escape.

'Is it a real fire?' I ask someone, bleary-eyed.

'We are not sure just yet,' says the staff member as he ushers everyone along, speaking to another colleague quickly in Greek.

A few minutes later, a fire truck arrives and the other guests and I are gathered in the car park of the apartment, while someone does an inventory of the guests using a laptop.

'Good job the weather is so nice,' says a woman I recognise from the wedding. 'I wouldn't fancy standing out here in the rain.'

'Me neither,' I agree.

A group of us stand chatting for a few minutes, when I hear a familiar voice behind me.

'Oh my goodness, what on earth is going on?'

I turn to find Tasha and Owen, who have returned from their few days away.

Tasha glances all around, as the crew from the fire engine head in the direction of some smoke billowing out from a ground-floor window.

'And oh my goodness, where are Irene and Patsy?' Her hand flies to her mouth as she glances around, unable to locate them. 'They are not still inside are they?' she asks, panicked.

'No, no they aren't,' I assure her.

I suddenly feel cold, even in the warmth of the morning sun, and I pull my robe tightly around me.

'So where are they?' she asks, puzzled.

'At the hospital,' I tell her. 'But please, don't panic, it isn't anything serious.'

At least I hope not. I haven't actually spoken to Patsy yet, to have an update about Irene.

'What happened?' asks a concerned Owen, a frown crossing his face.

I tell them all about Patsy calling me, after Irene had taken a tumble.

'I'm sorry you weren't told, but Patsy didn't want to ruin the final day of your honeymoon. As it didn't appear to be too serious at first.'

'Typical Patsy.' She smiles. 'We were just popping in en route to our hotel to see you all and make arrangements for this evening. We will head up to the hospital now.' She turns to Owen. 'We can bring her home if the doctors discharge her. I will give Patsy a call. And thank you so much, Mia, for being there for them both.'

'No problem, I was happy to. We have become rather good friends lately,' I tell her. 'And I promise I would have contacted you if the doctor had any real concerns.'

'I know you would.' She gives me a hug. 'And don't worry, we are here now. I will give Patsy a quick call and let her know we are on our way. Catch you later,' she says as they set off.

The fire that apparently began in a kitchen has been successfully extinguished, and fifteen minutes later, we are all allowed back into the apartments.

'I hope it hasn't affected the kitchen too much,' says one of the residents. 'I could murder a coffee,' he says, and his partner rolls her eyes.

Once in my room, I quickly dress and am about to ring the hospital when Irene herself calls me.

'Irene! How are you feeling?' I ask, relieved to be hearing her voice.

'Oh, I'm as right as rain,' she says and I breathe a sigh of relief. 'I just wanted to thank you for coming here yesterday, even though I was wasn't aware of any of it, being zonked out.' She laughs.

'Not at all, I was happy to be there. So are you okay? What have the doctors said this morning?'

'I am being discharged. All the tests were negative, although the doctor has told me to keep an eye on my blood pressure when I get home, maybe see my GP. He is also the second doctor to tell me that I could do with losing some weight, so I intend to really try and make an effort.'

'Well I am pleased the tests did not reveal anything too serious,' I tell her.

'Oh me too, and it really has made me determined to look after myself,' she says positively. 'I'm lucky I never broke anything as I went down like a ton of bricks. But then, I suppose I have plenty of padding.' She chuckles.

She tells me she fell down some steps when she lost her footing in the glare of the sun, so it seems there was a reason for her fall.

'Anyway, Tasha and Owen will be here soon, so we will see you later. She is booking a table for dinner tonight for us all, so we can have a good old catch-up.'

'That's sounds lovely.'

'Oh, and is everything okay at the apartments?' asks Irene. 'Tasha mentioned something about a fire alarm going off when she arrived. I don't think she meant to, but she let it slip.'

'Yep, don't worry. It was nothing really, just a small fire in the kitchen. It's all been sorted now,' I reassure her. 'I'm so glad you are okay, Irene. See you later.'

'Me too, see you later, love.'

I decide to take a walk along the beachfront this morning

and enjoy a coffee and a toastie from a beach café. I watch a couple walking a dog, throwing a stick into the water as the black dog bounds after it.

A little further along, a guy who has been for an early morning swim comes striding out of the water looking a bit like Daniel Craig in a certain Bond film. It takes me a moment to realise that it is Andreas. After drying himself off he strolls towards the café.

'Mia, good morning.' He smiles as he spots me. 'Can I get you another coffee?' he asks, noticing my empty cup.

'No really, but thank you. One coffee in the morning is about my limit.'

He orders himself a fruit smoothie as he takes a seat opposite me.

'Are you not working this morning?' I ask him, recalling that he is taking a day off tomorrow.

'Yes, in around an hour.' He glances at his watch. 'My cousin will be there to open the shop as I sometimes like to take an early morning swim.'

Looking at Andreas, it is obvious that he likes to look after himself.

We chat easily, and he asks how Irene is doing, as his smoothie is placed on the table.

'She is being discharged today, thank goodness. All her tests came back clear,' I tell him.

'That is good to hear.' He smiles. 'I think Patsy will be relieved too.'

I tell him a little about the fire alarm at the hotel earlier.

'It seems you have had quite the drama these last couple of days then,' he says as he sips his drink. 'Tomorrow, I hope you can relax.'

'I am sure I will. I am looking forward to it,' I say, realising that I really am. He arranges to collect me in the morning, before he finishes his drink and departs.

As I sit relaxing in the sun a little longer, just watching the sea rolling onto the sand, I decide to give Mum a call.

'Mia, how lovely to hear from you.'

We have a nice catch-up and she tells me Gran has finally decided to go to the Thursday social club at the village hall, something I have been trying to persuade her to do for a while now.

'What made her change her mind?' I ask.

'Bingo.' She laughs. 'Although I think it is more down to the fact that her old neighbour who used to frequent the club no longer attends as she has moved out of the area to live with her daughter.'

'I take it Gran didn't like her?' I ask, which is unusual for Gran to dislike anyone.

'Couldn't stand her. She said she was, to use Gran's words, "A gobby cow". Although I think it may have been down to the fact that she used to flirt with your grandad, which he found quite amusing.' Mum laughs.

'Oh dear. Well, I am pleased Gran is going to the club. I know she has plenty of visitors, and you take her out shopping, but it will be good for her to spend time with people her own age, I guess.'

'My thoughts exactly. Anyway, how is the holiday going? I am loving the pictures you send me.'

I keep Mum updated with regular photos on Messenger.

'It's lovely, Mum. I have so much to tell you when I get back.' I might leave out the bit about going out with two different men though.

I can't wait to let Mum know that I have been singing on the karaoke and to tell her all about the lovely people I have met and the places I have visited.

After finishing our call, I walk the long way back to the apartments, along the beachfront. Maybe watching Andreas swim in the sea this morning and observing how he looks after himself has inspired me to get fit.

I pass restaurants that are beginning to fill with diners enjoying breakfast as well as a few joggers, headphones on and racing along before the sun gets too hot. It's just so wonderful here, I wish I could stay for just a bit longer.

Strolling to the water's edge, I watch the foaming sea wash over the pebbles, before I pick one up and toss it into the water. Then I give myself a reality check. My apartment thus far has been paid for, so to stay here any longer I would have to pay for it myself, as well as reschedule my flight. I idly wonder if I could earn some money singing? Or perhaps Andreas could give me a job in the shop? But then, what good would that be, with nowhere to live long-term? Not to mention the fact that the summer season will eventually come to an end, when everything will quieten down.

No, I must face the fact that my time here is coming to an end, and if I want to return here any time soon, I had better start seriously looking for a job that pays a regular wage.

I tell myself that many people probably feel this way after spending time in a wonderful place, as I throw another stone into the foamy water.

Taking a right turn from a stretch of beach that leads to the apartments, I pass a restaurant and look forward to spending time with everyone this evening. Bryn and Ash will be joining us too, which means it should be a lot of fun. I guess it's time to count my blessings and make the most of the time I have left here.

TWENTY-SIX

I head to my room to update my social media, before I get ready for later. As I sit on my balcony, it occurs to me that Christos hasn't been in touch, either to ask me out again, or to check if Irene is okay, which I find a little disappointing. Perhaps he has reached the conclusion that we are never meant to be together. Besides, I am going out with Andreas tomorrow, so what would I say if he did get in touch?

I upload some photos and do a little talking video of the view from the balcony, and to my delight a wedding procession walks past.

A couple have seemingly married at the little chapel at the end of the road, and are being showered in confetti and good wishes from restaurant owners standing at the front of the restaurants as they pass. I'm thrilled that I can record the whole thing, giving my followers a real glimpse of a traditional Greek wedding.

A few hours later, I have showered and changed and I am in the reception area with Irene and Patsy as we await our taxi to the restaurant.

'I look like I've gone ten rounds with Muhammad Ali,' says

Irene, stroking the impressive cut above her eye. Her make-up has calmed things down a little, but it is still apparent she has sustained an injury. 'And please tell me you have heard of Muhammad Ali, or I really will feel ancient.'

'I have actually,' I reassure her. 'But only because my dad has told me he is the greatest boxer that ever lived.'

When we arrive at the restaurant a short time later, Tasha squeezes us all tightly.

'Oh, Auntie Irene, you look better, but are you sure you are okay?' She frowns slightly. 'I think you had us all worried for a while.'

'Oh, I'm fine.' Irene bats away any sympathy.

'Well, I am pleased to hear it. I was really concerned.' She frowns.

'Well you needn't be, because I am fine. Anyway, I am more interested in hearing about your time in that villa on the secluded island,' says Irene. 'But not the censored bits obviously.' She winks and Tasha laughs.

'Oh, it was bliss,' she says as Owen orders some drinks.

'I could easily have turned into Robinson Crusoe and stayed there forever.' He sighs, before planting a kiss on Tasha's cheek.

They are so loved up; I wonder if I will ever meet anyone who looks at me in that way.

'We never exactly had to hunt for our own food though,' Tasha says with a laugh. 'The chef came in and cooked us delicious evening meals. We did our own breakfast though.'

'Some days we never surfaced until almost noon, and skipped it,' Owen says.

'Too much information,' Patsy replies, putting her fingers in her ears and laughing.

We are sitting looking at the menu just as Bryn and Owen arrive.

'Blimey, you look rough,' Owen comments to Bryn.

'I am a little,' he admits. 'I made rather a night of it last night after winning a quiz. It's taken me all day to feel human,' he groans.

'In other words, he's been asleep all day,' explains Ash. 'Which meant I could get on with finishing a song I have been working on.'

'Ooh interesting, what type of song?' I ask.

'It's a kind of ballad. Something I think would really suit your voice, actually. You can hear the instrumental if you like.'

'Sure, I'd love to.'

He shows me a video of him strumming the most beautiful guitar melody.

'I have kind of scribbled down the lyrics for you to look at,' he says to my surprise, as he takes a piece of notepaper from his pocket.

'But I don't want to dominate the evening, so maybe you could look them over and tell me what you think? I will send the guitar video to you as well,' Ash tells me kindly.

'Perfect, thanks, Ash,' I tell him, excited to maybe try and sing the lyrics to the music.

Talk turns to our time in Greece, and we fill Owen and Tasha in on how we have been spending the last few days while they have been away.

'The Jeep safari sounds like fun,' says Tasha.

'It was, as was the boat trip. Oh, and Lulu says to say hi and to thank you both once more for your hospitality. She really loved the wedding, as did we all. It was such a special day.'

'It was, wasn't it?' Tasha curls her hand around Owen's. 'It's a day I will always remember.' She smiles. 'And it was lovely to meet Lulu, she seems so lovely,' says Tasha as she picks up an olive.

'She is. I guess I have good taste in friends,' I say, and she makes a little heart shape with her fingers.

My mind flits back to the day of the wedding at the hotel, where Christos worked his charm on me. The thought of his kisses still makes me go weak at the knees, but as he hasn't been in touch, I decide to push all thoughts of him to the back of my mind.

'So this is it then, our last supper together,' says Owen as our drinks arrive. 'I hope you can come over and visit us in the not-too-distant future though,' he tells me. 'All of you, I mean. Not you though,' he jokes to Bryn. 'I get to see enough of you.'

'Charming,' says Bryn.

'I would love to. I had better get saving though,' I tell him.

'Oh, it would be amazing if you could,' says Tasha. 'I would love to show you around my favourite places. And the beaches are pretty wow.'

'I'm not sure I could do that long flight,' Irene says sadly. 'Life's unfair sometimes, is it not?' she comments. 'Here am I with the money, but not the youth, while you are the other way around,' she says to me. 'Sorry, sweetie, I hope that didn't sound too rude,' she continues a second later, having thought about it.

'No offence taken,' I assure her. Even though she's right. I am young and I have an irregular income, which is a situation no one really wants to be in. I think it is maybe time for me to start really thinking about my future.

We order food, and talk and eat until the last of the diners have left the restaurant. When a waiter begins to stack chairs onto nearby tables, I think it might be time to order two taxis.

'I hope to see you soon.' I hug my oldest friend when the taxis arrive together, and try to hold back a tear in my eye. 'I am so happy I was able to be a part of your wedding.'

'I'm so glad you came.' She hugs me a tiny bit harder. 'I will Zoom call you soon, I promise.'

'I look forward to it, and I can't wait to see the wedding photos.'

We say our goodbyes before our taxis head in opposite directions, and I suddenly feel overcome with exhaustion. It will be straight to bed when we arrive back at the apartments as

I have an early start in the morning. As I stifle a yawn, I realise I am really looking forward to my day out with Andreas.

Even so, I check my phone one last time to see if I have any messages from Christos, but he is keeping his distance.

'Are you sure you are okay?' I ask Irene as we step out of the taxi. I noticed her nodding off a little on the short journey back.

'Just tired. I think it was all those drugs they gave me at the hospital.' She smiles.

'So no nightcap then?' asks Patsy.

'Not for me.'

'I'm joking,' says Patsy. 'I'm tired too. I think all these late nights are catching up on us.'

'Not to mention sleeping in hospital guest beds,' says Irene to her cousin. 'Thank you for being there for me. Both of you.' She turns to me. 'I feel blessed to know such wonderful people.'

'I couldn't agree more,' I tell her as we link arms and walk into the apartments together. I also wonder why a part of me hopes that Christos will not contact me again, and remove the dilemma I face. At least until I have got to know Andreas a little more.

TWENTY-SEVEN

The next morning, I wake early and check my phone. There is still nothing from Christos, and I wonder whether he was just after a quick bunk up the other night when he came here. Even if we had ended up sleeping together, would he have bothered to contact me again afterwards?

I get myself ready, choosing shorts and T-shirt for my day on the beach, along with a straw hat. Before I know it, it is time to head downstairs to meet Andreas outside. It occurs to me that I am really looking forward to seeing him, and although there are not quite butterflies dancing around inside me, a gorgeous warm feeling has taken its place.

'*Kalimera*,' he says with a smile. 'You look quite nautical,' he comments as he appraises my navy-and-white striped T-shirt and white shorts.

'Well, we are going to the seaside I guess.'

I hop into the car and we make our way to a place called Akrotiri. We stopped there briefly on the Jeep tour, but only near the lighthouse. I am looking forward to discovering a little more of the area today.

'So tell me a little more about your singing?' asks Andreas as we drive. 'Were you ever professional?'

'Well I did get paid for performing, so technically yes. Although I would call it more semi-professional, I guess. I had gigs here and there, but no agent or anything like that.'

'You have a beautiful voice,' he says kindly. 'At least what I heard of it the other night, but I was a little drunk I think.' He turns to me with a cheeky grin.

'Charming, I must say,' I reply, and he laughs.

'No, but seriously. It is wonderful to use a talent to make a living, although maybe I ought to take my own advice.'

'The sculpting you mean?'

'Yes. I'm a grown man, yet I seem to be blindly carrying on working for my father,' he says.

'Then maybe it's time to think about yourself, although I know it isn't always that easy. Especially if you are involved in the family business.'

'I think my father sees my sculpting as more of a hobby, even though he would still give me the money for a studio to work from, if I asked him.'

'And you don't want his help?'

'Not particularly. I would like to build my business alone. I guess pride is a terrible thing.' He shrugs.

'Not really. I think there is a lot to be said for building something for yourself without a handout. That's what I call a real achievement.'

I can't help but think of Christos then and how his father gave him a head start.

'My parents don't have much, but then they can't really help with a singing career anyway,' I continue. 'Although I have to say that my dad did work extra hours so I could have some singing lessons as a teenager, which I am truly grateful for.'

'That's nice,' says Andreas. 'Your parents could obviously see your talent from a young age,' he says kindly.

Before long we park up on a small high street lined with several tavernas, one or two villas and a pharmacy. Andreas takes a bag from the back of the car. 'In case I find any treasures,' he explains.

The view from here gives us a glimpse of the glorious blue sea below. The ruins of a Venetian castle stands over the town, the Greek flag blowing proudly at the centre.

We pass a few more cafés and tourist shops as well as a beautiful church, with six bells on its tower, dazzling white in the sun.

'We can access the beach by some steps,' says Andreas as we walk, the heat beating down on us.

The village is a jumble of white houses, an occasional blue-domed church and reminds me of a smaller version of Fira.

'Do you mind if we have a look inside the castle ruins before we head to the beach?' I suggest. 'I imagine the view down to the sea will be quite something.'

'Sure,' he says, before we stop at a shop and buy two bottles of cold water.

Climbing the ancient cobbled steps, I can't help but think of the people of long ago who stood here keeping watch for invaders.

After the short climb to the top, the view as expected is spectacular. I take in the houses that slide down to the sea, along with the view of Fira and the caldera. I stand and simply stare for a few minutes, taking it all in.

'So you like history?' he asks as we make our way back into the windy narrow street.

'I suppose I do, yes. I especially enjoy visiting a castle. My grandfather took me to quite a few when I was small,' I explain, recalling the days out that I have fond memories of.

'Then I guess that is something we have in common,' he says. 'And if you like history, there is an archaeological site not far from here that has an ongoing dig,' he tells me. 'Maybe you would like to visit that some time. The ruins are very well preserved.'

'That sounds lovely.' I smile.

We walk on until we are standing at the top of some steps that lead to a small rocky beach below.

'We can grab a cold beer shortly if you like,' offers Andreas. 'I think that heatwave has definitely arrived, as it feels hotter much earlier in the morning,' he comments.

The steps down seem to go on forever, but eventually we arrive at a stretch of rocky beach that looks out across some water with a few boats drifting in them.

The tiny harbour is host to a couple of tavernas and one or two shops. A shop selling scarves along with jewellery made from sea shells catches my eye, the objects displayed outside on a wooden table, and I stop and take a look.

Another shop sells painted wooden door plaques and seascape watercolour paintings. Ruins of houses can be seen dotted around the area and even one or two abandoned fishing boats, yet it manages to look charmingly rustic.

At the far end of the small beach, Andreas finds a bench partly shaded by a huge tree and sets down the cooler box.

'Looks like you have thought of everything.' I smile as Andreas twists the top off two cold bottles of lemonade and hands one to me.

'Maybe we will get that beer later.'

'No really, this is fine,' I tell him as I take a glug of the refreshing lemonade.

He sets out slices of spinach and feta pie, dips, olives, and two fat juicy-looking peaches.

'This is absolutely lovely,' I tell Andreas as I eye the impressive picnic. 'I can't remember the last time I went on a picnic. We don't often have the weather back home.'

'I cannot imagine living in a place without sunshine,' he

tells me as he sips his drink. 'I thought it better to sit here on the bench, as the small beach is very rocky.'

'It's fine here.' I smile. 'Does it get cold here in the winter months?' I ask him as I dive into a slice of feta pie, my paper napkin catching flakes of the delicious filo pastry.

'A little cooler, although we do get cold winters from time to time,' he informs me. 'Although not generally.'

Glancing around at the shimmering sea, and the dazzling blue sky above, it seems hard to imagine it during the winter months.

We finish our delicious picnic, and take a walk along the sand and shingle beach, Andreas occasionally stopping and picking up a stone or a piece of interesting-looking glass, often discarding them.

'Look over there.' I point to a piece of driftwood at the water's edge that resembles a snake as the foamy sea water washes over it.

'Well spotted, that is a nice piece,' says Andreas, picking it up and dropping it into his bag.

Half an hour later, Andreas has found some green-and-blue coloured sea glass, another piece of driftwood and some interesting-looking pebbles.

'What will you do with the wood?' I ask as we walk. 'I imagine it isn't the type of wood to fashion a sculpture?'

'You are right, I mainly use olive wood for that. This type of wood I can use for picture frames, maybe an interesting lamp stand. Here, let me show you something.'

He takes his phone from his pocket and shows me a picture of a stylish black table lamp, with a driftwood base.

'You made that? It's very impressive.'

'Thank you. I sold that in the shop.' He smiles.

'Well then, you really ought to think about opening a workshop,' I encourage him. 'You could take commissions for one-off bespoke pieces, which is what people love.'

'It is true that people like exclusive pieces,' he agrees. 'Especially if they have money to spend. Perhaps I ought to take your advice, and look for somewhere to work, and sell some of my products.'

'Hopefully you make the decision sooner rather than later,' I tell him. 'Life slips by so quickly, we often end up doing things that don't really set our heart on fire.'

'That is very poetic,' he says as he stops and faces me. 'And also, very true. But you must remember to use your gifts too.'

His comment makes me think of how easy it is to give other people advice, rather than address our own needs.

We walk quietly, enjoying the fresh sea breeze and looking for beach treasure, until we finally reach the foot of the steps that lead back up to the main street.

'This is the bit I often forget about,' I say, glancing upwards at the many steps. 'But what goes up, must come down, I guess.'

I can feel the pull on my calves as I walk, resolving to do a little more hill walking when I get home, but it isn't as bad as I feared. Soon enough, we are back on the high street and heading towards the car park.

Driving back, I feel completely relaxed, and not quite ready to head back to the apartments. I realise I haven't thought about Christos once today, and a quick glance at my phone reveals that he obviously hasn't thought about me either. Which, I realise, I actually don't mind. I have enjoyed my time with Andreas so much that I really don't want the day to end.

'Would you be interested in seeing some more of my sculptures?' asks Andreas, as we approach Fira. 'If you do not have to rush back, that is.'

'I don't, and I would absolutely love to,' I tell him, feeling pleased to be spending more time with him. 'It makes a change from "would you like to come up and see my etchings?"' I laugh.

'Etchings?'

'Yes, you know, drawings.'

'People say that?' He laughs. 'I have never heard it before.'

'They used to, according to my mum. Then it changed to "are you coming in for coffee?" After a night out usually, which was often a code for "would you like to have sex".'

'Oh my goodness, I am not trying to do that.' Andreas looks aghast.

'I know you are not.' I burst out laughing. 'Although there is no need to look so horrified at the thought.'

'No, of course, I am not. Nothing would make me happier. Wait, no that is not what I mean,' he says, shaking his head and tying himself up in knots, which makes me laugh even more.

'And joking apart, of course, I would love to see your sculptures. If the figure in the shop is anything to go by, then I am sure they will be amazing,' I say, still smiling.

'Then I hope I will not disappoint you,' he says as we drive.

Just outside Fira, we take a left turn and drive through a village, before approaching a long road, dotted with several villas. When we eventually arrive at a stunning white three-storey house, with floor-length glass windows, my mouth falls open.

He pulls the car into a huge gravel driveway that has room for several vehicles.

'This is your family home?' I ask. The house in front of me is truly stunning.

'It is. Maybe now you can see why I have not left home yet.' He smiles as, like a gentleman, he opens the car door for me to climb out.

A pristine lawn has a stone water feature at the centre, and two small lemon trees stand in pots on either side of the dark-grey front door.

Inside, the stylish rooms look like something straight out of a glossy magazine, with cool, clean lines and shades of taupe and dark blues on the walls. A table in the hallway is set with a large pot of white flowers, their sweet fragrance filling my nostrils as I walk past.

I think of the celebrity house programme with Abbey Clancy that I am certain this place could feature on.

As we head into the vast kitchen with cream glossy units, Andreas offers me a drink. We take our glasses of fresh orange juice upstairs, where he leads me to his bedroom. It has a balcony leading from it that gives a glorious view of the sea.

'Oh wow,' is all I can manage to mutter as I take in the view from his room. 'I can only imagine waking up to that view every morning.' I sigh.

He slides the patio door open and invites me to take a seat on one of the comfortable padded chairs outside.

'I think I could sit and stare at this all day.' I sigh as I sip my drink. 'You really are so lucky to live in a house as beautiful as this.'

'I believe I am,' he says. 'But money isn't everything.' He shrugs.

'Would you mind if I take a photo?' I ask him.

'Sure, go ahead.'

I snap a photo from the balcony of the vista below, the white buildings tumbling down towards the water.

'Don't worry, I won't take any inside as it is your family home,' I reassure him. 'But that view is too good not to capture,' I explain.

'For your social media?' he asks.

'I don't know,' I tell him truthfully. It almost feels too personal sharing the view from his home.

It occurs to me then that I barely took any photos of my day out today, as I was too busy enjoying myself. I truly was in the moment, savouring my surroundings and, of course, enjoying the engaging company.

'Anyway, let me have a look at the things I came to see,' I say, draining the last of my orange juice.

'Of course.' Andreas stands. 'Come.'

At the far end of the bedroom, a long shelf displays several wooden figures, and a huge mirror above it has a beautiful driftwood frame.

'Some examples of my work,' he says proudly, showing me the objects on the shelf.

I study his work in admiration: a smooth trinket bowl, a tree and one or two more face sculptures.

'May I hold it?' I ask, pointing to the perfectly carved tree.

'Of course,' he says, taking it from the shelf and handing it to me.

'It's really beautiful,' I tell him. 'And it looks quite intricate. Did you hand make this?' I ask as I turn it over in my hands.

'I did. It takes many hours, but I enjoy it. I find it very relaxing,' he says.

'You did this too?' I stroke the mirror frame, then automatically check my reflection, wishing I had reapplied some lipstick.

'I did, with some driftwood from the beach we visited today, actually.'

'You are very talented. Have you thought about selling your work online until you find some premises?' I ask. 'Although maybe you would need to put some more pieces together first.'

'You mean like these?' He opens a cupboard that is crammed with objects that range from small dishes to larger fruit bowls. A wooden jewellery box encrusted with sea glass catches my eye.

'That is so pretty,' I tell him. 'All of your work is amazing. How do you make these?' I ask, stroking one of the bowls that is pleasing to the touch.

'On a lathe,' he informs me. 'My grandfather left it to me after he died. It is in a garage, which is currently my workshop. He enjoyed making things as a hobby when he was not out on his fishing boat.'

'What a lovely skill to pass on. Although your hand carving of the faces and the tree is also seriously impressive.'

'Thank you,' he says. 'I appreciate that.'

'Do you mind me asking, will you be selling the tree?'

'I will be, I suppose,' he says.

'Then may I buy it? I think it would make a lovely gift for my friend's fortieth birthday.'

'But, of course, and thank you.' He smiles. 'I am flattered that you would give it to someone for an important birthday.'

I ask him the price, but he tells me we can sort it out another time as he slips it into a box and I place it in my bag.

Glancing at my watch, I can see it is very late in the afternoon, so think I ought to be on my way. There appeared to be no one else at home when we arrived, but I imagine his parents will return home shortly, after being out on their yacht for the day. Their yacht!

'I have had a wonderful time today, Andreas, but I ought to be heading back,' I say, draping my bag across my shoulder. 'Thanks for showing me your work, you really are very talented.'

'It is nice to have an appreciative audience.' He smiles as he leads me from the bedroom.

Walking along the landing, we hear giggling from the other side of a bedroom door.

'Is someone home?' I ask as we pass the room.

'Probably my brother.' Andreas rolls his eyes. 'Maybe we will leave the introductions for another day though,' he says, raising an eyebrow.

'Maybe that's for the best.' I smile, feeling pleased that he would like to see me again.

It really has been the most unexpected day, and I enjoyed myself far more than I could have imagined. We reach the top of the stairs, when suddenly the bedroom door swings open, and my heart stops. Because there standing in the doorway, with a blonde woman in tow, is Christos.

TWENTY-EIGHT

Time seems to stand still for a moment as I glance from Christos to Andreas in utter confusion.

'Mia, what are you doing here?' asks Christos, looking completely shocked.

'She is here with me,' says Andreas, a puzzled look on his face. 'Wait, you two know each other?'

'We have actually met, yes,' I tell him. 'At the nightclub,' I add, wishing that the ground would swallow me up.

'I see,' says Andreas, staring at his brother.

I can feel the heat creeping up my cheeks as Christos looks at his shoes and scratches the back of his neck.

'Is there something you are not telling me?' says Andreas, glancing between us both suspiciously. 'Only I have seen that look on my brother's face before.' He almost spits the words out as he glares at Christos.

'What? No, not really,' I say, my heart beating wildly. 'Christos has just shown me some of the sights.'

'I bet he has,' says Andreas under his breath, his jaw twitching.

Christos, I notice, seems to be hiding a smug grin from his brother.

The blonde behind him shoves him and tuts loudly, and as she steps onto the landing, I recognise her at once as the woman he was chatting to at the club the evening I went there with Lulu.

It feels as if all the air has been sucked out of the room as I take in the scene. I need to get out of here fast.

'I must be going,' I say, already heading for the stairs.

Andreas stands still for a moment, before he follows me to the front door.

'Let me drive you home,' he says, his voice tight.

'No, really, Andreas. I spotted a taxi rank in the village on the way in, I will be fine. Thank you for a lovely day,' I mutter.

I turn on my heels about to set off, when he takes me gently by the wrist.

'My brother is no good,' he says. 'At least around women. He uses them.'

I still can't take in the fact that they are brothers!

'Well, he never used me,' I tell him, thankful that I never slept with him. 'I am not in the habit of sleeping with the first man who pays me some attention. Especially on holiday.'

'I wasn't suggesting that,' he says more softly.

'Thank you again for today, Andreas. I truly did have a lovely time but I really think I ought to leave.'

As I head down the path, he makes no further attempt to stop me, so I walk purposefully towards the taxi rank in the village, holding back the tears that are threatening to spill over as I do so.

The image of Christos walking out of the bedroom plays around and around in my head as I walk, not to mention the look on the face of Andreas when he realised I had been out with his brother. I meet two men on an island heaving with people, and I end up going out with both of them, who turn out to be brothers! I tell myself that today was nothing more than an innocent trip to the beach with Andreas, yet deep down I wonder if I wanted more? What an absolute mess.

I find a taxi and back at the apartments, I head to a bar across the road and down a large gin and tonic before I return to my room.

I have two more days here, and I don't want the recent events to put a dampener on things, so I decide to concentrate on the one thing I am good at.

I grab my phone from my bag and find the recording of Ash playing the guitar, before I unfold the paper with the lyrics. Over the next hour, I fit the lyrics to the song, pausing and correcting it, until it sounds pitch perfect.

I record it all and play it back, thrilled with how it sounds. Without hesitating, I send the recording to Ash to ask him what he thinks of it.

A short while later as I am tidying my apartment, wondering how one person can make such a mess – although the apartment is rather small – my phone rings.

'Mia, you are bloody brilliant,' says Ash excitedly. 'Your voice suits that song perfectly, as I suspected it would. We should upload this to my YouTube account.'

'Do you really think so?' I ask, thrilled by his words, yet worried about how it will be received.

'Absolutely I do. Honestly, Mia, you sound amazing,' he assures me.

It sounds like such a big deal. The most I have ever done is sing at one of those recording studios with a friend, when I was gifted the experience by Gran. Putting it out there in front of all those people feels terrifying. I'm sure Ash told me that he has almost a million followers on his YouTube channel.

As I recall though, the guy who was mixing the tape at the recording studio did tell me I ought to maybe think about pursuing a singing career. Perhaps it's time I stopped hiding my light under a bushel, as Bryn said, and really get myself out there.

'Sure,' I tell him. 'If you think I'm good enough.'

'Believe me, you are,' he says excitedly. 'And what you must remember is that you are singing without any enhancements from studio equipment. People like that live lounge kind of feel,' he assures me.

'Then do it,' I say sounding far more confident than I feel.

The following morning, I take an early morning beach walk, my thoughts still swirling from the events of yesterday.

Before I know it, I have reached the far end of the beach, when I spot Andreas sitting at the beach café nursing a drink. I find the sight of him gives me another lovely warm glow inside.

'Mia.' He stands and waves me over when he sees me, and I make my way towards him.

'How are you? Please, let me get you a drink?' he offers.

'Sure, I'll have a coffee, please.'

I take a seat as he orders me a drink from a waitress who is clearing a nearby table.

'I'm sorry you had to encounter my brother like that yesterday,' he says. 'It must have been embarrassing for you.'

'I was a bit surprised, yes, but don't worry, I don't think we ever really had anything in common,' I tell him, realising I really mean it. Christos made my pulse race sure, but he did little other than talk about himself.

'It was just such a shock to discover that you were brothers,' I tell him.

'I can imagine.' He manages a smile. 'But we are very different.'

'I kind of gathered that.' I smile as my coffee arrives. 'And I have to tell you, we went out on more than one occasion,' I say, figuring it best to get the truth out there right away. 'He took me out on the family yacht. We went snorkelling.'

'That is his signature move,' he says, shaking his head. 'And it seems a lot of women are impressed by that. I think my father is a fool to let him use the yacht, although sometimes I think he is unaware of it,' he tells me.

'I won't lie, it is a pretty good way to impress a date,' I say as I sip my coffee. 'But it didn't impress me enough to want to sleep with him,' I tell him, although I have my fingers crossed behind my back because truthfully I was in fact more than a little tempted.

'It would be your business.' He looks me in the eye. 'But he is not ready to commit to one woman.'

'So it would appear,' I have to agree.

I think back to how Christos told me his father owned many businesses in Fira, including shops. I never imagined that the guy who worked in the gift shop would turn out to be his brother.

'I'm glad I ran into you,' I tell him sincerely. 'I really did have a wonderful time yesterday. And please believe me when I say, it was nothing with Christos, really. He invited my friend and I to the nightclub, and I guess I got caught up in all the glamour.' I shrug. 'But you know, we never really talked.'

'I can imagine. My brother likes to talk about nothing but himself,' he says, raising an eyebrow.

As I lay in my bed last night, I realised it wasn't Christos I had regrets about not seeing again. Especially after seeing him in his true light. I was thinking of Andreas and how he makes me feel.

'And I enjoyed yesterday too.' He smiles that easy smile as he looks at me, and I feel something warm inside. 'Apart from how things ended at the house.' He pulls a face. 'But how about we draw a line under it all. Maybe try again.'

'What do you have in mind?' I ask, feeling completely relieved.

'I was wondering how would you feel about us spending a little more time together before you leave? There is something I would like you to see. A place not far from here, near a beach I know of. When are you free?'

'Well, I'm free now, so...'

'Perfect. I have my car.' He picks his car keys up from the table. 'Shall we head off?'

'This all sounds intriguing,' I say as I follow him to his car, wondering what he is so keen to show me.

'I will not keep you in suspense for long, and don't worry, I am not going to kidnap you or anything.'

'That's a relief, as my family don't have a lot of money, so I wouldn't rely on getting any ransom money,' I joke.

I realise then that he belongs to a family that certainly doesn't need ransom money.

'Do you have another day off work then?' I ask as we drive along, wondering why he isn't at the shop today.

'Just the morning,' he tells me. 'My cousin is now happily working until lunchtime every day. I think she is happy to earn some money before she goes back to university,' he explains.

'Ah, is that the young woman I saw at the shop the other day?' I ask, recalling the pretty woman with the long dark hair.

'It is. She is studying art but enjoys working in the shop, which I am grateful for as she has a way of displaying the merchandise to its best advantage.'

'Oh, I agree,' I say, thinking of the beautiful displays when I called in with Lulu.

As we drive, I ask Andreas about the island in the height of summer.

'I got the impression you thought the cruise ships were a bit of a nuisance,' I tell him as we head out along a coast road. 'I won't lie, I found that a bit surprising as surely they are good for tourism.'

'You would think so,' he replies. 'People on cruises have all their needs catered for onboard, food, entertainment, etc so yes, they may buy a coffee or lunch here and there, or do a little shopping when they dock, but that does not really help the economy,' he explains. 'Don't get me wrong, we are proud to have visitors to the island, the problem is the sheer numbers that descend all at once,' he explains. 'It literally puts pressure on the ground. Many footpaths and steps have had to be rebuilt,' he tells me.

'I don't suppose we think about that when we visit places,' I say, mulling over his thoughts. 'Especially as so many people are travelling these days.'

'Which is a wonderful thing, but maybe people ought to think about coming here in the autumn. I personally think it is a much nicer place to visit at that time of year,' he advises. 'Before the season ends. The island looks beautiful then.'

'I will remember that next time.' I smile.

'So, you will return?' He turns to me.

'I am certain I will. It is easy to see why people fall in love with Santorini.'

'I am pleased to hear it.'

I lean my arm on the open window as we drive, the breeze gently blowing my hair as we pass a strip of sea.

Eventually, we cut onto a beach road, passing a couple of gift shops, a beach café with people sitting outside having breakfast, and a surf shop that hires out boards and sells beachwear. This little row of shops leads directly onto a gorgeous sandy beach with a good number of sunbeds. A building at the end of the row of shops stands empty.

'Gosh, what a gorgeous place. I would never have known it even existed,' I say as I glance around.

'It is a little gem, and very busy in the height of summer. It is not very well signposted from the main road, although there is always a lot of passing trade, especially from tourists.'

He leads me to the uninhabited shop, next door to the surf shop.

'So, what do you think?' he asks as we stop outside.

'About what?' I ask, puzzled.

'I was thinking that maybe this would make an excellent workshop for my sculptures. And, of course, I could sell them here.'

'Wow, you are thinking of buying this place? I can't think of a nicer location,' I say.

'I already have.' He grins. 'Come on, let me show you inside.'

Stepping onto the wooden floor of the abandoned space, I can at once imagine Andreas sitting in a corner working, his art displayed on shelves around the studio. At the end of the room a large window lets in light, and gives an enticing glimpse of the beach beyond.

'It's absolutely perfect,' I tell him as I walk around the room.

'I think so too.' He grins. 'And this particular beach has lots of treasures, including plenty of driftwood.'

'So you are finally going to go it alone? What does your father think about you not running the shop?' I ask.

'He is fine. As I say, my cousin is keen for more hours. In fact, my father has agreed to work in the shop himself a little more,' he reveals. 'Although maybe it is my mother's idea.'

'Your mother's idea?'

'Yes. She says retirement does not really suit him and he cannot spend all his time on the family yacht.'

'Because that sounds like hell,' I say, and he laughs.

I think of the day on the yacht with Christos, but push the thought to the back of my mind.

'My mother is a social butterfly with lots of hobbies,' he continues. 'My father, not so much, so I think she feels better if he is occupied. Secretly I think he agrees.' He smiles. 'He is already looking at new suppliers for the shop, he always loved it there. My mother says he can relax when the summer season is over.'

'My gran always says that people need a purpose in life,' I tell him. 'Which I guess is true.'

I head back towards the window, captivated by the view of the rolling sea as Andreas produces a tape measure from his pocket, ready to measure a wall.

'I think that maybe she is. And you know? I guess I have finally realised that my purpose is to create things for other people to enjoy.'

'I don't doubt that for one minute, you have a real talent,' I say.

'Thank you. And surely your purpose is to bring the gift of your voice to people,' he says as he joins me at the window, and we both glance out across the sea.

I can feel his presence as he stands next to me, taking in his calm, masculine demeanour, and his woody cologne. He is tall, and more rugged than Christos, whose manicured look is probably a result of spending hours in barber shops and salons. Not for the first time, I wish Andreas was the only Greek man I had met here in Santorini.

'Shall we make a move?' Andreas asks, although I would honestly be happy standing here for a while longer.

'Sure,' I reply, a little reluctant to leave.

'Or maybe you would like a walk along the beach before we head off?' he suggests.

'I would love that. And you never know, you might find something interesting.'

We go for the door handle at the same time, and when our hands brush, I'm surprised to feel a jolt of something between us.

We walk quietly on the stretch of northerly beach that has a strong breeze. I watch a young boy with an older man, laughing gleefully as his kite takes to the air. One or two swimmers are braving the waves and enjoying a morning swim.

'I can see why the surf shack is there,' I comment, noticing the foaming waves as we walk. 'Do you enjoy water sports?' I ask.

'I like to jet ski occasionally, although I prefer swimming,' he says as he bends down and picks something up from the sand.

'That's pretty,' I say as I watch him turn over a piece of green, marbled sea glass.

'It is,' he says, sliding it into his pocket.

As we stroll along, I realise how much I enjoy the company of Andreas, and don't want our day to end. I also think of the feeling I experienced when our hands collided, and wonder if he felt it too?

At the far end of the beach, Andreas finds an unusual-looking gnarled piece of wood in shades of brown and cream and lifts it from the sand.

'I should have brought a bag,' he says, dusting the sand from one of nature's treasures.

'One moment,' I say, diving into my shoulder bag. 'Another thing my gran says is always carry a spare bag.'

I fish out a string bag I bought from an artisan market back home.

'This gran of yours sounds like a remarkable woman,' he says as he happily carries the bright-pink string bag with the piece of driftwood inside.

'She is. I spend a lot of time with her. She's funny too,' I tell him, thinking of some of the hilarious conversations we have had.

'My grandmother was funny.' He smiles. 'And you could always rely on her to give her honest opinion,' he remembers fondly. 'I miss her.'

I don't even want to think about the time when my own grandmother is no longer here.

As we walk and talk, I realise my phone has been firmly in my pocket the whole time. I should probably be taking some photos for my social media accounts, yet I don't feel compelled to do so.

Having not eaten breakfast, when we arrive back at the beach café, Andreas offers to buy us some breakfast.

'Sure, but I insist on paying,' I tell him as we take a seat outside. 'I never did thank you properly for saving me from a fall that day in Fira.'

Andreas protests, but I insist. I am heading home in a couple of days, and I still have plenty of euros left. The sensible part of me thinks that I could change them into sterling when I return home, but as I don't know when I will travel abroad again, I might as well enjoy myself while I'm here.

'So what will you do for work when you get home?' asks Andreas as he tucks into the daily special, an omelette with chunks of village sausage and feta. I ordered the same thing too, and it is absolutely delicious.

'I have a couple of options,' I tell him, which is not entirely the truth, but fingers crossed something will turn up. A recent chat with Mum revealed that the Royal Oak back home is, in fact, reopening at the end of the month, so hopefully I can secure a few paid gigs there.

'What would you do if something turned up here?' he asks, in between mouthfuls of food.

'Here?' I frown. 'I don't see how I could ever get a job here. It might be nice over the summer though.' I idly daydream. 'I'm pretty sure I could get used to spending mornings like this in the sunshine.' I say, as I glance around the idyllic location..

We sip our lattes and Andreas is quiet for a moment before he speaks again.

'Perhaps I could help you with that. If you wished to stay here a little longer, that is.'

He looks at me with those gorgeous brown eyes framed by long black lashes, and it is as if I am really seeing them for the first time.

'You could help?' I ask, puzzled. 'I mean, I would love to stay here a while longer, but I don't understand?'

'A friend of the family owns a smart restaurant in Oia, with a piano bar. It is in a sublime position to watch the sunset,' he tells me. 'He is looking for a singer this summer, three, maybe four nights a week. I think your voice would suit such a venue perfectly.'

'Me!' My mouth falls open in surprise.

'Why not? Didn't you once tell me that we ought to follow our passions?' he reminds me.

'Well, yes, of course we should, but a job singing here in Santorin? I'm not sure I could do that.' I shake my head.

'Why on earth not? You say you have experience of singing in public back home? And I heard you at that karaoke bar, and you were amazing,' he says kindly.

'Thank you, and, yes, I do have experience but wow, here in Santorini, really?' I let his words sink in as I wonder what is actually stopping me from staying out here for a while longer.

'Well, at least think about it,' he says. 'And it would not be for another month, so you could maybe go home first if you have things to sort out,' he says. 'I will happily pay your plane fare back here.'

'You would do that?'

'I would.' His hand reaches over for mine and I feel a rush of affection for this lovely man. 'If it is what you want.'

During the drive back, I mull over Andreas's words, wondering if I could actually make it happen? Lots of people do seasonal work, but then where would I stay? Any money I earned surely wouldn't cover the cost of accommodation too. Perhaps it is nothing more than an impossible dream.

'Can I see you before you leave?' Andreas asks as he drops me off back at the apartments. 'If you think about what I have suggested, I can take you to the restaurant in Oia to meet my friend.'

'Do you mean to audition for a singing job?'

'If you decide it is something you would like, then yes,' he says.

'Sure. He is hardly likely to hire me without hearing me sing, I guess.'

Although I do have a recording of me singing something to the music Ash wrote, I remind myself, although I am not sure how well that has been received.

I don't have to wait long to find out though, as back in my apartment I take my phone from my bag and charge it up after the battery had died. As it springs to life, I notice two missed calls and several messages from Ash.

As I slowly scroll through the comments of me singing, I almost burst into happy tears. The comments are nothing short of fantastic, many people asking Ash who I am, and where can they watch me perform.

'Finally,' he says when I give him a call. 'I was beginning to think you had vanished off the face of the earth.'

'Sorry, I was out on a beach and my battery died,' I tell him, realising once more that I hadn't been preoccupied with taking photographs. 'Oh my goodness, Ash, I can't believe the response!'

'I can. It's had two million views already and you are currently viral on my TikTok.'

'You are joking!' I gasp.

All the hours I have invested uploading videos of eateries and shops, and my singing views have gone through the roof. Maybe I should have listened to my friends all along.

'Nope,' he says. 'You are being discovered and appreciated, and rightly so,' he tells me kindly.

'Oh, Ash, I can't believe it. And it may have just given me the confidence to take on a little singing job.'

I tell him all about the possibility of doing the summer season at the restaurant here in Oia. 'If I can sort out somewhere cheap to stay, that is.'

'Oia, hey that sounds amazing,' he says. 'And when you come home, I'm sure people will be queuing up to hire you,' he says.

When we finish speaking, I do my little running on the spot happy dance, which I realise I haven't done in a while. Suddenly life seems full of possibilities and it feels so good!

TWENTY-NINE

'But you are coming home with us tomorrow?' asks Irene as we enjoy a penultimate breakfast at the Sea Breeze.

'I'm pretty sure I will be, yes,' I tell them, having finished a breakfast of fruit and pancakes. 'I want to go and see my family, and my brother is home this coming weekend,' I tell Irene and Patsy. 'But if things work out, I will return in a few weeks to start the job in the restaurant.'

'Ooh how exciting!' says Patsy. 'We might even come out again and see you, before the season ends, what do you think, hey, Irene?'

'We might do just that,' she agrees. 'Life is for living after all, and none of us know how much time we have left.'

'I'll drink to that,' says Patsy, and we clink our coffee cups.

After breakfast we opt for a beach day together, so nip back to the apartments to grab our towels and change into our swimwear.

After applying sunscreen, I settle down onto my sunbed with a book, when my phone pings with a text message. It's from Ash telling me to check his YouTube account.

'How many million?' asks Irene as she sits up to take sip of her drink. I show her and Patsy the video.

'Three million and rising,' I tell her.

'And what are people saying?' asks Patsy.

'Have you been signed up by anyone yet?' asks Irene.

'I'm not sure there are any record producers watching, but so far people have been very complimentary,' I tell them, much to my relief.

'Well, that is hardly surprising, you are brilliant! Oh, Mia, this might be the start of something big,' says Irene. 'What made you change your mind about you sharing a video of you singing?'

'Truthfully? I'm not sure, but perhaps hearing Ash play that music he wrote made me realise we shouldn't let our talent go to waste. He has a talent for writing songs, and without singers to perform those songs, they would never come to life, would they?'

'They would merely be poems,' says Patsy, nodding.

'That's very true,' I agree.

'Have you told your parents all about the job offer?' asks Irene.

'I think I will wait until I get home the day after tomorrow,' I say as I sip a delicious fresh fruit mocktail. 'Then if it all works out, I will tell them that I will be returning here for the summer holidays.'

'Yes, maybe that isn't something you should tell them over the phone,' Irene agrees. 'Oh, but I am sure they will be thrilled for you.'

'I'm sure they will.'

In fact, I am certain they will be, and Gran especially will urge me to follow my dreams. I feel blessed to have such a supportive family and can't wait to spend some time with them when I get home. Especially as my brother will be home for a while too.

I upload some photos to my socials, as even though I have not been as preoccupied with my phone, I have a loyal following who enjoy seeing my content.

Scrolling through my pictures brings back all the memories of Santorini, although a picture on the yacht alongside Christos feels almost like seeing a snapshot of me with someone I barely knew. I decide not to post that one to my social media.

I linger over some of the other photos as I upload them, smiling at the sight of the donkeys in Fira, and the day of the picnic at the beach with Andreas, that includes a picture of us raising our soft drinks as Andreas pulls a funny face.

The photo taken from the family home has me wondering if I will ever set foot inside that house again? Then I wonder why such a ridiculous notion has popped into my head.

I know that I will see Andreas again though, as he has promised to take me along to the bar in Oia when I audition for the job.

Having completed my uploads, I sit on the balcony chair and feel the warmth of the sun on my skin, thinking of what an eventful few days it has been. I still can't believe that Christos and Andreas are brothers, and find myself idly thinking of how that could work, if I somehow did grow closer to Andreas. Then again, he has never been anything other than courteous towards me, but perhaps that is because he is nothing like his brother.

As the sun beats down and the sound of music pumps out gently from a bar across the road, I concentrate on topping up my tan. The soothing effects of the sun soon have me drifting off into a glorious snooze.

THIRTY

A little after six in the evening, Andreas calls me and asks if I am free in around an hour.

'I am sorry it is a little short notice, but I wondered if you would be up for that trip to Oia later?' he asks me.

'Do you mean to audition?' I ask, feeling a sudden ball of nerves in my stomach.

'Yes. I realise it isn't much time to get some songs together, but there is a resident pianist, and one or two musicians,' he says. 'They would be mad not to fall in love with you,' he says, before quickly adding, 'With your voice, I mean.'

'Do you really think so?'

'I am certain. When I explained you were going home tomorrow, my friend was keen to see you before you leave,' he explains.

'Of course, then yes, I would love to go to Oia,' I say excitedly. 'And thank you for setting that up for me,' I tell him gratefully.

'It is my pleasure. And, of course, it will be the right time to enjoy that famous sunset,' Andreas reminds me.

'Sounds wonderful,' I say, imagining sitting in a bar and

watching the sun go down. A singing audition in Greece though? This might just be the craziest thing I have ever done in my whole life.

I quickly shower and change and in no time at all Andreas has arrived. He looks handsome this evening in a peach-coloured shirt, and some dark jeans. On his wrist, he wears a leather rope bracelet, in contrast to his brother, who is never without his Rolex on his wrist.

'You look nice,' he comments on my knee-length white dress as he opens the car door for me to climb inside.

'So do you,' I return the compliment.

The drive to Oia is short and beautiful as we drive along the mainly empty road, passing fields of grapevines and rugged mountainous scenery, interspersed with pink and yellow villas. As we climb higher, we enjoy wonderful views below, and my stomach begins to churn. Shouldn't I be looking for a singing job back home, and looking for a place to rent? And didn't Dad say another local pub is reopening and that they would be looking for singers? Maybe I could combine that with another part-time job to earn a decent living wage.

I tell myself that the work here would only be until the end of the summer, so I guess I would at least have the experience to look for something when I get home.

We pass a row of donkeys on the white pavement below a cobbled stone path that leads up to a church, before the road becomes busier with cars and quad bikes, as we near our destination. Thankfully my nerves have begun to give way to a feeling of excitement.

'No going back now then,' Andreas says with a smile as we pull up outside a white building that looks seriously cool. A sign above the door has the words 'Theo's Bar and Restaurant' in black writing against a silver backdrop. Two marble sculptures of Greek goddesses sit either side of a heavy black-wooden door at the entrance.

'This place looks expensive,' I say to Andreas as we approach the door. 'And it appears to be closed.'

I almost suggest leaving, as once more my nerves get the better of me. Am I really good enough to sing in a place like this?

'It only opens at eight o'clock,' he tells me as he rings a bell. After a brief conversation on an intercom, a man around the same age as Andreas appears at the door.

'Andreas, welcome.' He shakes us both warmly by the hand as Andreas introduces us.

Stepping inside onto a marble-floored reception area with a chandelier overhead, I glimpse the restaurant ahead, ready for service. Orange high-backed velour chairs contrast perfectly against white walls adorned with black and white art.

The guy who greeted us is called Mikail and he offers us a drink, before leading us to a room a little further along a corridor.

The spacious room has a piano in one corner, and a patio door leading to a large outside area, filled with chairs and tables that give dramatic views over the island.

I take in the bar on one side of the room and the sumptuous sofas dotted about.

'Wow, this is gorgeous,' I say as I look around the beautiful room.

'This is the piano bar, as you might have guessed.' Mikail introduces me to the resident pianist. 'People like to relax here after dinner and listen to some music, which, of course, is why you are here.'

Could I seriously be hired to sing in a place like this, over the summer? Even the thought of it has me pinching myself.

'We have a set of songs we can suggest, but if you have anything in particular, we could take a listen,' says Mikail.

'Okay,' I say.

'In the meantime, we would be happy to hear you sing today, if that's okay?'

'Yes, and I would be happy to go with your suggestion for a song today,' I tell the pianist, who is introduced as Nicos.

He suggests 'The Long and Winding Road' by The Beatles, which is thankfully a song I have sung several times before and suits my voice perfectly.

The piano man plays his intro, and I can feel the adrenaline kick in. As I begin to sing, I feel as though I am soaring above the mountains as I give the vocals everything I have.

The three men in the room are silent for a moment when I finish, and I think I see Andreas wipe away a tear from his eye.

A slow smile spreads across the face of Mikail as he slowly applauds me.

'You were not joking when you told me she was good.' He turns to Andreas, before shaking me warmly by the hand. 'That was wonderful. The question now is surely, when can you start? I think you could work with Mia, yes?' He turns to Nicos the piano man.

'It would be my honour,' he replies kindly.

'Wow, really? That's it? I'm hired?' I ask, my heart thumping.

'You are. That is okay, isn't it?'

'Yes, of course, it's more than okay, it's wonderful, thank you! So am I right in thinking that the post will start in July?' I ask.

'Yes, it does,' Mikail replies with a smile. 'I suppose I was being impulsive when I thought of firing our current singer so you could start sooner,' he says to my surprise.

'Are you not happy with him?' I find myself asking.

'Not always, but not because of his singing,' he explains. 'He has the voice of Michael Bublé, but unfortunately the drinking habits of a drunken sailor,' he reveals. 'He has me on edge, turning up late and sometimes has me wondering if he will turn up at all.' He sighs in frustration. 'But, yes, you can start one month from now if it suits you?'

He tells me I will appear four nights a week, between nine and midnight, with a break in between. The salary he suggests is far more than I was expecting.

'Oh and, of course, accommodation is included if you need it,' he tells me.

'I'm sorry, what?' I say, hardly able to believe my ears.

'Staff accommodation. Literally just down the slope,' he says. 'Sorry, I didn't mention it to Andreas at the time, but a room has only just become available. One of the restaurant staff has had to return home earlier than expected,' he explains.

'I can't believe it,' I say, genuinely shocked by the offer of free accommodation. 'To tell you the truth, I think that paying for a place to stay might have been a stumbling block,' I tell him.

In fact, it would have been highly unlikely despite the very generous payment I am to receive for my performances.

'Then now you have nothing to worry about.' He smiles. 'That is assuming you would like the job?'

'Yes. Yes, I would love to perform here, thank you so much,' I tell him, my head spinning. Have I really just accepted a job here in Santorini?

'Perfect,' he says. 'Welcome on board. I will email details of your contract. And if you arrive a couple of days before you start work, you can go through some songs with Nicos.'

'Yes, of course, and thank you,' I say, hardly able to believe what is happening to me right now.

I head outside with Andreas in a complete daze.

'My gosh what just happened?' I say, realising I am shaking slightly.

'What happened is that someone has rightly recognised your talent,' he says. 'I am so happy for you. And now, let us find somewhere to celebrate.'

Around the corner is a small bar with football shirts all over a wooden ceiling, once more with a stunning vista.

'Not quite as glamorous as the last place, but shall we grab a beer?' suggests Andreas. 'The sun will be setting shortly, so we are lucky to get a seat anywhere around here at this time.'

'This is perfect,' I say as we head inside.

It isn't long before the bar is crowded out with visitors hoping to bag a seat to watch the legendary sunset.

'You know, I think we ought to toast both of us actually,' I say to Andreas when our beer arrives.

'You do?' says Andreas.

'Yes. You have the beach workshop and I have a singing contract, which feels weird when I say it out loud.'

'Well deserved. And, yes, perhaps we ought to toast our respective future careers,' he agrees. 'Not everyone has the opportunity to do what they truly desire.'

'To us,' we say as we tap our glasses together.

There is a hush in the bar as the sun begins its descent and the view from up here is nothing short of spectacular.

The sky fills with a rainbow of colours, and as the sun begins its final descent, the surrounding buildings seem to be bathed in an orange hue, giving it a truly magical feel.

'This is perfect.' I sigh, resting my head on Andreas's shoulder as we watch together, lost in a moment that I will remember forever.

When the conversation in the bar resumes, I feel slightly embarrassed to have leaned on him like that, but he didn't seem to mind. At least I hope he didn't. Watching the sunset here has been the most extraordinary way to end one of the most exciting days of my life.

'Would you like a coffee before we leave?' offers Andreas.

'No, thanks, I will be awake half the night if I do, but you get one if you like.'

'I am okay.' He smiles. 'Perhaps it is that I don't want to

leave just yet,' he says and it occurs to me that I am in no hurry to leave either.

His eyes meet mine and as he leans closer, I prepare myself for his kiss as a waiter drops a glass on the next table and it crashes to the floor.

'Although maybe we ought to get going,' he says. 'There are so many people here this evening, the roads may get busy later on.'

'Of course,' I tell him. I suddenly feel a little tired anyway, no doubt coming down from the adrenaline rush I experienced earlier when I sang at the restaurant.

I have to stop myself from drifting off to sleep on the journey home by chatting to Andreas, and taking in the surrounding landscape that has been plunged into darkness. As we leave the lights of Oia, the road becomes even darker, the only light from passing villas or the occasional bar or restaurant.

It is almost eleven when Andreas drops me off at the apartment.

'I can't thank you enough,' I tell Andreas as we stand beneath a sky studded with bright stars. There is still a buzz from the restaurants across the road; the sound of chattering and laughter ringing out can be heard. 'I would never have thought of looking for a job here in Santorini.'

It makes me think that contacts can be invaluable when it comes to securing any type of work.

'I was happy to help, although you were only hired because of your talent. Believe me, Mikail only hires the best people,' he tells me.

'Thank you.'

'So would you like a lift to the airport tomorrow?' Andreas offers.

'Surely you can't keep taking time off from the shop?' I say.

'My cousin is more than happy to work,' he reminds me.

'It's kind of you to offer, but I have a hire car that I can drop off at the airport,' I explain. 'I will be travelling back on the same flight as Irene and Patsy, so I will take them to the airport too.'

'I see,' he says, glancing down at his shoes for a moment. 'Then I guess this is goodbye.'

'For now,' I correct him. 'It won't be long until I return.'

Just then I hear someone call my name as Irene and Patsy come bounding across the road.

'Oh, my goodness, you're back,' says Irene excitedly. 'So how did it go?'

'I will leave you to it.' Andreas smiles, before wishing us all a safe flight, and saying he will be in touch, before he climbs into his car.

As I wave him off, I can't help wondering what might have happened if Irene and Patsy had not appeared when they did.

'So go on, tell us how it went,' insists Irene as we link arms and head into the apartments.

'Well, you are never going to believe this, but...'

THIRTY-ONE

'I still can't believe you have landed yourself a job here,' says Irene the next morning as we pack our cases into the hire car. Thankfully, I hired a large car with a boot that can comfortably store our three cases.

'Me neither,' says Patsy. 'But you go for it. I wish I had taken up more offers when I was young.' She sighs.

'The world was a different place then,' Irene reminds her. 'Once you had chosen your career path, that was that, you were pretty much stuck with it forever. I loved working as a nurse though,' she reflects.

We had said goodbye to the staff at the Sea Breeze earlier, and are thrilled to see them standing outside the restaurant and waving us off as we drive past. I give a toot of the horn in response as we wave our arms out of the windows.

'I will really miss that place,' Irene says sadly. 'Everyone was so lovely. The food portions were so large it was pointless trying to diet.'

'Nobody watches their weight on holiday, Irene,' says Patsy, lighting up a vape that smells of blueberries. I ask her to keep the window open as I am not fond of the smell.

'I realise that, especially in a place like Greece where the food is so delicious,' agrees Irene. 'I will be joining that slimming club as soon as we get home though,' she says with determination.

'And I might actually have a go at quitting these vapes when I get home,' says Patsy.

'You would think it was New Year with all these resolutions.' I laugh. 'Although I can add to that as I resolve to concentrate more on my singing.'

At the airport, having dropped the car off, we wait around for our check-in desk to open and the pull to return to Perissa is so strong I almost walk off in search of a taxi, before giving myself a reality check. I have no money to stay on here just yet, plus I am keen to see my family and to tell them that I have secured a singing contract and will be returning here in a few weeks. I hope they will be happy for me, and maybe they will decide to take that trip to Greece after all and watch me perform. That would make me so proud and happy.

I'm sitting looking at my phone, when I suddenly hear a familiar voice call my name.

'Andreas, what are you doing here?' I ask as I stand to greet him.

'I just wanted to say goodbye to you properly,' he says, taking hold of my hand. 'I felt I didn't do that earlier.'

Irene and Patsy are watching the scene unfold, while pretending to hide behind the novels they are reading.

'And I was wondering,' he continues. 'How would you feel about us spending some time together when you return?'

'You came all the way here to ask me that?' I smile, feeling thrilled by his presence.

'So, what do you think then?' he asks.

'I think I would like that very much,' I tell him.

'You think?' he says as he moves closer.

'I am sure I would like to spend some time with you. Is that better?' I say, my heart beating as he pulls me to him.

'Much better,' he says, before his lips finally meet mine. And the wonderful thing? I still get those tingles but without any feelings of uncertainty. I trust Andreas. It just feels right.

'I am looking forward to you returning already,' says Andreas as we stand together, his arms around my waist. 'I hope you do not change your mind about returning, once you get home.'

'Of course I won't,' I assure him. 'Besides I don't want to go breaching my first contract as a singer, do I?'

He gives me a final kiss, before our fellow passengers make their way to check-in, signalling that it is time to leave.

'Bye, Andreas. I will see you again soon,' I say, giving him a final hug before he departs.

Sitting on the plane, I am about to switch my phone to airplane mode, when a text comes through from Andreas, telling me he forgot to wish me a safe flight, and I smile to myself as I thank him.

Christos has remained silent since our impromptu meeting, which is unsurprising really considering what happened at his home. Once more I think of how relieved I am that I never slept with him, despite the obvious chemistry between us. Since meeting Andreas though, I have barely given him a thought. Seeing him with another woman revealed his true colours, and despite my initial surprise, I am glad it happened.

'Fancy a gin and tonic?' asks Irene later when the drinks trolley trundles along the plane. 'One last treat before the diet starts at home.' She laughs.

'In that case, shall we have some Pringles too?' suggests Patsy.

Seated in our row of three, we sip our drinks and chat about the highlights of our holiday.

'I have two really,' says Irene. 'Tasha and Owen's beautiful wedding and lunch in that fancy house near the beach.' And Patsy agrees.

'Honesty really does pay off,' she says, thinking of the day she found the rightful owner of the pretty necklace. 'I still can't believe they had staff to serve us food and drinks, I felt like a celebrity.' She sighs with pleasure.

'Oh, I agree,' says Patsy. 'I think I could easily develop a taste for the finer things in life, after trying that lobster.'

'Maybe you ought to develop a taste for tinned tuna, it's more in your price bracket,' Irene says with a giggle, and Patsy playfully nudges her.

'And remember me telling you we were offered a reward?' says Irene. 'Well, the owner managed to sneak a hundred euros into my bag, even though we refused to accept it.'

'Did she?' Patsy looks shocked. 'You never said.'

'How do you think I have paid for those extra cocktails?' She giggles again.

'Well, I imagine it was nothing compared to the cost of the necklace, I suppose,' says Patsy.

'And she is lucky that it was you who found it,' I say to Irene.

'How the other half live, hey.' Patsy sighs.

Her comment makes me think of Andreas, and how he said that money isn't everything and that it cannot really guarantee happiness. I think there may be some truth in that, but I guess it depends on the individual. Some people adore money and riches above everything else I realise, as annoyingly Christos pops into my head.

'So how about you, Mia, what was your highlight?' asks Patsy as she opens her tub of Pringles.

I think of all the wonderful experiences, starting with, of

course, my oldest friend's gorgeous wedding. Surprisingly though, Christos doesn't feature in my top holiday moments.

'The wedding, of course, not to mention the stunning scenery and the wonderful restaurants,' I tell them. 'Oh, and the Jeep safari. Lulu and I both really enjoyed that.' I smile to myself. 'But the night in the karaoke bar was a real highlight for me. It gave me the confidence to realise I really am a good singer, even if I say so myself.'

'A great singer,' says Irene and Patsy agrees. 'Who has only gone and bagged herself a job in a piano bar in Oia.'

'I know!' I almost squeal.

I think then not of the time I spent on the luxurious yacht, but the day I spent with Andreas at the beach, and the delicious picnic he had thoughtfully prepared. I recall how he really listened as I spoke to him. And then, of course, there was that most surprising kiss as we said goodbye.

'What's the soppy grin for?' asks Irene, which I didn't realise I had on my face.

'Oh nothing. It's just that being here has reminded me that we really ought to use our talents and follow our dreams.'

'I'll drink to that,' says Patsy and as we tap our little plastic glasses together, I look forward to the future with a new-found confidence.

THIRTY-TWO

Mum is stirring some custard to go with the home-made apple crumble, the day after I arrive home.

After arriving late last night, I had a lovely lie-in and I am now handing out the little gifts I bought in Santorini, and my family thank me.

'Ah, I love a snow globe, thank you, love,' says Mum.

'Yes, me too,' says Gran, giving hers a little shake and smiling fondly. 'Although I don't suppose they have snow in Santorini.'

'Maybe it's ash from the erupting volcano,' I suggest when Mum shakes hers too and she laughs.

As we chat, I notice Mum has set the table for five people, rather than four.

'Are we expecting someone else?' I ask as Mum looks at an incoming text on her phone.

'We are. And they should be arriving any second now,' she says as I hear the sound of a key turning in the front door.

'Lewis!' I scream as my brother walks into the room. I rush to him and crush him in a hug.

'Nice welcome, sis.' He grins, before hugging everyone else in the room.

'So tell me all about your holiday,' says Lewis as we tuck into delicious roast beef. 'You have a nice tan there,' he notices.

'Oh, it was wonderful, but tell us all about what you have been up to first,' I insist. 'Then I have some news for everyone.'

'Well, you will have to go first now,' says Gran, putting down her knife and fork. 'You can't leave me in suspense, it's not good for my digestion,' she tells me.

'Alright then.' I take a deep breath. 'The thing is, I will be returning to Greece next month for the rest of the summer.'

You can hear a pin drop in the room, before Mum is the first to speak.

'What?' Mum frowns. 'But I don't understand. Surely you can't afford to do that, without any money.'

'And don't you think you ought to be concentrating on finding a job?' says Dad, mildly exasperated, and I hope I haven't gone and ruined the happy mood in the room.

'That's the thing, I have actually found one,' I tell Dad. 'It's only temporary though.'

'Well, that's something, I suppose. Are the wages any good?'

'Oh, they are.' I smile. 'Very good. It's just that it happens to be in Santorini.'

I tell my family all about the job I have secured for the summer season, and Mum claps her hands together.

'That's great news! Oh, I'm so glad you are pursuing your singing again,' she says excitedly.

'Me too, love, that sounds like a smart place too,' Dad says with approval.

'Yeah, nice one, sis, that really is great,' adds Lewis. 'Let's see the photos of the club,' he urges, so I grab my phone and do just that.

'Oh, very nice,' says Dad, looking proud. 'Very nice indeed.' He nods approvingly.

'Gran? What do you think?' I ask, noticing she is a little quiet, despite congratulating me.

'I think it's absolutely marvellous,' she tells me. 'Yes, I will miss you, but oh what an opportunity.' She smiles warmly. 'If I had my time over again, I would say yes to more things, I can tell you.'

'Oh, thank you.' I hug my gran, who is sitting beside me. 'It isn't for another month, so let's enjoy the time I have here,' I say.

'Let's do just that. And I think we ought to open a bottle of something to celebrate,' says Dad. 'Don't we have a bottle of Prosecco somewhere from Christmas?'

'And maybe we can finish off with this,' says Lewis, lifting a bottle of good brandy from his rucksack nearby.

After our delicious lunch, we are sitting around in the lounge chatting. I show my folks more pictures of the piano bar in Oia, and some of the unofficial wedding photos.

'Oh, doesn't Tasha look a picture,' says Mum. 'And Owen looks so handsome. I can't wait to see the official photos.'

'Smart venue,' says Lewis, looking again at the photos I took of the piano bar in Oia. 'I'm sure you will have a great time working there.' He smiles as he hands me back my phone.

'And I will come and visit you, Gran. I'm home for six weeks now, remember, so any little jobs you need doing around the house, I'm your man,' he tells her and I can't help wondering whether he will be happy to cut Gran's toenails.

'You might regret saying that,' she says with a wink as she sips a cup of tea.

Dad is about to protest, I'm sure, but maybe thinks twice about doing some DIY at Gran's, as he remembers his slight back problem. He does offer to mow the lawn though, as gardening is something he enjoys.

'So where will you be posted to next?' I ask Lewis as we tidy the kitchen and load the dishwasher.

'Cyprus,' he tells me. 'Which isn't actually that far from

Greece, so I might have time to pop over and see you sing.' He smiles. 'In fact, I know a bloke who runs a tribute bar near Paphos if things don't work out. He could sort you a job,' he says as he places some cutlery in a drawer.

'Not sure about being a tribute act,' I tell him. 'But thanks anyway.'

'Not a problem.' He smiles.

I have fond memories of Lewis and myself growing up together, even though he could never stay indoors for long, always seeking out people to play football with, or go off somewhere for the day. Sometimes, he would allow me to trail along with him to the park, but only if one of his friends had one of their siblings with them too. He always looked out for me if he was around, but it came as a surprise to no one when he decided to spread his wings and join the army.

It seems Lewis's arrival home couldn't have come at a better time with my imminent departure, although Mum and Dad have never been the type to insist we stay around for them, although I have been immensely grateful to have spent time here since I lost my job and flat.

Mum finds the Prosecco in a cupboard, and after Dad cracks it open, we sip from paper cups, also left over from Christmas, to avoid any more washing-up.

'Here's to our Mia,' says Dad. 'And Lewis. We are bloody proud of you both,' he says as we raise our paper cups, and Mum holds back a tear.

'And you know, that Greek holiday we have been thinking about, perhaps it might be possible this year,' says Mum. 'Do you reckon you would be up for that?' She turns to Gran as everyone raises their cups in the air, after Dad proposes a toast.

'Just you try and stop me,' says Gran, and suddenly, all feels well in the world.

THIRTY-THREE

The following week I am preparing for the evening out at the opening of the furniture store with Lulu.

As expected, once I had tipped Phil off at the catalogue about her birthday, he ordered in some food and fizz, and had a whip round for a gift.

'It's gorgeous, isn't it?' Lulu shows me the pretty silver bracelet, dotted with pearls.

'It really is. They are a good bunch,' I say, fondly recalling my colleagues at the catalogue phone line.

We sip our drinks as people wander about, some I recognise from social media, who stop to say hi.

'They are, I am blessed to work with such good people. I still miss you being there though,' she says kindly.

'You have Phil though.' I nudge her and she laughs.

She has been out on two dates and I couldn't be happier for her. It's so lovely to see her dating again after being single for so long. My friend deserves nothing but happiness.

'I still can't believe we went roller skating,' she says, laughing. 'It took me right back to my youth and I was thrilled that I managed to stay upright.' She giggles. 'Thankfully so did Phil.'

I am also happy to report that her children took her out for a meal before Tom went on his travels, and downloaded some photos of them all together which went into a thoughtful gift album, along with some of her favourite perfume.

'They have been fending for themselves a lot more,' she tells me as we help ourselves to some canapés offered by a passing waitress. The buffet table is impressive with various dips, wraps and a selection of Korean tapas that include savoury pancakes, and delicious crunchy salads.

'Which I have to say is down to you,' she continues as we load our plates up. 'When I suggested a rota, they kind of looked sheepish and said that wasn't necessary, and promised to pull their weight. Up to now, they have stuck to their word.'

'I am so pleased things have worked out,' I tell her.

The evening entertainment is slick and professional, the fire-eaters and acrobats drawing an amazing response from the assembled guests.

As the evening wears on though, I don't feel quite the level of excitement I usually do at such events. Everything seems to be about appearances, and who has the biggest following, and I get the feeling there is a definite pecking order. Especially when I notice a particularly well-known YouTuber hardly mix with anyone, apart from the owners of the club.

Almost everyone around me has their phones out recording, which, as this is a freebie, I ought to be doing the same in order to do a review. I pan my phone around the room, and take the obligatory photos of the cocktails and food, having already snapped one or two of the entertainment, but not nearly as many I would normally.

'You okay?' asks Lulu later as we head out into the night in search of a taxi.

'Yes, fine,' I tell her. 'It's just, oh I don't know, I wasn't really feeling it tonight, exciting as it was,' I tell her truthfully.

'I had a lovely time though, I am so happy you invited me,' she says.

'Oh, don't get me wrong, I have massively enjoyed spending the evening with you,' I tell her. 'I was referring to the social media aspect,' I explain. 'I enjoyed just being at an event and wished I didn't need to think about reviewing it later. You know how I love spending time with you,' I say as we approach a vacant taxi.

'I know that.' She smiles. 'And I wonder if things have lost their appeal slightly, now that you are off to Santorini again shortly.'

'Who knows?'

'I am so excited for you, Mia, no one deserves this more than you,' she tells me. 'I wish I could come over again and hear you sing, but I guess there is always next year.'

'You think they will offer me more work next year?'

'They would be mad not to.'

'Thanks, Lulu.' I know that Lulu has always been one of my biggest supporters when it comes to my singing.

As we make our way home, I think about Lulu's comment about my lack of excitement over my social media. Surely posting content of my singing in Santorini would send my followers wild, maybe even increase my followers by tenfold. The thought of it should be sending me wild with excitement, yet it doesn't.

I think back to the laid-back attitude of Andreas, who despite being part of a rich family enjoys his beachcombing, and creating beautiful things. He lives in the moment, and barely glances at his phone.

'Maybe fame and fortune isn't everything after all,' I mutter.

'What was that?' asks Lulu.

'Oh, nothing really. Just thinking out loud,' I say as we drive on.

THIRTY-FOUR

Andreas greets me at the airport with a lingering kiss that confirms how much I have missed him. He looks so handsome and smells so good, I could stand here in his embrace forever.

'So are you excited?' he asks as he loads my suitcase into his car.

'I am. Nervous and excited,' I tell him as we climb into the car and make our way to Oia. It's late morning and I stifle a yawn after an early morning flight.

'I imagine you will be busy later, so I was wondering if I might show you something now,' Andreas says. 'If you are not too tired that is.' He smiles. 'And breakfast is on me.'

'Then how can I refuse?'

We make our way along a familiar road, and it feels so good to be back here, beneath a blue sky.

Presently, we pull up at the beach, with the beach shack and other shops we had visited previously.

As we stand outside the once abandoned building at the end of the row, a slow smile spreads across my face.

A sign above the door has the words 'Nature's Treasures'

written on it and Andreas takes a key from his pocket, and lets us inside.

'Oh wow, it looks beautiful,' I say, glancing around at the transformed space. The walls have been painted white, with driftwood shelves displaying his work.

A wooden island in the middle of the space has some bowls and trinket boxes displayed on a long silk turquoise drape.

'Has your cousin helped with the displays?' I ask.

'How did you guess?' He smiles.

In the far corner of the room stands the lathe where Andreas works his magic. The smell of wood feels so comforting.

'Has business been good?' I ask as I wander around admiring his work.

'You know it really has,' he tells me. 'People are so happy to find a handmade gift. I have had one or two tourists commission gifts to collect before they leave,' he tells me proudly. 'But more importantly, I am doing what I love.'

As we stand by the window gazing out to sea, his hand reaches for mine and I recall the first time we stood in this very spot.

'Shall we get that breakfast now?' he asks. 'And then I will take you to Oia.'

'Sounds good.'

'Oh actually, wait. Before we leave, I have a gift for you.'

He goes to a drawer and pulls something out before handing it to me. It's the jewellery box I first saw at his house, embellished with pieces of colourful sea glass.

'For me?'

'Yes, of course. I recall you admiring it at the house. It was actually one of the first things I ever made,' he tells me. 'I was so mad with myself for forgetting to give it to you before you left, so I brought it here.'

'Thank you, Andreas, it is truly beautiful,' I say, kissing him gently on the lips. He takes me in his arms then, and kisses me with a passion that takes my breath away.

'I've missed you,' he whispers.

'I've missed you too,' I tell him. 'More than I ever thought I would.'

'Shall we get that breakfast then?' He takes me by the hand as we walk outside. 'Then I will take you to Oia. I have a few things to do today, but I will call you later,' he says.

'Let's go,' I say, feeling the excitement in the pit of my stomach as I head towards my future as a singer.

'How do you feel about covering a song a male artist normally sings?' asks Nicos as we run through some songs the afternoon before I make my debut.

'I could do, do you have something in mind? It would have to be something I am familiar with though at this stage.'

'I agree,' Nico says with a smile. 'Although I wasn't thinking of for tomorrow, but something to consider in the future. It's just a thought as you sang your audition song so beautifully,' he says kindly.

'I guess you're right,' I tell him. 'And I think I have the right pitch for "Bridge over Troubled Water" sung by Art Garfunkel.'

'Yes!' Nico agrees emphatically. 'A favourite of mine which I have played many times on the piano.' He smiles. 'I think we are going to get along just fine. Now, how about a drink?'

Sitting in the seated area outside as the sun beams down, I count my blessings once more. I would never have thought about even looking for work here, without the support of Andreas. I think of all the missed opportunities we have in life, because we are afraid to put ourselves forward. But then, I guess, I would never have known that this place existed if it wasn't for Andreas.

I quickly settled into the accommodation provided, chatting

to the four other staff that include bar and restaurant staff, as well as another singer, who is truly talented according to the other people here.

The house has a small terrace off the garden, where the staff were enjoying a late breakfast when I arrived, and quickly welcomed me, inviting me to join them.

'Thanks, Nicos,' I say, finishing my drink. 'I think I might go for a walk along the beach now, although perhaps I ought to be practising my songs?'

'I would say you have rehearsed enough,' he tells me reassuringly. 'There is such a thing as overdoing it. It's important to relax before a performance,' he advises.

'You're probably right,' I say before I depart.

It's late afternoon when I walk along the beach, busy at this time of year with people swimming and children running along the rocky beach shouting and laughing. Families are enjoying picnics on blankets spread out, as others lie on sunbeds reading or soaking up the sun.

I have read online that there is a bookshop not far from here that I will look forward to exploring. Apparently, they have a roof terrace and seating area for reading, and I think it might be a good way to enjoy some downtime. The whole village looks so inviting, with its white buildings and familiar blue-domed churches dotted about.

Andreas sent me a good luck message earlier, and said he will call me when he finishes work at the shop.

We kept in touch regularly before I returned, via texts and video calls, and I am deeply happy that he came into my life. He is so funny and kind, I can hardly believe that Christos is his brother.

There has been no talk of Christos thankfully, other than Andreas telling me he is currently in Ibiza and that he is no longer allowed to use the family yacht. It seems he had a party that ended up with someone being drunk and falling overboard.

Luckily, they were fine, but the police had been called and their father had been enraged.

I walk to the edge of the water, and gaze out into the far distance as I take a deep breath. Tonight I will make my debut at the club, and I am determined to enjoy every single minute.

'Did you feel nervous before your first performance?' I ask Saskia, a bubbly blonde singer when I have returned to the shared house.

'I did,' she says. 'Which is silly really, as I've done loads of concerts back home, but Theo's is a bit posh, isn't it?' She laughs. 'At least that's what I thought. But believe me, later in the evening, no one is posh after they have had a few cocktails.' Which puts me at my ease.

'Really, you will be fine,' she says kindly. 'You have the voice of an angel; I heard you practising in your room earlier,' she lets slip.

'Thank you. I was trying not to, as Nicos said it's important to rest my voice, but I don't know what to do with myself,' I admit.

'It's only natural. But really, once you have done the first performance, you will be just fine.' She winks.

I have chosen a simple knee-length red dress for this evening's performance, and a single solitaire necklace, and before I know it, I am striding into the cocktail lounge where Nicos waits at the piano.

When he plays his note, I feel the familiar butterflies in my tummy before I begin my first song. Thankfully, it is received with rapturous support and over the next hour, as the lounge begins to fill with people arriving after dinner, I relax into my set. I even have a little chat with the audience in between songs.

When it's time to take a break, I find myself in a side room, and almost shaking.

'I would say you went down a storm,' says Nicos kindly as

he makes himself a coffee from a machine. 'It seems you are a natural in front of a crowd.'

'Thank you. I hope so. I really enjoyed it,' I say, feeling exhilarated.

'Want one?' He offers me a coffee, but I decline and have some bottled water instead. I think a coffee would send my already adrenaline-filled body through the roof.

'And you can relax now,' he tells me. 'At this time in the evening, people are in high spirits.'

'You mean, they will have had so many drinks, it doesn't matter what I sound like?' I laugh.

'Not quite. But perhaps the pressure is off a little in the last hour.' He grins.

I am just returning from the bathroom, when my phone rings. It's Andreas.

'How is it going?' he asks me.

'Andreas, hi, really well, I think,' I tell him. 'At least the applause has been good, so I think so.'

'That is wonderful, I knew you would be a hit,' he tells me kindly.

I can hear chatter in the background and he tells me he is out with friends. I can't deny a tiny stab of disappointment that he isn't here this evening for my debut, but he said he was busy today and perhaps he already had plans that he couldn't get out of.

'I will see you very soon,' he tells me. 'Good luck with the rest of the evening.'

'Thank you.'

Quickly glancing at my phone before I am due back on stage, I smile at some voice notes from my family, wishing me the best of luck. I dearly wish they could be here to watch me, but know that maybe isn't possible right now, especially with Gran's mobility problems.

Returning to the lounge for the last part of the evening, I

notice some of the younger groups have drifted off, maybe in search of a nightclub, but the lounge is busier than ever with couples, and groups of slightly older people sitting around chatting.

As I grab my microphone ready to resume my set, I scan the room. There is no mistaking the bloke at the back of the room, with a phone in front of him, seemingly ready to record me, and a warm feeling washes over me. Andreas lifts his hand and waves.

The evening is coming to a close, when I turn to Nico and ask him if we can change the last song of the evening.

'Sure.' He smiles. 'Especially as it is one of my favourites.'

When I begin to sing 'The Long and Winding Road', I slowly walk towards Andreas, who is now clutching a bunch of gorgeous red and white flowers and the audience burst into applause.

I can feel a lump in my throat as I sing, but somehow I manage to keep my composure.

'You are amazing,' says Andreas as he hands me the flowers, and I could die of happiness as I take in the whoops and cheers all around. I did it. My first paid performance in as long as I can remember and it felt so good.

'I will second that,' says Dad, walking towards me, and this time I really do burst into tears. Especially when I see Gran's wheelchair being pushed by Lewis, and Mum walking beside them.

'But how? I don't understand.' I choke back more tears as I embrace my family. 'Are you really here?' I say, literally pinching myself.

'I told you I was busy today,' explains Andreas. 'Collecting your family from the airport.' He smiles and I feel a rush of love for this amazing man.

'It wasn't so bad you know,' Gran tells me. 'No waiting around at the airport, straight through I was with this.' She taps the arm of her wheelchair. 'I might even see a bit more of the world before I meet my maker, if I don't have to wait in queues.' She laughs.

'Maybe next time get an electric wheelchair,' jokes Lewis. 'Good job I have big guns to be able to push you around,' he says, flexing an arm muscle, and she shakes her head, but with a smile on her face.

'So where are you staying?' I ask in a daze, still hardly able to believe my family are here.

'In a villa, not far from here,' says Dad. 'It was a last-minute bargain, and Andreas kindly paid for our flights,' he reveals.

'You did?' I stare at Andreas open-mouthed.

'It was my pleasure,' he says. 'And as it is your evening off tomorrow, I have arranged for you all to have dinner at my family home.'

'Seriously?' I can hardly take it in. 'Your parents are okay with that?'

'Of course, they love entertaining. If you would like to accept, they would be honoured,' he says, placing his hand on his heart.

My family eagerly accept the kind invitation, and I can't help wondering what Gran will make of his family home. Will she think it needs more colour?

'I would love you to meet my parents,' whispers Andreas as we head outside. 'My mother says that given the amount of time I spend talking about you, she thinks she knows you already,' he says as he threads my hand through his, giving me a warm fuzzy feeling.

'Everyone back to the villa for a nightcap then?' asks Lewis. 'I've bought a bottle of Metaxa brandy at the airport.'

'Ooh now you're talking,' says Gran with a wink.

'Lead the way.' Andreas smiles and right now I think that all of my dreams may have just come true.

A LETTER FROM SUE

Dear reader,

I want to say a huge thank you for choosing to read *Not My Greek Wedding*. If you did enjoy it, and want to keep up to date with all my latest releases, just sign up at the following link. Your email address will never be shared and you can unsubscribe at any time.

www.bookouture.com/sue-roberts

I hope you loved *Not My Greek Wedding* and if you did I would be very grateful if you could write a review. I'd love to hear what you think, and it makes such a difference helping new readers to discover one of my books for the first time.

I love hearing from my readers – you can get in touch through social media or my website.

Thanks,

Sue Roberts

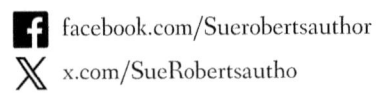

facebook.com/Suerobertsauthor
x.com/SueRobertsautho

ACKNOWLEDGEMENTS

As always, I would like to thank everyone involved in the production of this book. A special thanks to my wonderful editor Natalie Edwards, and every single one of the incredible staff at Bookouture. The graphics and design team, never cease to amaze me with their gorgeous book covers. This one may actually be my favourite!

In this story, I have touched a little on social media that almost everyone has some involvement with these days, especially the younger generation.

I must thank Olivia Foley, for her insight and inspiration for this book. Olivia is an avid traveller and some of her recommendations for holidays are well worth noting, especially her amazing visit to the Wadi Rum desert when visiting Petra. Mia would have loved that experience!

Check out Olivia's travel pages at the top of her TikTok page @Oliviamaifoley.

Also, thanks to Sophie Paterson, a performing arts student currently attending LIPA (Liverpool institute for performing arts) who I talked to about overcoming nerves when performing live. She told me that being part of a supportive group of friends, and having the best tutoring at an outstanding sixth form college really helps.

Thankfully, unlike Mia, Sophie is happy to show off her talent and some of her singing can be viewed on TikTok under Sophiep.performs. Such talent for a sixteen-year-old, and a name to look out for in the future!

As we live in a world often dominated by social media, I thought I would make this the subject of this book. Many people have found success on various social media platforms, and I say good luck to them! It often involves a lot of hours uploading content, and is maybe not as easy as some people may think to earn a living in this way.

I was thrilled to set this book in Santorini, a place I have visited on several occasions, and it holds a special place in my heart. I hope the book may have inspired some of you to visit there one day.

Finally, thanks to ALL of you readers and book bloggers. What would us authors do without you? It means the world when you enjoy one of our books and shout about it to others.

I am always happy when a reader reaches out (On social media of course!) and I will always reply. Leaving an Amazon review is also greatly appreciated. Much love to you all.

PUBLISHING TEAM

Turning a manuscript into a book requires the efforts of many people. The publishing team at Bookouture would like to acknowledge everyone who contributed to this publication.

Commercial
Lauren Morrissette
Hannah Richmond
Imogen Allport

Cover design
Debbie Clement

Data and analysis
Mark Alder
Mohamed Bussuri

Editorial
Natalie Edwards
Charlotte Hegley

Copyeditor
Jane Eastgate

Proofreader
Becca Allen

Marketing
Alex Crow
Melanie Price
Occy Carr
Cíara Rosney
Martyna Młynarska

Operations and distribution
Marina Valles
Stephanie Straub
Joe Morris

Production
Hannah Snetsinger
Mandy Kullar
Ria Clare
Nadia Michael

Publicity
Kim Nash
Noelle Holten
Jess Readett
Sarah Hardy

Rights and contracts
Peta Nightingale
Richard King
Saidah Graham

Printed in Dunstable, United Kingdom